FAREWELL,
SILVER BIRD

FAREWELL, SILVER BIRD

Karolina Kolmanič

tP
Texture Press
2016

Farewell, Silver Bird
Copyright© 2016 Karolina Kolmanič

English translation by Amir Klement Kolmanič

Published in the United States by
Texture Press
1108 Westbrooke Terrace
Norman, OK 73072

For ordering information,
visit the Texture Press website at
www.texturepress.org

Cover and book design by Arlene Ang

ISBN-13: 978-0-692-69703-0
ISBN-10: 0-692-69703-9

May the book resonate in the hearts of my dearest family members and in all courageous, tolerant and humane souls. Cruel was the war that sowed death in my homeland. In the worst of times, the people kept their humanity and rescued foreign lives, even at the cost of their own. The triumph of good over evil should today and forever guide the world.

FOREWORD

The timing of this book's publication is extraordinary. It coincides with two significant dates for Slovenia and the United States in the month of April, namely with the Slovenian-American Friendship and Alliance Day on April 2 and the date of the official recognition of independent Slovenia by the United States of America on April 7, 1992. In addition, Slovenia celebrates this year (on June 25, 2016) the 25th anniversary of Slovenia's independence.

This year's commemoration of the Slovenian-American Friendship and Alliance Day took place at the site where 72 years ago an American B-17 aircraft was downed by German artillery and eight crew members died while en route to Austria to bomb industrial installations. Incidentally, these facts are very similar to those in the novel. This year the commemoration was attended by Slovenian President Borut Pahor, U.S. Ambassador in Slovenia Mr. Brent Hartley, Slovenian Defense Minister Andreja Katic, the U.S. defense attaché in Ljubljana and many others. On this occasion, the President and the ambassador delivered speeches and U.S. Air Force planes overflew the site.

TABLE OF CONTENTS

YESTERDAY

A train station in Upper Carniola. A young woman steps off a train. A tall, broad-chested man offers her both hands. A firm handshake and warm kiss ease the impatience and quiet yearning of two young hearts long eager to meet.

The train whistles off into the cold winter eve. The wind blows and delicate flakes of snow sprinkle the faces of two beings walking up a narrow path.

A man wearing a black fur hat carries a small suitcase and leads the way as he breaks a path. A woman, wrapped in a white kerchief and wearing a black fur coat, carefully shifts her feet, for a layer of ice underlies the freshly fallen snow. The path widens. They continue side by side. The woman clasps the man's warm hand and says:

"France, we've been walking a while now."

"The house *is* far from town, but it's wonderful, you'll see. I looked long to find the perfect little corner where we could spend these short vacation days of ours and our New Year's holidays."

"It's nice that you think of everything. I could use some rest. You know the way from Belgrade to Ljubljana is long and arduous."

"I figured you'd be tired when you got here, so I took care of everything. Look, the villa's over there. I left the light on, or we'd never have found it."

"Is it always empty?"

"Not always. The owner sometimes rents it out to passing tourists. No rush in the wintertime, though; there aren't any skiing resorts nearby. That's why I managed to get it. It's ours for the entire week—if you've the time, of course. I know I do. After my vacation I'll be driving to Ljubljana for work. Either way—we have three more days of vacation ahead of us. We'll see then."

"Dear, let's not discuss that now, and anyway, you know I only have five days off—the ones left over from October, when we spent those few warm days at the beach."

"And we're spending *these* few in a winter idyll. And I plan on making it even nicer. Look, the house! Take care; quite a few steps to the top."

"They're untrodden and clumsy. Obviously nobody cleaned the snow from them all winter."

A fairy-tale house amid a spruce forest. The light casts its thin rays on the silvery snow, and the warm house is an inviting shelter. Above the entrance rigidly hang icicles. The large, wrought-iron door creaked when France opened it.

"After you, my dear Silva!"

"Oh, how pleasantly warm! And so tidy! But I think I fancy this fireplace most of all. We'll turn out the lights and warm ourselves there. France, you awaited me like a princess in a fairy tale! How splendid!"

"We're having dinner soon. I've prepared everything. Just be sure not to criticize my skills. You know I'm clumsy even though I keep house myself."

"Don't worry, I won't breathe down your neck. We'll be fine today. Tomorrow, I'll take over things. I'll cook, and clean as well."

"No, we won't be working much. We'll make love; that's why we're here."

A passionate kiss interrupted their exchange. Then, stillness again. After dinner, the light went out.

In the fireplace, thick beechen logs crackle pleasantly. Silva walks to the window:

"It really is romantic. On the hill there a little house, behind it another. Look at these lights. It reminds me of home."

"Home is what our past is all about. You still know how tirelessly I chased you, and you, stubborn as you were, would always reject me. Good thing, too. I know you loved me, and that you weren't afraid when I threatened to leave you. Other girls were … And gave up every time. The young me didn't mind at the time. I looked and looked, but couldn't find another girl like that. So my desire drove me back home, where I found you. And now you're mine."

An orange beam of light faintly illuminates the large room. The unfolded couch waits in the corner …

Silva slowly lays down her clothes. The room's reddish glow lends the light blue lingerie a violet tinge. France stares for a minute or two, as though a film about a seductress were playing before him. Dark hair falls down below her round shoulders to partly reveal a pair of full breasts … Once, his gaze would have faltered, but now he was still and could admire a while.

"Silva, you're beautiful. No artist could hope to capture the image into which nature has made you. You can see how I must restrain myself, can't you? I want to see you in all your fairness. Silva, I love you …"

Only now did he become a man thirsty for kisses, hungry for love. He was as he had been at the beach. Two unfulfilled bodies sway rhythmically … The sweet melody that unites them yearns for reprise until exhaustion defeats them. Only now do they again hear the crackling of a dying flame in the fireplace, only now notice that a gloom blankets the room. Bodies relaxed, souls at ease and content.

"Nice, dear?"

"Indescribably … sweet. But it could be better still if I told you …"

"Told me what?"

"Oh, nothing …"

"I'll throw some logs on the fire and put on a record. I've got the one you like."

"No, not now. I'd rather not think about goodbyes."

"I'm sure; neither would I. That's why we shall listen to *"Pretty Is Our Day …"*"

A cold wind howls and gusts furiously at the flimsy door. Its untamed song creates dissonance with the harmonies of the record and the two hearts inside. This is happiness. Neither of them thinks that it's also ephemeral. They live for these moments; not for yesterday, nor for tomorrow. Perhaps Silva does … she has to. Just not right now.

The next morning, France gets up first, restocks the firewood and makes breakfast. Silva is still groggy and tries to sleep a little longer. At once, a call comes from the kitchen:

"Silva, I've forgotten; hard- or soft-boiled eggs?"

"None at all. They don't agree with me lately."

France falls silent and begins to dawdle. Now Silva's had her of fill of sleep.

"I've got to tell him … But now, in the morning? This is silly. Any other woman would have written it down by now or found out at the first opportunity, but here I am still waiting. Waiting for what? We love each other. Is that not a sure sign of a future together? And yet … tonight. I'll tell him tonight—at midnight … Yes, it has to sound as good as it can."

France brings a breakfast-laden tray and Silva's thoughts evaporate. She asks, as mundanely as she can:

"Have you invited any guests for this evening? We're not spending New Year's alone, are we?"

"Of course not. I've invited two friends and their girlfriends. There will be six of us. I've got everything figured out: food and drinks. It's up to everyone else to bring their high spirits. You and I have plenty to spare ourselves."

"I'll prepare the cold cuts and all that."

"Good girl. But don't overwork yourself; you need to be fresh and rested come evening."

"Why's that of such significance?"

"It'll be the first time my friends see you. You have to make a good impression. Anyways, I'd best stop prattling. You'll be the prettiest of all ... It's just that I'd like you to relax. Don't be so very serious."

"Picking the fairest of three girls really is nothing difficult, whichever one it happens to be. The judges will have an easy task."

"I'm also bringing a spruce branch and candles, or it's no celebration and we won't know it's New Year's at all. We'll decorate. Next year we'll have a fir tree as high as the ceiling and we might not be alone anymore."

He squeezed her gently. There's something Silva wanted to utter through ardent lips, but the words would not come.

In the afternoon, the wind had ceased. White stars had slowly begun their descent toward Earth. Silva grabbed a broom and swept snow from the steps that ran down the hill to the path. She stopped on the last step and looked up. The house they now called home is a true miniature luxury. Its former owner had enclosed the property and the surrounding forest in a tall iron fence. A chain and rusty padlock kept the old wobbly gate to this paradise locked. France told her that a rich man from Zagreb had had the whole affair built for his girlfriend.

He had met with her here even before the war. The owner of the house and the woman both died during the war. The house and its garden, rock garden and swimming pool fell into other hands entirely.

The Kamnik mountains rise skyward, high in the background. On the nearby hill there are no buildings, save for the few farms huddled along its rightmost edge. Through the window, a ruddy light pierces the twilight. The scene reminds Silva of a winter postcard.

She returns inside. Her feet slow on the stone stairs. She begins to count her steps—she passes two-hundred before she tires of counting. The thought dawns on her: this was once a refuge for wild lovers whose reputation or position forced them to hide away. Today, she will try to reimagine all that was long ago buried here. The house will come alive. She will breathe all her love into it, all her womanliness and hospitality. At midnight, yes, precisely at midnight, she will say what she already should have. If the company is right, she'll say it aloud, and if not, she'll whisper it into France's ear. The lights will go out while the fireplace radiates its light and soothing warmth. Champagne will rustle in crystal goblets …

When she got back, France was in the kitchen.

"I was thinking of renting the house for our entire vacation in the summer. Wouldn't that be swell? Fresh air, short trips into the hills, swimming in the pool before the house. Have a look at pictures in the room. That's how the house looks in the summertime—all vines and flowers. The blue pool conjures the sea."

"We'll think about it. Summer's still so distant! Winter still has snow to pile on us. If we're snowed in, we'll have a hard time leaving this fairy-tale cottage."

"I think we'll stay here. We'll prolong our vacation and delight in our contentment. We'll have everything we need: the love we have for each other. Sometimes I still think myself an unsated man, so let us love unreservedly."

"For the moment, certainly. I cannot imagine a more perfect way to celebrate."

France's hands once again gripped her full, shapely form. His voice quavered, and Silva could feel his heart beating rapidly. She felt fresh and rested herself. Saying something probably wouldn't have been the worst idea.

In silence, their bodies fused and tensed like a guitar string.

"Instead of the night, sweetheart," he whispered in her ear. And that was all. During unions like this, any loud utterance is an unnecessary one …

The large wall clock has struck eight. On the platform in front of the house, the thumping of shoes intermixed with indiscernible hollering and gleeful laughter. The company's arrival was boisterous: two men and three women. The men put down their bags. The girls begin to lay out food on the table. As soon as they were acquainted with Silva, the visibly youngest among them, Adela, began to gabble:

"We barely made it up; there are so many of these damned stairs. And what's more, they're slippery! If it hadn't been for the wonky railing, we'd have found ourselves lying in the snow more than once."

"Even with the fence there, you ended up in the snow three

times. Just admit it," said Tone, a smiling man of about thirty with an athletic build and handsome face.

"Is it at all strange, when you wouldn't stop trying to trip me?" she shot back.

"He wouldn't have dared if your Goran had been here with us," returned Tone's fiancee.

France, who was taking care of the coats, chimed in:

"Oh right, the door is still open. Say, where is Goran, anyway?"

Adela blushes faintly and says:

"I don't know, something's got into him again. He simply did not want to come. He said he would later. He's so difficult when he's stubborn. But anyway - let's not let him ruin our night. Let him sulk; I intend to dance."

Maria, the calmest among them, a dark-haired woman of roughly twenty-five, glances at her fiance, Miran, then says to Adela:

"Dance? Oh, well have a look at her, then - only if we lend you a dancer. You're at our mercy now."

"Oh, how cocky she is! I presume that, in the interest of democracy, the ladies will as well be allowed to vote? I shall choose whomever I please. And if you decide to be stingy, I shall have to bring a gentleman. There's one downstairs I've already arranged with."

"You know we're only joking. We won't be breathing down anyone's neck tonight, nor shall we think twice before speaking," says Tone's Milena with a hint of self-importance.

The generously laden table beckons. The soft music compels the feet to move, while drink slowly beguiles the mind.

The first dance. Adela goes to the gramophone and laughs:

"Now you'll all dance the way I want you to." And it was true: now she shifts the needle on the record, now she adjusts the revolutions. It's all rather amusing at first.

"Not that way, Adela. You'll destroy our favorite record," Silva remarks.

"Forget the records! They've loads like this and better for sale at the store. I'm having a blast watching you, how slowly you adapt to the new rhythms. Watching is fine and dandy, until it becomes tempting to join in."

"You'll have your chance. Don't worry! We three fellows should be more than enough to tame you," Rick was first to oblige as he stepped forward.

After that, there was indeed a trading of places.

Silva changes out the beautiful Viennese Waltz record for another. Adela is turning with France and is smiling sweetly. The grey eyes beneath her well-proportioned eyebrows dart about the room, then stop on France's face. France looks at her, continues to dance, then turns to face Silva. He can make nothing of that searching, uneasy look.

Once the dancing has reached its conclusion, everyone takes their seat at the table. Miran remembers:

"Where have we got our playing cards, boys?"

Milena objects:

"Oh no, we're not playing now. There will be plenty of time for that later."

"If we continue to guzzle our drinks so diligently, soon we won't know *how* to play. Why, only France is drinking in moderation. He can play for all of us. Of course that means he'll be able to play dirty at cards. But not at anything else …"

"Lads, someone has to stay sober. Who'll show you the way to the valley? We'd all break our legs," France speaks his excuse.

"Do you really think we'll be going home soon? We've got two days' time. We'll eat, drink and make love here," Milena interjects.

"If my Goran actually manages to show up, that is. Otherwise there shall be no loving whatever! I'm no saint to watch you here in your opulent bliss. Nay, the very mention of it makes me want to leave, and if I so much catch sight of it, it drives me mad."

"Oh, stop it, Adela. Your tongue is about all that goes mad," Marija says in her defense.

The atmosphere grows increasingly tense. Wine intoxicates heads that are already. The bodies of beautiful women in revealing dresses offer themselves. Miran speaks:

"Silva, would you be a dear and make us some coffee to

calm us down, or I fear we just might burst."

"It isn't time for coffee yet, it's normally drunk nearer morning, but I'll make some if you wish. Everyone for coffee?"

"Of course, go ahead and brew us a whole pot. And fetch us some cake, will you?"

Silva makes her way to the kitchen. Her work is accompanied by the unpleasant feeling that she has unwillingly been made hostess, instead of being in the the company of the guests herself. With some reluctance, she reaches for the pastries and places them cursorily on the plates. She finds and prepares the cups she had forgotten about earlier. She puts on the coffee and returns to the room some fifteen minutes later.

It was dark. By the fire's glow, she could only briefly make out two figures sitting on the couch. Strangely, everything suddenly went quiet. The door leading from the living room to a smaller chamber was ajar; even from there, unintelligible voices were all she could hear. Her legs became heavy, and she returned unnoticed to the kitchen. A minute or so later, someone walked through the anteroom and past the kitchen door. A door from the anteroom led into a small room, which was ice-cold. Her disquiet was growing: Until now, all four of them had been gathered in a single room ... now, somebody had departed into the lonely dark. Would their love keep them warm? They were the only ones left there now ...

She cautiously left the kitchen. She came to a halt in the corridor before the little room. Passionate words and restless movements betrayed the couple.

"France ..., you're ... divine. I can't ... forget. You love ... me. Goran ... is nothing."

Silva's vision was blurry. Her heart was pounding, her knees were buckling. Her mouth is tightly shut; her chest draws no breath. She is as cool as ice. She must concentrate and listen all the way through. She had never heard such dialogue ... And now they were bartering for her ... proud Silva. Disgusting!

"It's true ... You're a woman, Adela ... Untamed ... passionate like a tigress ..."

"And Silva ... Do you love her?"

"Leave that ... I can't ... think clearly ... Not, not when

I'm with you … You're always … the same … intense. I'll always look for you …"

Not another word was spoken … only actions. Silva grits her teeth to stop herself from screaming. She could scream and it wouldn't change a thing. They have been meeting and will continue to do so - they have become physically attached to each other and have been for who knows how long. Her relationship with Goran was merely an excuse and he a helpless puppet.

A puppet, but is she not one herself? What is she doing here? Get out of here! And quickly, or someone might be woken from their sweet dreams … Perhaps by the aroma of coffee …

She immediately fetches her purse. She hastily tears a page from her calendar and nervously scrawls:

"Cheated and offended, I am leaving. Know, however, that I am giving birth to our child in June."

She carefully gropes down through the darkness and manages with difficulty to join foot to stair. No light issues from the house; even the fireplace has spent its flames. Everything has darkened. Even the stars have conspired against her. There is no brightness to be found anywhere to show her the way and ignite so much as a spark in her desolate soul. The cold cuts into her face and weighs so heavy on her chest that breathing has become a chore. There, the stair ends here, now for a few more feet of pathway. Then comes the road and the houses by it, houses with lights, great bright lights that tonight illuminate the people and their homes. Yet every light within her has been snuffed out … Tears stream down her cheeks and seem to freeze in the process. She does not wipe them away, as tears wash away the pain.

The snow squeaks beneath her slippery soles; her arms occasionally swing in the air to help her catch her balance. Straight ahead along the path … right to the station. Her perseverance is with her; she would not have lasted were it not, not earlier, before the door, not now, walking in a foreign place on the brink of midnight. Down there lies the station …
It's lit. It represents the only hope in this all-devouring darkness.

There are no passengers at the station. Because she does not know the timetable, she asks the only employee ambling there.

"Excuse me, is there another train headed for Ljubljana?"

"In ten minutes," responds he, looking her over and nodding in a somewhat peculiar fashion.

She cares not at all now about what he thinks of her; she is herself incapable of thought. Her brain petrified and went utterly numb as she witnesses that scene, which is sure to never leave her consciousness.

When the train came whistling in from Upper Carniola, she breathed a sigh of relief. She squeezed into the corner of the cold compartment and shot a glance through the foggy window at the hill where she had only two hours ago happily expected a grand declaration of love.

In the living room, a lamp was burning.

"So the merrymaking has only just begun … or ended. I had no idea that France was so bold or drunk. I had never known this side of him," she whispered bitterly to herself.

Belgrade had now become her city more than ever before. She no longer wanted to so much to know about Ljubljana, or anything else. Everything that had once been so precious had now withered away. Only in her a new life was sprouting, and because of this new, unwanted life, she will sooner or later have to quit her job. She will have to stow her snug uniform. The airplane, her white butterfly, will have to take off without her. Another person will walk from person to person, offering coffee, newspapers … Someone else will have to encourage the frightened passenger who is on her first flight. And the pilots, her friends, brothers in distress and off-duty admirers will wonder where she's gone. And it had all been so wonderful … It is true that she had once silently wanted a quiet family life, which is why her nights in the air over the sea were so relaxed. But now, a sudden horror befell her: She will lose her blue skies, have a fatherless child and be forced look for a job in some little rural town. A fall from white clouds onto the hard black ground!

"No, that's not what I want! And my child must die because

of it! I shall find a doctor this very day," she says to herself again and again to squelch her nature, her very self, as she had never given the idea any consideration. This grotesque resolution in no way comported with her inner voice. She was loath to think about death, whether her own or anybody else's. Yet now, everything had perished: a quiet home on the edge of Ljubljana, a serene family idyll with France and a child by her side ...

France is gone ... He still exists, but not for her. Adela has torn him from her ... Perhaps solely for the sake of carnal pleasure. In that regard, Adela was formidable ... He could not refuse her. She could only guess how many times they had deceived her. But then why had he even bothered to call her to his side? He had in fact mentioned something to her: she was *serious*, he had said, by which he had perhaps meant to say that she was cool. She was not; she was simply incapable of giving up until the end.

Oh, drive away these thoughts! It's all in the past now! There is no more New Year's, no more villa, no more anything. Everything has faded from consciousness; her thoughts have become frozen solid by the tall old building, her footsteps have stalled. Her eyes traversed the sign, and her brain registered reality: Gynaecology Clinic. Two months have passed since she was last there. Now she is here a second time, and with completely different intentions ... There are at least twenty women in the waiting room. She'll wait. She is a persistent woman, and she will manage just fine in this confined space where the dry, warm air uncomfortably intermingles and settles in the lungs and on the soul.

She sits without a care and looks only from time to time to the door, through which women enter at quite a fast rate. Then, for a time, none come through. The woman sitting next to her shifts anxiously in her seat and, in a low voice, says:

"She's been gone for a long time. If it doesn't work now, her marriage is through. This hope is the last thing keeping them together. The husband sorely wants a child. He told his wife he'd go elsewhere if they wouldn't have one. He's a wealthy man and worries that his fortune will end up in someone else's hands."

"Oh, how can he be so selfish!? There are plenty of other children, and as for his wealth, he can always give some of it to the poor. If he hasn't got any children, there are others who've got too many," mused the woman on the far end of the bench. In that moment, an elegant woman of around thirty walked into the room. Her face was pale, her eyes large and sad, and her gestures languorous, all of which signified in her defeat. Her eyes met her friend's and she shook her pretty head. They all understood …

The silence has settled between those white walls and robbed the women in the waiting room of any shred of courage they had summoned up in conversation earlier.

It wasn't until a good hour later that the nurse called Silva in. She took a moment to nervously run her hand over her luxuriant hairdo, swallowed, and attempted to gather her thoughts. In vain, for they had all dispersed.

She let out a good few coughs, as though to, at least temporarily, smother the bitterness that would behind these white doors infest the entirety of her being.

The doctor, whose head of rich, black hair was already interspersed with silver strands, gazed through his spectacles and examined Silva from head to toe. He might as well have been reading her mind, for he said:

"Please, have a seat."

Silva sits down, sees the doctor's placid expression and straightforwardly says:

"Please, I'm pregnant." With the utterance of this one amelodic, colorless sentence, she at once felt unburdened and relaxed.

"I may even remember. I'm the one who told you."

"And now, now I'd like to … *cancel* my pregnancy … You know, doctor, the boy is not serious. I cannot rely on him any more. And besides …" she spoke incessantly, so she would not have to begin anew.

"My dear girl, I can only offer you my words to help you, my advice. Nothing more. The committee makes these decisions. The only question is whether it is not yet too late. Why did you not come sooner?"

"Sooner? Yes, well … I did want to come sooner, it's just … We were discussing the wedding."

"And now? Can nothing be mended anymore? You young people are like a flood. Once the water stills, it settles back in its riverbed and flows calmly onward."

"No! I don't want to! I cannot. I know the word *forgiveness*. But he did not even ask me for that. A woman must be proud as well as loving."

"I won't resolve your arguments; I will not even get involved in them. That is not my job."

"I understand."

"Are you certain you've made your decision? Have a look inward ... You know, these walls say nothing of the fates of our visitors.. Yet this is precisely where bitter truths are learned. The eyes of many a child must forever close because of one misstep on the part of the mother. I would not want you to follow that course. There was someone just today with whom I had to share this very observation. But now it is too late. Many women are granted motherhood, though some are only granted it once. If that opportunity is neglected, it is gone forever.

Do as you believe is right. You're a healthy, adult woman. Rash decisions in life are seldom successful. Sleep on your decision. Tomorrow the sun might be shining and everything might be brighter, including your thoughts."

"I'll do my best to listen to you. I'm sure you can see how I waver ..."

"I'm not sure. Perhaps one day you'll come back angry with me, or perhaps you will return to thank me."

Silva makes her way back. She is somewhat confused, yet relieved. She has stayed a hard sentence on her child. The hand swam through the air and stopped before eyes that in the cold, wintry morning yearned for sunlight. And there, somewhere in the distance, the sun was dimly shining ...

This is how Silva spent her winter holidays—without much rest.

The next morning, she went to work. She was a good quarter

of an hour early to the airport as usual. She chanced on Mira, her lively, tall, fair-haired coworker, who on the occasion opened wide her arms and heartily greeted her:

"Hey, Silva! How did you spend your holidays? Is there a lot of snow in Slovenia? Did you do any skiing?"

"Well, aren't you impatient!? How can I answer when you've got so many questions all at once? It was … all right. What else can I say? I haven't skied yet because the company wasn't right."

"Let's go upstairs. There'll be more time to chat. I have to tell you that Milan was a tad disappointed that you just disappeared the way you did," Mira revealed to her somewhat furtively.

"Milan? What? Why? Last time he only asked me if I wanted to stay in Belgrade, and that was it."

"What did you tell him?"

"That you had gone home. I didn't mention your romantic rendezvous. You can tell him about that yourself if you want to."

The machinery started with a deafening buzz.

The great white bird has come away from the earth. The passengers sit quietly. Some look about and are frightened, while other read their newspapers with confidence. Most simply lean to this side or that and nap in their seats.

As the aircraft rises above the clouds, of which only the shadowy side is visible to the passenger, Silva follows them with her eyes.

"When everything is so dreary, why would the clouds be any fairer and better? Everything conforms to the time and place. Still, I cannot help but feel sorrow at the sight of these glum companions of planes. As soon as they burst, one's eyes can relax above the beautiful panorama that unfolds as we sail over cities; over rivers that criss-cross like silver threads among the peaks and forests. But it's all final now, Silva. You will fly over worlds familiar and foreign only a handful more times, and then land on ground—on solid, steady ground!"

Suddenly, Silva sees on the seat before her a pale woman. She immediately steps to her and asks:

"Pardon, are you alright? Can I get you some coffee or tea?"

"I don't know which would be better. I already took a tablet downstairs, but it hasn't helped."

"Have a sip of this, it'll help right away. Is this your first time travelling by airplane?"

"Yes, it is. I'm also quite afraid," she finally admitted.

"It's a nice, peaceful flight. There's no reason to worry. The weather is favorable as well."

She took a stroll all the way to the captain's cabin. The passengers were calm. She stumbled upon Mira, who said to her:

"Our examination is in fourteen days. Have you begun preparing?"

"Oh, that's right. I'd forgotten that the year is almost through. But anyway, I don't think things like hygiene and healthcare and things like that will give us too much trouble. I mean, not much can have changed since last year, right? I might not even bother taking it."

"What do you mean?" Mira asks, bemused.

"Exactly what I say."

Thus, Silva migrated from the blue heights to the ground. She found work at the same airline, though the work she was doing was completely different. For her, the flights were over … except for the distant thundering of departing white airplanes—she still heard that daily at the same time as before. At first, that sound thudded in the ears and seemed to mar her very being. Her eyes follow the plane until it is veiled by a curtain of clouds, then she feels a stinging sensation in her eyes and a warm trickling on her pale cheeks … She sat and began to sort her correspondences and respond to them. Loud, hard footfalls in the corridor signaled that a man was coming. As there came a knock, the door opened.

"Good day, Silva! How are you feeling amid that mountain of papers?" he asks briskly.

"It's nice of you to have come, Milan. Not many people wander here. Almost all mail is brought and taken by a courier. You asked me how I'm feeling. I suppose I'm managing; I hope I'll get used to it. Have you also brought me work?"

"No, not today. I've come ... I've come to ask you out to dinner with me tonight," he said, embarrassed.

"I don't know. I'll have to give it some thought. Is there something you're celebrating?"

"No, but I wish there were. I wanted to invite you out for New Year's, but you just ran off on me."

"Oh yes! New Year's is already behind us now. It's almost time to think about Easter."

"You haven't given me an answer yet," he persisted.

"Alright, why don't you call me, just in case," she said to him without taking much time to consider.

The cold wintry evening stretches on endlessly. Silva sits by the electric furnace in the dark and weighs: should she go or decline the invitation? Milan, a round, chubby man never represented ideality to her. But what good were ideals now? An ideal had betrayed her and left her high and dry. Perhaps she would find more of a human streak in Milan, she thought, so she slowly rose, turned on the light and began to embark on a journey into the unknown.

When there came a ring at the door, she was already prepared for sweet vengeance and forgetful dalliance alike.

"Come in, have a drink!" She invited him in.

"Thank you, but we can do that at dinner."

They got in the Fiat 600 and drove off. They exchanged few words on the way to the restaurant. Milan was very emphatic in his expression, just as she had always known him to be. And she, with the exception of everyday things, had nothing to say.

The compact but elegantly furnished restaurant was virtually brimming with guests. In the fore corner sat a few gypsies who were churning out some unknown melody of theirs.

After dinner, they danced together for the first time.

"I'm happy, Silva. I am allowed to call you that, right?" he whispered in her ear.

"You are; why wouldn't you be? We could have long ago dropped the cold formalities."

"I love you," he did his best to sound gentle.

Silva says nothing. Her feet follow the beat, her eyes stare blankly. Her body is locked into a rigid armor; only her legs yet move freely. Something is meant to awaken now, to react. But she knows nothing, neither in spirit nor in body. Vacant, grim, futile ... She tried to form a smile, to appear happy. She could not. Perhaps the memory of France was too vivid, perhaps the offense he had caused her ran too deep. But neither notion had anything to do with Milan.

The pair return. Milan holds the steering wheel with only his left hand; his right hand seeks hers. The car stops before her apartment.

"May I escort you up?"

"No, Milan. Another time. Forgive me, I'm very tired today. There will be another time."

"I hope so. If you were to agree to it, we could dine together every evening," he said, seeming not the least bit affronted.

"Good night, Milan. We'll work something out."

And thus they began to go out for dinner together. Nothing special happened between them. Silva was perplexed by this secretive relationship, which after a week had not progressed beyond gauche hugs and kisses. She now began to look for fault in herself: perhaps she truly is nothing more than a pretty ice sculpture. Had she not detected a similar sentiment in France before? It would be impossible for a man not to find her desirable if she were normal.

She resolved that she would not object if Milan wanted to come into her apartment with her tonight. Her studio apartment was directly adjacent to the third-floor elevator, which made it easy for her to steer clear of prying eyes.

Saturday evening. The time is nine o'clock. The two are back at the house. Silva hesitated briefly, then said, directly:

"If you wish, I'm prepared to make coffee tonight. We can always get sleep tomorrow."

"Very well, but it was your idea. After the first time you refused me, I decided I would wait for you to invite me in yourself."

"Is that so? I didn't know that," she says with a smile as she opens the door to the apartment.

"You've got a comfortable place here," he notes as he looks

about the apartment.

"If it had central heating, I'd never want to move out."

Now that they were both here, Silva suddenly became excited at a thought that she had endeavored all week to relegate to her subconscious. She must tell him the truth: at any rate before he himself notices. Maybe today, perhaps tomorrow, or never. She will see in what way the matter develops.

She is preparing coffee in the kitchen. Milan has turned on the radio in the living room. She has returned to the room with a tray and the warm smile of a hostess. She has barely set the coffee on the table when the doorbell rings. Both of them wince.

"Don't get that," Milan suggested.

"I really should. It could be someone from the bureau; it could be post from home," she voices her decision and heads toward the door.

Without asking who it is, she opens it.

"Good evening, Silva."

"Good evening. What is it you want, France?"

"Well, you don't have to be quite so rude to me, you know!"

"I'm only as rude to you as you were to me then. What do you want?"

"To speak with you."

"Now? At this hour?"

"Yes of course, now. This is, after all, the third evening I've looked for you; you're never home."

"I'm afraid you're an unwanted guest tonight," she returned and went to slam the door in his face."

"I don't care about that at all right now. We need to talk."

"All right, go ahead."

She opened wide the door into the room.

"Good evening," he extended an ironic greeting to Milan.

"Good evening!" replied the latter as he turned to face the evening guest.

"Milan, this is my former boyfriend!"

While Milan seemed to be fidgeting with something, France's eyes blazed angrily. Milan gets up. France's disdainful look pauses on the shorter, stout figure that moves now in the direction of the door. The tension in the air was palpable until Milan said:

"Good night, Silva!"

"Good night! Give me a call tomorrow!"

"I've come to apologize, but now it seems there's nothing to apologize for. I see you're living quite the life of comfort here, and that you've got company to boot." He tried in vain to sound composed.

"I do. Did you perhaps think I'd be retiring to a monastery after you'd played me like that? I still don't know whether you invited me into your home that night purely to insult me or whether you'd lost your mind."

"Silva, that sort of thing can happen to anyone. As a bright woman, you could understand that. Alcohol bewitches the mind, but, sadly, not the body."

"You weren't that drunk. Not drunk enough to forget what you were doing."

"And therein lies the evil; if a man is too drunk, there's nothing more that can possibly go wrong. Besides, I'm not convinced talking was all you did with that friend of yours."

"France, I don't intend to speak about that."

"Silva, how could you trade me for a pansy like him! How could you not value yourself more highly?"

"Milan is no pansy! You have no right to insult him. His spirit is twice what yours is and overshadows even that athletic physique you so flaunt. We're friends, that's all. One must have someone, a companion."

"There can be friendship between a man and a woman only once the flame of passion has already died down."

"That's *your* theory! You always made your own claims. And you're wrong now too. There's nothing between him and me, that's to say, there hasn't been so far."

"Darling, does he even know your situation? I can't believe I'm about to say this … Is he even … capable of being … a father?"

The final few words were fired through trembling lips and hit their mark.

A redness flooded Silva's face and she had to exercise

considerable restraint to prevent her hand from connecting forcibly with his blushing cheeks.

"Go, France! Please leave! Not a word more about this; about anything! You and I are through! You know who I used to be and where we went together and how we lived then. Now it's over. Look, there's the door!"

"No, I'm not leaving!"

"If you have a shred of dignity, you'll go. What was until now somewhere alive, you've completely destroyed. It can't be fixed now, so you need to go."

He straightened, looked her once more in the eyes, which in that moment held no tears, but also no hatred. She watched him calmly as she walked him to the door. In an instant, she slammed it shut, as though by doing so she wanted to shut away and destroy everything that once bound them.

She stayed awake throughout the night. As morning neared, her thoughts strayed from the real to a series of warped, nightmarish, continually shifting and fantastic hallucinations.

The next evening, she did not go to dinner. Her mind had numbed, and there were no more wishes in her anymore. She did not want to see Milan or France. The latter least of all. She fell asleep while reading a book.

At the office, in the amplitude work that she had there, her thoughts scattered. Suddenly, she received a telephone call from Milan.

"Yes, do come! No, he's left ... for good," she said calmly into the receiver.

And so, he entered her apartment. As they drank their coffee, they avoided the more difficult questions that Milan burned to ask and resorted only to small talk. Silva waited for him to do just that and had her answer ready, yet the questions did not come.

After the first kiss, Milan became unexpectedly aroused. Silva did not resist. Silently, she nodded as the excited man whispered a few impassioned words in her ear. Piece by piece, underwear dropped onto the chair. Milan observed this ritual closely, as he considered it necessary to heightening of his desire. The lights go out. Two bodies find each other in one embrace.

Silva is disappointed. Her whole body feels strange, stiff. Not a single string of passion rings or vibrates. What's with her? Milan's heavy body lies as though lifeless by her side. He, too? Or only he? No, there exists no mutuality here; they cannot find each other … Only disappointment, which stymies her every word and is expressed only by means of a steady sighing.

One of them must break the silence. Milan feels that the guilt is his.

"Silva, I feel awful about this. This happened to me all the time … Which is why I didn't succeed anywhere … It's easy to see … I'm very unhappy … I dared not approach you for fear that I would lose you."

"Don't say that, Milan! It might improve one day. We'll get used to it. You're giving up too quickly. You see, we all have our misfortunes."

"Even you?" he asks with relief in his voice.

"Yes, even me. My bad luck just happens to be of a different kind."

"I was thinking that you, as a woman, were incapable of being completely detached. And I … cannot be certain I will ever be able to make you happy. I love you. But love cannot take place exclusively outside the bedroom. I'm worried you'll become frigid at my side. I've consulted the doctors, but it was no use. It's killing me. I want to make a home for myself, a family, but …"

"Milan, you saw it last night. He was my boyfriend once, and not so long ago. We loved each other before he wounded me deeply. I do not carry much of our love with me anymore, but … I am pregnant. With his child …"

"Are you speaking the truth or did you make all this up just now?" he asked her in an indeterminate tone.

"The truth, my dear! This I wanted to tell you the day before yesterday, before *he* arrived. I did not wish to string you along that you would continue inviting me to dinner every evening. If I'm to be completely frank with you, I should let you know that I only became attached to you because of your honest nature. Now you know. Think about whether we can continue to be friends."

"When are you expecting?"

"At the end of June, perhaps in early July."

"And why did the two of you break up?"

"That's a rather lengthy story. I don't enjoy digging up old memories, so please be so kind as to spare me that. Now he's come for reconciliation, but we've only become more distant."

"Was I the cause of it?"

"Of course—our meeting vexed him so that he's rolled the burden of fatherhood onto you."

"Silva, I would be a happy man if that were true, but sadly it might never be."

"Milan, we owe each other nothing. I was afraid of telling you this, but it came naturally and without much difficulty. You see, I've accepted the fact that I'm going to have a baby. As for men, they will only occasionally have the privilege of being my friends."

"Even I?"

"Yes, even you. Milan, go home and think everything through on your own time. If you can overcome your own self-importance and manly pride, then you'll be free to come over. Provided, of course, that it is love and respect that bring you to me, not pity. Bear in mind the notion that
I will soon begin to change. My slender figure will grow round, my face will pale, perhaps my skin will become strewn with nasty brown spots. Will it not bother you that the heart of another man's child beats inside me? If all that is something you'll want, you'll need, in addition to patience, a healthy measure of nobility. I won't hold it against you if you decide never to show up again."

"You're right—we've given each other too much to think about to make a decision right away. It's midnight. I'll go home and give everything a good thinking-through. Silva, if I'm not back soon, I promise you that we will never mention any of this to anyone and that I will live as is expected of a family man and father. I will care for the child and everything will be all right."

"You see how easy it is for mature people like us to come to an agreement? Everything is considered and thought through, though I am a little concerned it may be a little *too* rational."

The two bade each other farewell with a kiss. When Silva was alone, she felt satisfied with having confided in Milan and, if she were to be honest with herself, had to admit that she even somewhat enjoyed Milan's powerlessness. Why, she knew not herself. This is that selfsame mark of blackness that surfaces from the depths of even the most noble soul. And revenge ended up proving pointless …

A week went by. Milan was absent. He did not call her on the telephone, nor did he come to her. During the day, she did not think of him, and in the evenings, she would grow bored. She did not love him, and since that last failed attempt, she even found the thought of him unpleasant. But he was a human being, one who had been there, who had shown her the city and conversed with her. Only a month ago she had been in the company of acquaintance and friends, yet now she had torn herself therefrom and confined herself to solitude.

Her fingers reached autonomously for the telephone dial. She called Maria.

"We're celebrating the day after tomorrow. My parents are having their silver jubilee. I had just today intended on coming to invite you," a voice sounded from the other end of the white receiver.

"Will there be many guests?" Silva asks, bearing Milan in mind.

"If you mean Milan, we can invite him."

"No, not at all. We've had an argument. I'll be there, of course I'll be there."

Satisfied, she replaced the receiver. The news of the invitation brought her joy, as did the knowledge that Milan would not be there. At the end of the day, one might have thought that she had orchestrated everything herself.

The biting January north wind chills her face as Silva makes her way to Mira's home. Mira resides in the luxurious city district by the park. When Silva approached the iron fence and opened it with a creak, she involuntarily remembered that one particular night in Upper Carniola. Mira's home is inviting and all of it is well-lit—even the five steps that lead to the main entrance. Two tall stony statues, each capped with a layer of snow, stand guard before the old villa.

Mira and her father are welcoming guests. Another memory, though not a painful one. In good spirits and prepared for a dance, she sat at the table. She had been assigned a place next to a young man who might have been a first-year student at university. He introduced himself as Saša and shared with Silva a few things about his parents. When someone placed a waltz record on the gramophone, several pairs lined up on the dance floor in the large foyer. At some point in the middle of the dance, Saša mustered the courage to ask Silva for a dance. She got to her feet, adjusted her lavish light blue dress and confidently stepped onto the floor.

The young man danced terrifically and even Silva was in the mood to glide across the parquet all the way to the dining room.

Then they danced more, on and on. Every once in a while her eyes would stray to the luxuriantly lit dining room, from behind the tables of which the eyes of Saša's father were following her; perhaps those of his mother were, too. Silva tried to read their thoughts: they were afraid that she would seduce their well brought-up son. Who knows what grand plans they had already arranged for him?

The assemblage of tables beckons the guests to dinner. Couples slowly take their places at their tables. Silva has arrived last. Mira and she were talking. At the conversation's end, Mira asked:

"Saša really knows how to dance, eh?"

"He does. He's yet a young man and ought to be limber. Who are those people?"

"They're Slovenes. The father is a representative of some company or another and the mother works in a pharmacy. Their only son will be graduating this year."

"And how did find themselves here at your place?"

"We Slovenes always find one another somehow. They know my father, and he invited them."

Every right hand has a crystal glass raised to the health of the celebrants and then clinks it with that in a neighboring hand. Silva's gaze lingers on the eyes of Saša's father, who had earlier introduced himself to her as Rajko. This is followed by the tedious clanking of cutlery, after which the guests fall silent and devote their hungry eyes to sating their hunger.

It was Rajko who asked her hand in the next dance. He moved so wildly and youthfully that his greying hair would fall across his forehead. Beneath this wrinkled forehead hid a pair of dark, blazing eyes. Across his upper lip, a thick, brownish tuft of hair, trimmed short, formed the man's whiskers. He was light on his feet, in one moment Squeezing Silva tightly to himself, in the next stepping out of reach, only to make his approach time and time again. Silva knows that a forty-five-year-old like him yearns for the past and chases his own youth. He no doubt envies his handsome son her.

She was right. During a slow tango, he drew himself close to her and directed them both toward the corner beneath the maple steps. She briefly felt the presence of something new and intoxicating in her body. An eerie chill ran through her as she felt the powerful male creature by her side. His eyes were entirely cloudy. The pair could no longer see their surroundings. There was nobody there. Silva caught herself thinking evil thoughts, quickly gathered herself and skillfully led the dancer back into the light.

"Not like that, mister Rajko," she expelled from herself with difficulty.

The man had also stilled himself. A minute or two later, he pressed himself tightly against her body and whispered:

"Miss Silva, where do you live?"

"That's an odd question. You aren't by any chance a detective of some sort, are you?" she said in her most sarcastic vein, knowing full well what he meant.

"I would like to know. I would pay you a visit someday."

For a time she ponders, then, in a flash, as though some sweet melody of desire had resounded again in the distance, she told him clearly:

"Raičeva 15 … On the third floor."

"Thank you, you're a real sweetheart. I really do intend to visit you one day."

The record has ended. Silva stops for a moment in the kitchen. Her hitherto unidentified moral reservations prevent her from sitting at the table with him. Nothing has happened thus far, and this reassures her. Nevertheless …

Mira escorted her to her place. Mrs. Lea, which was the name of Mr. Rajko's spouse, was conversing zealously with her husband. Silva could not detect any dis-ease; though Rajko did not dance with her again.

Dancing with Saša was nothing like dancing with his father. Gently he held her hand, except when he accidentally brushed up against her voluptuous bosom and moved away completely in embarrassment.

His eyes sometimes wandered to that area of ample feminine whiteness amid which was hidden a golden locket.

At the table, Saša's mother engaged in conversation with Silva.

"Young lady, we know that you speak English very well. Our boy, on the other hand, has so much difficulty with the language, that we ask ourselves if he'll ever manage to finish school. Would you be prepared to give up a few hours of your time for him?"

"I do speak English. How good a teacher I would make, I truly do not know. You see, one does not easily take on such a responsibility."

"At least give it a try with him. He had help last year too, but his professor relocated. He's been struggling on his own ever since."

Not feeling particularly enthusiastic about the work she was being asked to do, she accepted anyway. On Wednesday evening, Saša came to see Silva. Under his arm he held a packed briefcase.

"Have a seat, make yourself right at home," she told him, "we'll find out right away where the trouble lies."

"I don't find conversation difficult. Grammar is where things become problematic. Tenses in particular."

"Grammar, that's just a bunch of logical thinking. I also disliked it in secondary school."

Silva searched all the hidden drawers of her memory for various scraps of pedagogic and methodic knowledge that she accumulated during her time at university.

"First, I'll show you how it works in a few specific examples. We'll be changing sentences from the present tense to other tenses."

"All right I understand now. And how do we handle special cases?"

"We will learn that. You cannot grasp everything in one day."

An hour and a half later, they concluded their lesson.

As the young man was leaving, he managed to utter, with some embarrassment:

"My parents told me to ask you if you'd rather come to our house for the lessons. Our apartment is big and warm. I'm most used to working in my own room."

"I could, though I would have to come a little later. Let's have our first lesson on Friday afternoon, shall we?"

Saša's parents live on the third floor.

Silva arrived at the top of the stairs a little out of breath because the elevator was, just as in her building, out of order.

Saša's mother warmly welcomed her in, led her to the dining room and offered her a coffee with cream and a pastry.

"Oh, we cannot simply begin with food. I must keep an eye on my figure, you know."

The woman looked over the girl in a white pullover and black skirt and said in a tone of flattery:

"You really have no need of all that. You cut a figure so fine it may as well have been chiseled by hand. Though if memory serves, we were not plagued by overweight when we were young, either."

The boy grasped the material quickly. As a result, Silva felt she had to say, before leaving:

"He has a very good grasp of it, Madam. I think he was having trouble because he wasn't studying regularly."

"What do you think, does he perchance not even need help?" the mother asked.

"I'll come over like this once a week to make sure there's nothing he doesn't understand."

"Thank you, we'll take care of the payment later."

"We'll make no mention of payment until he's improved his grades!" she replied before leaving.

On her way home, she came across Mira and five of her coworkers from the airport. "Ah, here you are roaming the streets, and we've left no stone unturned to find you," Mira told her, a smile on her face.

"That's right, dear girl, you're coming with us now. It's Goran's birthday," Ivo, the pilot, chimed in.

"How did you slip past us like that? Ever since you've settled with those bureaucrats, you don't even want to know us friends of the blue skies anymore."

"Don't hold it against me - I honestly couldn't tell left from right among all those papers. But it's better now. You'll see that I'm still the same old Silva."

"Right, you can show us all tonight. Goran, where are you inviting us?" Mira went on.

"Let's eat at *Pri ribi*. They have nice service there and the gypsies keep their bellows busy."

"Boys, there are five of you. The two us won't be dancing with all of you," Silva pointed out.

"Goran, hop in your vehicle and and bring Marina and Vesna back with you."

The restaurant *Pri ribi* transformed into a veritable beehive of activity. The merry disposition of the young couples had spurred the other guests to the dance floor. Silva spent the entire evening dancing. She felt good in the company of her friends. She did, however, remain detached. She wants to form no attachments. She likes all of these boys equally well, is as kind to one as to the next and bears each of them the same smile. She wants to be everyone's friend and nobody's lover. That's the only way she can please everybody. Everybody but Goran. While the pair dance, he embraces, squeezes, kisses and trembles with excitement by her side. Perhaps that enticing exhilaration of the body will return. But it doesn't ... It appeared only once - when she was with old Rajko.

At the table, it was melancholy that filled her. It came from some deep within her soul. All that jolly company, all these people whom she knew would in a month or so be thoroughly disappointed. They will look at her with pity when she will no longer be able to dance with them , and wonder who the father is. Maybe they'll even suspect one another, but they will never learn the truth, the truth she will not reveal even to Mira.

In the heat of the night, nobody wanted to give thought to merriment's end. Yet when the clock struck twelve, it was time to go home. One final slow dance. Silva enjoys it, her face still aglow from some hidden satisfaction. Goran kisses her eyes, her neck. She feels him next to her in all his masculinity, but nothing within her stirs. Her inner disquiet urges unceasingly to be let out and makes her ever more certain that of the relaxed dances left to be had, this will be the last. This is the swansong of her youth ... She therefore extends everyone her farewell hurriedly and avoids Goran, who is waiting for her in his car ...

Once more she sits in her office. Because she stayed awake nearly the entire night, she wishes someone would bring her a coffee. Sips of the warm and fragrant beverage reinvigorate her and so enable her to return to work.

The telephone rings. Being accustomed to receiving at least as many as ten calls every day and each time concerning nothing but an order, her hand reaches automatically for the receiver.

"Oh, Goran! How nice of you to remember. I feel well. How are you?"

"I cordially invite you to a dance that is to take place tomorrow evening. We've danced a great deal, but not quite enough."

"Thank you, Goran. Really, I shan't come. I danced yesterday. Now I've had enough and do not wish to dance any more.

Don't ask why. You'll find out some day."

"I'm sorry, Silva."

"I am too. I always wanted to belong to *all* of you, not just to one of you. We all understood one another too well for me to risk harming our camaraderie."

"I will still call you. Perhaps you'll be in a better mood the next time I do."

"Perhaps. But I cannot promise you anything."

She never heard from him again. He remained only a respectful comrade to her, and they would meet on occasion. He would walk down the street, see and greet her, then simply walk away, as though he was embarrassed to have forgotten himself that one time.

By chance, the two met in the shop. He was buying a gold women's ring.

"Silva, please come and help me pick something out," he asked of her politely.

"If it were for me, I'd have a hard time choosing. The only jewelry I wear is my necklace."

"A memento?" he asked.

"A memento," she answered calmly.

"When buying precious stones, you must take into account the color of the person's eyes," she said didactically.

"You don't say?"

"What color are her eyes?" she asked without a trace of embarrassment.

"Well, you know her - Marina. Now then, let's make a selection. It's her birthday."

"Marina, Marina ... oh yes, I know. Take the one with the blue stone. It's beautiful, she'll be very happy. Is it the one from then?" she asked him with a hint.

"Something like that. Forgive me, you know I tried with you as well."

"I know, but I think it was more the alcohol speaking than

your heat. I understand and I don't hold it against you."

"There, you're a smart woman. All women should be like you."

"When you're not all hurt or offended, you can be too."

On Friday afternoon, Silva remembered that she must visit her pupil. Making sure to not forget anything, she was getting ready to leave. Finally, she stepped before the mirror; she looked herself over and noticed that a tight belt is still capable of concealing well her condition. There is not yet any sign of pregnancy. In addition, she feels good. The tight-fitting crimson dress gave her a slim-enough look. Her strands of lush hair, flowing freely across her shoulders, lent her somewhat pale face a touch of romance. To complement her dress, she quickly applied lipstick of the same colour. For whom? This she does not want to consider. She'll make use of these remaining few weeks and be presentable to the world.

With a light touch, she presses the doorbell. From the corridor, she hears the approaching of heavy footsteps. Mr. Rajko opens the door.

"I have come to see what my pupil is up to."

"Come right in. You may leave your coat here."

He turned deftly and took off her coat. The door to the living room is open. There is not a soul in sight.

"Is your son not at home?" she asks surprisedly.

"He'll be here. I also am waiting for him."

"And where is the Madam?"

"At work. The afternoon shift is hers this week."

"I'll wait a bit, and then I'll be off. The boy can give me a call."

"We can have one drink, make a toast."

"If you insist. But not something too strong. I don't drink spirits."

"Let's see, we have maraschino, chocolate liqueur and brandy. Please, choose."

"I'll have half a glass of maraschino, please."

"Cheers, miss Silva!"

His eyes very soon became cloudy once more. The corners of his eyelids sank, and his hand reached to lightly touch her.

"Cheers, mister Rajko!" she uttered reluctantly. She emptied her glass and in a flash had risen to her feet.

"Thank you. I must be going now!"

"No, no, wait … Sit a while longer. I want you to be here," he stammered as he clutched at her hands.

"Let me go. It is important to remain calm! It is precisely in times of temptation that we must control ourselves."

"What? What do you mean by that? You too?"

"I am also only … only a woman, human. Which is why I must now get away from here! I'm sorry, but you're a married man and I'm …"

He slumped back into his chair helplessly. He did not go after her.

She ran to the anteroom, grabbed her coat, turned the key and vanished.

The snow falls and pleasantly cools her heated cheeks as she walks alone toward the narrow street. She feels a kind of mental contentment for having done the right thing; whether the deed was the intelligent choice, she does not know. Not until the chilly wind blew along the street did her perturbed temperament still.

Her return home was nearly a run—some internal force stimulated her feet as well as the rest of her body. To ease her mind a little once she was back home, she donned a long blue robe and began to tidy her room. Carefully, she shifted books from shelf to shelf, wiped away the dust and then put them back in place again. The radio was softly playing a foreign but mellifluous melody. She opened the drawers as well and in one, atop a pile, found her mother's letter. Large, clumsily written words were laid out before her. Whenever she recalled her home, it was never without a measure of nostalgia. To think of all the things she experiences alone in a wide, alien world while her mother lives a quiet life in a cottage among the vineyards …

When was it that her mother wrote this? Ah, she forgot to

write the date. The postage stamp indicates January 27th. Now she will write her mother a reply. But what will she write? How can she disclose to her the truth of her situation? She'll have to reveal it at some point, she won't be able to conceal it forever. But what will she tell her mother? Countless times she has heard her say:

"The boy will harass and beg you until you give in to him. Yet when something befalls you, it is *you* who must seek *him* out for aid."

Mother was basically right in this. But in one sense she was wrong: she, Silva, seeks help from no one, even if the thing mentioned back home only in hushed whispers had already befallen her.

She read the end of the letter:

"And be a good girl. You're surely adequately clever; God knows you've been in schools long enough."

Her mother's advice had come too late. A shame, for she has brought poor mother only shame.

The small, cosily lit room had grown warm. Silva sat and began writing. She has decided to write her mother a wholly ordinary letter; she would still have time for everything else. Why unsettle her mother and brother before she needs to?

From the kitchen she could hear the bubbling of water. She rose to go to brew herself some tea. On her way to the kitchen, the doorbell rang. She cannot for a moment explain her hesitation to open the door. The doorbell, however, knows no mercy and its ringing grates her ears.

Swiftly, she turns the key and opens the door just a crack.

"Good evening, miss," says a man at the door.

"What brings you around here at this hour? Come in, then, for a moment."

"I've come to tell you that the boy has improved his English. He was quizzed this afternoon," he spoke in an apologetic tone.

"Would you like to sit? Forgive me, I'm just preparing supper."

"If you permit me, I would."

He sat in the armchair and waited for her to come. From the kitchen she brought a tray, placed on it two glasses, filled the one intended for her guest, and poured herself only a sip.

"You won't have any yourself? Ah, I remember - you don't drink. You see, that's why I've brought you something different."

"Pretty box of chocolates. But why do you have it with you?"

She set herself down on the couch. Only then did she notice that the collar of her robe was undone a little too much. The man's eyes again lost their shimmer. He did not say anything. Silva got to her feet and headed for the kitchen to fetch the tea; she wanted, for his sake and for her own, to remove herself for a moment.

The man stands up abruptly. His hands and arms take tight hold of her waist and his right hand loosens the top of her robe. His lips meet the pale flesh beneath her neck.

Her knees buckle. They cannot seem to steady … She should say something, but the entirety of her body is frozen in a sweet longing for union. For an instant, everything disappears. The faint pain she feels is obscured in this magnificent moment of pure devotion.

Only several minutes later do the two rest. One of them has to sever the silence, though doing so suits them both.

"I'm ashamed of myself. Never, believe me when I say this: never have I experienced this. I was afraid of you from the very moment we met. You should not have touched me then."

"Silva, we won't be ashamed. We have satisfied our bodies and quenched our natural drives. I haven't felt that in almost ten years. It must have been fate, whether good or ill, that caused our paths to cross, because I thought I was a completely impotent man. Even at our first dance you managed to kindle in me all the forgotten passions of my youth. I love you, Silva. Perhaps not just for that, but on account of something ineffable."

"Is that love? No, dear man, it is only passion."

"Let us not bother with it; they can call it what they please. I am content and know that you are, too."

"My God, is it not awful? You have a wife, a son. I am torn between the voice of conscience and the voice of my body. Eventually, one or the other will have to perish."

"Do not remind me of my son. When he went to see you last

time, I almost went mad. I was jealous of him, even though I had no reason to be. And jealous I shall be of any man who would touch you. I want you to be mine and mine alone, though I know I do not have that right."

"So is that why he wasn't allowed to come here anymore and why I had to come to your home instead? And here I thought it was your wife who feared for her son. I never thought that it was to be a married man who would reveal to me all the secrets and delights this life has to offer. I always condemned women who kept the company of married men. Now I understand them. How old are you, Rajko?"

"I think that following all of this, that is of no consequence. But if you really wish to know, I am forty-three."

"You'll have to forgive me; my opinion of a man of that age was mistaken. No young man could ever awaken my inner woman the way you managed to. And believe me when I say that there were times when I suspected there might be something wrong with my womanhood."

"Nonsense! Your presence could no doubt melt an iceberg, let alone a mere man! When first I laid eyes on you it was clear to me that yours was a fertile but unploughed field."

Every other day Rajko would come to visit Silva in her apartment. Pleasant evenings, filled with the thrill of arousal and therapeutic tranquility, came and went at a steady pace.

The evenings that Silva spent on her own she fulfilled with thoughts of Rajko. Gradually there swelled inside her warm emotions in addition to bodily passions. She contemplated whether she loved him. There was no answer. Love is familiar only with mute speech. Nevertheless, there must be some force at work to explain why she was powerless to resist. But how and why would she? By opening the door to him, she had given him license to do as he desired. Aside from providing each other with pleasures, the pair also conversed a great deal. At his side, Silva matured from girl to woman. She was clever enough to know what she was doing. She is taking the husband from some wife; she could hear the light voice of her conscience, which calmed her with the fact that her boyfriend had also been taken by another woman. But this is no excuse. Lea had not wronged her. Revenge always comes at the expense of someone else. She had loved her boyfriend and had been prepared to sacrifice much for him, and now she was pregnant with his son. Rajko's marriage, on the other hand, is tired. The passion that this man had awakened in her was poisoning her reason and robbing her of her vision. But to what end should she go looking for evil and then repent when she knows that it will come to her at any rate?

The cold wintry morning has turned the streets into a bright skating rink, while the trees have stiffened beneath sheets of frost crystals. She could feel the air's frigidity in her chest, and there was an undesirable prickling in her nose and a stinging in her eyes. People took careful steps along the street and stumbled across the salted pavement. A car stopped behind Silva's back. She heard the words:

"Silva, get in. You can hardly walk."

Milan opened the door and Silva, without a second thought, sat next to him.

"Aren't you bold to be driving when there's black ice on the road?"

"And aren't you bold to have sat down next to me? I do have winter tires, but sometimes the car will simply slide across the road. It'll be better with two of us in the car; it'll be a bit heavier."

"If that's what helps, then consider me willing, in this ghastly weather, to offer you my assistance in increasing the weight of the vehicle. Though, I have yet a ways to travel."

A little before the airport, Milan pulled over. Silva wanted to get out and thought that Milan had forgotten about their agreement. But he asked her:

"Silva, let's talk for a moment. Were you waiting for me?"

"I don't know. I was almost doubting that you'd come. Maybe it would have been better if I hadn't confided in you the truth back then. I could have
waited for both of us to fall properly in love. People in love often overlook things. But I decided to be honest with you and didn't want to leave you with a child like a cuckoo would. Believe me, I'm over it."

"I needed a long time to think things over and now, if you'd allow me, I wish to come with you. I didn't think only about you, but about myself as well. If you've got the patience for it, we'll fix our problems together."

"Everything you've said has been too coldly calculated. I am not like that. I'm not one for drab affairs.

"I'll come with you anyway, if I may."

"Come, then. But I won't be home today. Thanks for the ride. Goodbye!"

She spent the remainder of her trip to the office comparing Rajko to Milan. No, it was not possible to find any common ground between them. And did he really think that she, who had become accustomed to living a full life, would patiently tend to him whenever his strength would leave him? And beside that, he was committing so much time to consideration that it looked as though *she* might be the one dependent on *his* mercy. They could talk to each other, but it was out of the question that anyone whatsoever would be allowed to experiment with her body. She cannot go from one extreme to another.

"Is there something the matter, Rajko?"

"Let's sit down, I need to catch my breath. Your elevator is out of order again, as usual, so I had to properly pant my way up."

"Here, have a gulp of this! What brings you here?"

"Let's leave words out of it for now, dear. There is time for it all."

His firm hands reached over her willing body. His voice was shook and could barely form the words:

"Oh, Silva, how I love you!"

There was a quality to those words that was unusual, plaintive somehow. He dropped his shirt and from beneath the white fabric appeared a darkly overgrown chest. She had seen every part of him, but not by daylight. The skin that gave his body form was still smooth, his muscles taut, and in them was inexhaustible strength.

In silence she surrendered herself and listened in on the stupefying melody that the body sang.

Finished. Rajko remained resting on the couch. He brushed a few curls of hair away from his forehead without once lifting his gaze from Silva. She had covered herself up, and her head rested on a white blanket.

"Oh how I adore you, girl. And how I loved you. All my long faded dreams were revived by your presence. It feels as though it took me at least twenty years to find you. I pursued you without knowing who you were, what you were. Always you would evade me, but your image was constant in the distance , illumined with a mysterious glow of blue or rosy hue. I outstretched both arms to touch this pale silhouette that invited with such allure. I found you. We brought each other bliss, and now ..."

"What now? You spoke like a poet. Do I hear the prose coming?"

"No prose, only a drama in a single act and even that has an unhappy ending. Unless we can be strong enough."

"I don't understand at all. Why did you not mention this before?"

"To ruin even what we have left?"

"Enough! Speak plainly; don't mince words and don't beat around the bush. We're grown-ups."

"My wife found out ... She wants to speak with you. Don't expect her to mince words. She is sharp and quite direct."

"I don't know. Perhaps there are no kind words to be said about a thing like this. It depends only on the person's manners, on the way she expresses them. But I do not wish to meet with her. She has the right of it at any rate, anyone could tell you that."

"Silva, I don't want to lose you. I've become attached to you. And I can't go on living torn in this way. I'd like for us to sort out this matter."

"How do you mean?"

"I'm going to get divorced. We'll talk it over in a fair and humane way. I'm aware of what I'm saying, Silva. I want to a burn with passion, Silva, not feel after it's gone lukewarm. . And I'm not thoughtless, either. You have to believe me when I tell you that you're the first woman to interfere in my marriage, which is why I'm prepared to straighten things out so that you can be my wife for all the world to see."

The look in Silva's eyes was one of indescribable sadness as they fixated on Rajko's unflinching visage. She was fond of his proposal, but she could feel something foreign growing beneath her heart. She swallowed hard but could not prevent herself from breaking into tears:

"Rajko, I could pretend all you like now, about how I'm good and have no desire to ruin your marriage. But it isn't true. I love you and I would accept your proposal, but I cannot. There's something between us, something I can't talk about today."

"I know you can't make a decision right away. But if you truly love me, it suffices that you promise me we shall meet again."

"Go now. I'll call you."

"I suppose it is for the best that I leave. My wife might come looking for me here."

"Rajko, we've made something special out of three weeks of mundanity, and if that's all fate has in store for us, then it's enough. We ought to be grateful. It was wonderful, but one of us has to go … or both."

A void was left in the little apartment, along with the memory of something beautiful and consumed to the point of exhaustion. Gloomy and premature was the setting of the January sun that took with it the scant remnants of light that struggled to pierce the windows …

The next evening, she was expecting Milan. She knows that he will not fill the gap, but she also knows that she is now in need of a strong human hand. He was a good friend, someone she could lean on.

But he did not show up. It was Mira who rang the doorbell in his stead

Pale and frightened, she said from the hallway:

"Milan is dead. He crashed into a lorry. Icy road."

Silva felt dizziness coming on. She sat down on the couch. Mira brought her a glass of water. When she regained her composure, she said:

"I am sorry. I think he was on his way here."

Mira stayed. They talked about Milan and about everything else. The subject of Rajko was the only one they both avoided.

Silva attended Milan's funeral. As he was buried, everything else was buried with him.

One week later, Silva bade farewell to all of her friends. They looked at her with curious eyes and asked her about the reason for her hasty decision to leave them. She told them nothing. Why not leave everyone with good memories of herself?

She gave Rajko a call from the airport:

"I'm leaving. It's all done. There's nothing left for me here. I have nobody here anymore. I want neither to steal you nor to have you permanently. Stay with your people in your world, I am going to look for a new one."

"Silva, now that I'm having everything arranged ... This can't be ... Stay!"

She hung up before the voice that had previously befuddled her wits could seduce her. She was afraid of herself. She no longer had the resolve to overcome the temptation that recently dogged her.

It was the final flight in the body of the white plane. She sits in her chair motionless. Her lips are tightly sealed, and through them escapes not a single breath that haunts her inwardly. The young, dark-haired stewardess had exchanged her shift with her and was pouring her, who was now a passenger, coffee. She quickly empties the cup, then closes her eyes. Tears begin to slowly stream down her cheeks, tears for her white bird, for her good comrades, for a dead Milan, and tears for a great and forbidden buried love.

The clouds once more show the passengers their tenebrous backs. Silva observes them with prophetic words:

"Is it evil you foretell? Much repentance for minor sins?"

The domestic airport was bathed in an afternoon that was at once cold, sunny and bright. Perhaps it portended clear skies and felicity in her future.

"It is fulfilled. I have settled my score with the azure skies. I've slaked my yearning for him, one that dwelt in me ever since I heard the grim howling of that wounded airship during the war ... and the helpless descent with parachutes of its faithful helmsmen."

TODAY

The July sun blazes pitilessly. The pavement exudes heat and the faint smell of tar. Though the windows of the four-story building are shuttered, the employees inside drip with sweat. Three sides of the building that houses the tourist agency, which is what this particular bureau comprises, are caught by the sun's rays, as there is no tree nearby to ever shadow any of its walls.

"No coffee today?" crankily asks a plump official whom one would judge to be forty or fifty. She's the type of woman whose exact age one would never be able to guess. She glances sternly through her glasses and begins to search her papers.

"I'm not sure, it's probably not nine thirty yet," answers a younger employee and wipes her face with a scented tissue.

"Silva, it just hit me! Who are you looking ten years younger for? Fair hair really works for you—you could pass for a teenager. You're glowing!"

"Marica, stop! I had to do myself up. You know I had white hair covering my temples, so I whitened it. Forget about that. Just think, I'm going on vacation tomorrow. Home!"

"Hence the stylish hairdo?" Marica says, smiling.

"I'll get some rest at home; go for walks among the fields, through the vineyards and the forest. Tomorrow, no, the day after tomorrow, Tonček and I will go foraging for mushrooms, and then

… Oh, home, sweet home …"

"It's about time! My, that smells divine! What have you thrown together for us today: some gold, special, minas?"

"It's good, have a taste!" replies an agreeable girl in a white blouse and black miniskirt as she proceeds to knock on the door of the next office.

Silva takes a sip of the warm beverage when the telephone rings.

"Really, right *now*? They won't even let me drink my coffee! Get that for me, Marica!"

"Here, it's for you!"

"Come in here, we need an interpreter," says a voice through the receiver.

Silva walks to the elevator to find it occupied, and takes the stairs to the ground floor instead.

"Good morning," greets a foreign, tall, grey-haired man and gently shakes Silva's hand. "Do you speak English?" he asks immediately with an American accent.

"Yes, I do."

"I am Rick Harris," continues the foreigner, "if that rings a bell."

"Rick Harris … Hang on! I just might remember you!"

His eyes beam directly at her and he seems ready to help her out when she exclaims:

"Rick! Hello, Rick! So nice of you to have come! How on Earth did you find me?"

"I came with the tourists. I was at your house yesterday. You have a nice home. I wouldn't have recognized it, everything's changed so much."

"I'm curious who spoke with you," she smiled sweetly.

"Nobody. I showed this photograph around, this one here, and your brother soon recognized me. It took your mother a while, though. I then told them, more with gestures than with words, that I'd like to see you. It was then that your brother courageously told me: "She speaks English good." I'm not sure how he memorized that phrase, but I doubt he knows how to say anything else."

His blue eyes glowed occasionally, then reverted to staring mundanely from beneath their drooping eyelids.

"You wouldn't happen to have time for coffee or tea, would you?" Rick asks.

"Please excuse me, but my annual vacation starts tomorrow and I still have a lot of work to do. I'm sure you'll still be here. We can continue this later, if you wish."

"Vacation, bravo! They're giving me one, too. So then let's meet in the afternoon at lunchtime, if you'd like. I'll wait for you here. What time?"

"I'll be here, Mr. Rick, around two, give or take. But I'll be here. Thank you."

It's ten past two. Rick saunters along the spacious lobby and looks over the brochures, souvenirs, maps and pictures. The employees have left. The second shift has begun ??. Rick does not appear at all nervous, though he wonders why Silva still hasn't shown up.

At that moment he hears, from the far end of the lobby, a woman's footsteps, and, shortly thereafter, Silva comes into view. Rick, with all his masculine taste, estimates this elegant woman's age at thirty-five (though he already knows her age); her lithe gait, fetching, tall figure and lightly tanned face, embraced by light hair. Underneath gently arched eyebrows, her dark eyes are fixed upon him with what he knows to be critical scrutiny.

"If you please!" He opens the door to his grey VW.

"Thank you. I'll just leave mine here."

"Where did you leave it?" I think it would melt on this asphalt platform if left here all day in the Sun."

"No, there's a sliver of shade for employees on the north side. We park there."

With difficulty, they managed to find a table in the corner of a garden restaurant.

"Recommend something good!" says Rick as they look over the menu.

"I will. I've already decided."

They exchanged little during lunch. Silva's eyes only occasionally met Rick's blue eyes, and she could not glean anything particular from them. From the first look she could tell that Rick cut a full, handsome figure, and that his hands were well cared-for, a thing she had always valued. His face is still well preserved, smooth, sunburnt; teeth in order. His suit is light grey and his hair more so. This monotony is enlivened by a blue tie that agrees with his shirt, white as snow. A charming forty-five year-old whose hair has grizzled too soon, her friend would say.

That was about it. She knew nothing about him, and in honesty did not care to very much. She had already met men like him, had fun with them and then seen them leave. She never mourned them. Rick is average just like the rest, albeit an average American.

"It was great. I've learned that your cooking is delicious. I've known this since then …"

"It wasn't delicious back then. Believe me, we used to starve, though that's something you never felt. Anyhow, that's in the past now."

"What'll we have to drink? Would you like a cold beer or something else?"

"Beer's not for me. I prefer juice or a Coca-Cola here or there."

"Where to now?" asks Rick, once he has paid.

"I'm going to my apartment. And you?"

"I'm staying at the *Turist* hotel, but I'll take you home, if you'd permit me, of course."

"Off we go, then!"

The roads and streets are almost empty. The people have retreated either to their apartments or to the swimming pool. Rick drives carefully and demonstrates his familiarity with the place.

"Okay, make a left here and then another after that. And we're here."

Silva, self-confident though she is, is not quite sure what to do when it's time to step out of the car. Should she invite him in …?

"We're here. You can stop there!"

"Nice building, and all in green. Is your apartment big?"

Because she can do little else now, she tells him:

"If you're not tired I'd like to invite you in for coffee."

"Gladly, I'd love to."

"Please, allow me to open the windows and let through a draught. Just the kitchen and bathroom and it'll be better right away."

Rick's eyes dart from object to object. They stop immediately on a hefty closet, heavily stocked with books. He stands and sees the many foreign writers Silva keeps: James Joyce, Cronin, Goethe. If she has read all this, he gathers while he sifts through the pages, she must be an emotionally mature and learned woman.

"Pardon me, I also went to put on the coffee."

"I've kept myself occupied. I was looking through your book collection, though that wasn't very proper of me. Now I'd like to hear a little about you. I'd like most of all to know where you learned how to speak English so fluently."

"I'm not sure it's quite that good. I took Germanic Studies. My German doesn't flow quite as well. Before I graduated I gave up everything and found a job."

"Here at the travel agency?

"No. I was a stewardess."

"You're kidding! That's great. So then you saw the world."

"Not as much as people imagine I did, but some of it, sure."

"But no more of that? How so? Forgive me if I'm being too forward."

"Have I got to tell you? I left before they could let me go. I'm none the sadder for it."

"You must have been a pretty stewardess. But then I suppose all those girls are sharp and pretty. And to be honest, I think you're still an interesting woman."

"Perhaps once. But let's please not discuss that. I'll fetch the coffee."

"Once … How distant that is. You were a girl then, a maturing, clever girl. I was a boy, full of idealism, though when you met me there was none left," he spoke through the open kitchen door.

Silva placed the coffee and saucer on the table, brought a pastry with her and sat on the couch across from him. Coolly, she filled the cups and offered:

"Let us drink, I believe it's fitting after twenty years."

"Right, there was no coffee at the time. At least not for you." He put down the cup and asked in another voice: "Forgive me, but I think you live alone here."

"You needn't ask me questions so cautiously. I am alone, Mr. Rick. But I'm not entirely alone."

She walks to the cupboard, opens a drawer and shows him a photograph. "This is my son."

Silva expects a little surprise at the very least, perhaps disappointment, but Rick remains placid and turns to her, saying:

"You know, he looks like you. Where is he now?"

"He's gone to his first summer camp this year. Otherwise, he lives at my house. There isn't enough room here us both, so once I pay off the car, I'll buy myself an apartment. Then he'll come to live with me. He needs a home and mother of his own, seeing as he doesn't know his own father."

"He doesn't? Odd, a father like that. The boy is so handsome."

"That's just the way it is. When it mattered most, it seems he forgot how to be a man. Later on I didn't need him anymore. He lives somewhere in Belgrade now. I ask him for nothing and do not write him back. Now you see that I had to leave behind the airplane and its heights. I fell back down to Earth. Here, I've already woken up."

"And today you're a reasonable, experienced, unapproachable woman."

He put particular emphasis on *unapproachable*.

"I'm not sure what you mean by that. Maybe you think I used to be stupid, green and oh-so easy back in the day. That's where you've got it wrong. I was merely in love."

"A thing you could no longer be?" he asks and softly reaches for her hand.

"That's not how it works with me, if that's what you think," she replies sharply and withdraws her hand.

"I like you, Silva."

"Thank you. Don't think that that flatters me any more than

it should. Men five times married seem to think that an older girl must warm up at any cost(??). I'm no longer counting on getting married. I'm fine as I am."

"Silva, allow me to speak in earnest. I was married once. This was my wife." His voice now trembles.

In it can be heard nothing ordinary, but perhaps for sadness or disappointment, as his hands clutch a faded photograph.

The silence has spread between them; it was quiet and more painful than it had been when Silva spoke about herself.

On the fourth day following Rick's arrival, it is still hot. The time nears midday. The car slides along the road towards the river. Silva is giggling. Now and then she turns and looks at the driver.

"You know, Rick, I can't believe it. Life is queer, don't you think? Who'd have thought we'd meet like this some day?"

"And that I would tame you, my indomitable stewardess. Now you'll lead me across your sea. I promise to be an obedient passenger - or pilot. Our first port?"

"Opatija, Rick. Hotel *Slavija*."

By an odd coincidence, the two managed to get a room in the hotel. They spent the first evening sitting on the terrace and gazing at the sea. The ships glistened like silver in the distance under the setting Sun.

"Care to talk a walk with me?" Rick inquires delicately.

"Let's. Can you hear the song ? You can't understand that, can you. I'll translate. It doesn't sound as nice in English. I'll play you this record when you leave; no, I'll dedicate it to you. Your eyes are blue like our sea. I loved that eye color … He had eyes like that too. We sat here. Above his eyes and his prominent forehead there was black hair."

"Silva, *I'm* here now. Please, focus. That's in the past.

"I understand. A good thing that everything ends sometime."

"You never said why you didn't reply to my letter."

"You're a clever one! When you had written me, I could barely read any English, let alone write. You wouldn't have comprehended any of it. Besides, what could you have written besides "thank you', which we all knew and understood. I suppose you meant it when you said it."

"I did, dear. Let's rest. I'm not tired, but I'd like to go to our room. If you're in the mood, you can tell me all about yourself and your family. I'm interested, believe me, since I've often wondered about you all, but it's always been a big mystery."

The lamp casts an unusual shape on the ceiling. A supine Silva retells all she can remember of her early years. Rick faces her and observes her lips' every movement. In his mind he walks with her up a hill, across vineyards, through hidden places. It's all just as it erstwhile was, only two decades later, and these two decades, which in the grand scheme of things are but a moment, have made him from a young pilot into a middle-aged man.

LONG AGO

"We lived in a cottage, as you knew yourself. I owe everything that has grown there today to my brother Ivan.

We were vintners. The cottage had a thatched roof, and a thicket that extended all the way to its back wall. We lived in the midst of vineyards, sunshiny vineyards, amongst ripening grapes and the song of the wind rattles. There was a cart track nearby, which was all dusty in the summertime, and mired in autumn so that our shoes would always sink deep into the sticky loam.

These sun-kissed vineyards also have, however, a darker side, one that we as children knew as well. We, the children of wine-makers! For on our hill also lived farmers' children and those of noble stock who would only come here to visit or for vacation. The large, light-colored storage sheds, which can still be found proudly standing on the hills among vineyards, were the property of the gentry, who resided either in the town or even across the border.

Our storage shed was equipped with a cellar, and a large room and kitchen upstairs. It was only ever opened when the gentry came, or when the space had to be cleaned. Our master had a shop in an Austrian city. Once I started going to school, my mother took me there to buy me my school supplies. This was a real luxury for someone in her first year, since the children of wine-makers rarely even had any supplies, unless they received them in school.

My mother always taught me to socialize only with my own peers and to leave the town children alone and not to force myself to fit in with them. I obeyed her.

My brother Ivan was still little at the time. In the morning, Mother would carry him in a basket with her to the vineyards.

In the afternoon, it was I who had to look after him. When I would return from school, which was a good hour away, work was the last thing on my mind. But at my house, nobody asked you what you thought about it. Work came first, personal needs came second. Man took the place of machine - he would toil in the fields, spray them and then harvest them. That was the reward for all his efforts.

A vintner is simple in his thinking and his actions. When injustice robs him of his sound reason, he gets drunk and swings his hoe at objects or perhaps at people. That's the type of person he is. Nobody can change him. The times today really have changed people somewhat, as well as conditions. Oh, but I don't want to think about all that. It was because of such rash anger that I lost my father.

Should I tell you about him? Must you be interested in everything that happened and was going on, there on your little hill thirty years ago?

I remember my father well. I know that he was strong, tall and that he even caressed me sometimes. Caressing and cuddling were not customary at home; the few times he allowed himself these were clumsy and he later probably remembered them with shame.

My mother was the daughter of a crofter. Her folks were not vintners the way we later were. They owned a cabin, a cow and a few chickens. It's true that this was poverty, but not the kind where you're directly dependent on a master who only keeps you around as long as he likes the look of and you are still able to work.

On the hill opposite ours stands, even today, a lovely farm. It belonged to the Korens. And my mother, a tall and thin crofter's daughter, was their day laborer. Her mother, that would be my grandmother Mima, had got her the job while Mother was still in school.

It was a waste of time and money for a wine-maker to send his child to and from the town square for six years. Mother did not, in truth, walk there every day, but the point stands.

When the spring came, the people were weeding Koren's vineyards. My mother was also among the workers. That day she had absented herself from lessons and was counting on being able to attend the next day when she heard, from behind her, the words: "Mima, your daughter is so big! But it's easy to see that she isn't performing her duties so well. It's your own fault for sending her to school. When did our people ever spend that much time in town!? She can already read and write, can't she? And she'll learn to drag a garden hoe right proper.

My mother swallowed hard, and my grandmother said: "The child is yet learning, let her go as long the law says she must go."

"Of course, if you want to have a proper young lady around the house, leave her be!" gruffly intoned Mrs. Koren, who had just brought with her lunch to the vineyards.

My grandmother had nothing else to say for the rest of the day. The keenness of Mrs. Koren's words did not even particularly bother her. People for miles around knew her as a thrifty and sharp woman who commanded no respect, but of whom they were afraid. Decrepit though she was, she did pay them - if not with money, then with foodstuffs. If anyone crossed her, she would scold them: "I had better never see you on my property again!" Later, she would longer come looking for apologies, but instead for workers. And again they went. My grandmother went, and so did my mother. In the evening, once they had retired tired from the vineyards, my grandmother said to Mother: "You see, Angela, there's no other way. I'm going to go see the headmaster and they'll be writing a petition …"

Mother understood what she meant, but all the same asked:
"What on Earth? What petition now?"

"So she won't have to go to school anymore. You can see it, it's difficult."

And so the decision was made. It *was* difficult, and to a child's mind unfathomable, but real. It's the kind of decision that too early robs you of your childhood, of all your dreams for the future, and casts you into the waves of life. Such was tradition in the Hills and it was one not easily uprooted. All of the Hill folk walked this path, and none deviated from it. The vineyards asked to see no report card, neither one with good marks nor with poor. They are familiar only with tough hands, a great big hoe, pesticides and autumn grape baskets. That is the unsung refrain of the vineyards.

The vineyards were being sprayed. It was the first time my mother had to drudge all day long. In the morning people would let out the occasional joke, but by the afternoon a tiredness would set in capable of suppressing any smile. Mother carried two large pails of water uphill throughout the day. She would pour their contents into a sprinkler carried on the back of an older man. If she hadn't known him from before, she wouldn't recognize him now, either. The rags he wore were sprayed green-blue and clung firmly to his sinewy body. Even his face was in places dyed either green or blue. At first, being exposed to that corrosive liquid caused stinging in the eyes, on the arms and everyplace else, but later the skin would adjust and no longer react to any irritation. Come evening, Mother succumbed to exhaustion. Her knees buckled, her arms seemed overstretched, as though they reached all the way to the ground. But the insatiable, never quenched sprinkler demanded attention. Mother was scooping water from a tall cement vat that was already nearing empty. Each time she had to stoop sharply over its edge. The grass surrounding the vat was slick from the wet. Once she again bent over into the vat with the pail in her hand, she lost her balance. She would have fallen too had France Koren not caught her. From above she could already hear: "Come on then, skinnybones, now is no time to take a bath! Bring the water!" Her face turned red, and her eyes remained downcast as France scooped the water and thrust the handle of the pail into her hands.

The months went by and had soon melted into two years. Everything was alive in Koren's vineyards. Bright, colorful and red kerchiefs and dirty and rotted black and green hats had been misplaced among the verdant and yellowed foliage of the grapevines. The harvest that year had been exceptionally bountiful. Koren's wife was downright aglow with happiness.

"Look, France, this is Father's plantation! It's borne for the first time this year. What a shame. I wouldn't mind still having him around either. But what can you do!"

"Moaning won't do you any good, Koren. God wanted it thus. Everyone has to die. Be glad that you have a strong boy like you do. He's done his duty in the army and will now bring you home a daughter-in-law."

"We'll see. If he finds anything good anywhere, I'll have no complaints."

France cast a furtive glance at Angela. Today she has on a white kerchief, from beneath which juts thick, dark hair that drapes a well tanned face. A once elongate and thin body had taken on curves, and a once unformed, bony leg had now become gently arched and healthily full.

"Dear little Angela, when did you become all grown up?" the question gnawed at France in his mind. No answer came, for he had not given the question voice. Someone in the row said:

"Mima, what a pretty daughter you have!" It was Mrs. Kavčič, the sister of Mrs. Koren and a wealthy farmer at home in the valley, who spoke before she had the chance to reply:

"What good is all of that!? Beauty fades, but money has its worth. Grooms don't simply fall from the sky if your pockets are empty.

Mima, who had earlier been interrupted, answered calmly:

"They don't need to. As long as she has a sound mind and a pair of functioning hands, she'll manage fine without a bridegroom."

Angela was cutting away heavy grapes and dropping them into the collectors' bushels. Then, France came to her.

"Come on, then, show me your stick so that I might see if you've carried more of them than Jožek!"

"Here, count the notches! There's a pretty little line of

them."

"Watch it, you two! France, I'm quite certain that your row is *here*! Jožek is busy hauling over there! We won't stand about here with our pails full!"

"Angela, we're pressing today. Are you coming over after supper?"

"I know that if there's picking, there's bound to be pressing, but that's a man's task. I'm off to sleep."

And off she went. France was waiting for her on her way through the vineyards. Once they had had their daily conversation, he declared to her words he had long since prepared.   They issued from his mouth impassioned, yet lacked all amorous sighing:

"Angela, you are always by my side: in the orchard, in the field, in the vineyards. I've fancied you for a long time. You have to believe these words."

An awkward kiss affirmed the declaration. This represented Angela's first encounter with love. She believed in it and she was happy. She was on her way back to the cottage. The moon in the sky, a jovial ditty from Koren's grape press and the breath of her first affection—it all coalesced into an inexpressible harmony the of which was happiness.

The young lovers saw each other often, but they only rarely spoke. Try as they might to conceal themselves, to curious eyes and ever attentive ears, nothing remained hidden. Mother Mima waited in vain for her daughter to reveal her feelings to her. The inhabitants of our dear Hills are untrustworthy. Mothers have trouble finding a way to the hearts of their daughters. At any rate, people consider it barely necessary to ever talk about themselves. As for the relationship between France and Angela, nobody was expecting it to last very long. Koren's mother believed this notion more strongly than anyone else. It was peculiar that even nana Mima was unhappy about this relationship when, at the same time, many a wealthy mother would love nothing more than to slip France her daughter.

The sons and daughters of these hills are hardy and resilient when the time calls for it, when is required. Angela and France, too, were like this. The late autumn had summoned the cold to the peaks while it enveloped the valley in a veil of mist. The Korens were lagging behind in their work. On a day wrapped in fog, when lesser farmers had already stored their produce, Mimi and Angela were again at the Korens'. They were shredding corn stalks. Mrs. Koren was not too kind, but she abased herself by asking for their help for fear that the snow would catch her unawares. As evening neared, France and Mihol, the farmhand, were driving the corn stalks home. On their last way up a steep incline, the horses came to a halt. France goaded them with his whip, but it it had no effect. They heaved so that the muscles in their abdomens tensed dangerously, then froze once more. Mihol had to come and pat them on the head for them to budge again.

"You see, master, sometimes even animals need a little whisper in the ear, not just girls."

"Perhaps you're right, Mihol. I shall take your advice."

After dinner, Mima rose to her feet and quickly set off for home, where a hungry cow, pig and chickens were expecting her. On her way there, she ordered her daughter:

"Angela, help unload the wagons and then come home at once!"

"I will, mother, it'll all be done in an hour or so!"

Following the completion of her work, Angela tucked a slice of flat cake behind her apron and trotted home. She was almost at her goal when France intercepted her.

"Let me go, I need to get home. And I saw Mihol going somewhere along the path earlier."

"Bah, who gives a fig for Mihol!? He's no concern of ours at all."

France held her tightly between his strong arms like a vice that she could feel the uneasiness of his body.

"Angela, you will be my wife. I love you ... You, nobody else, do you understand!? Even when I was in the army and you were only a child did I know this."

A comforting warmth, the result of friction between two bodies, made the ground beneath her feet more unsteady with every passing second. Disappearing was the boundary between wealth and poverty; between virtue and sin. Disappeared had the mirage of Mrs. Koren, who with her bony fingers had been counting her money.

Diminished had the illusion of love without passion; for the realization that these two terms are most closely connected demanded satiation. The cool, misty, starless night shined in two young hearts in the brightest of shades.

In front of the door to her home, Angela adjusted her kerchief and apron. Her mother was sitting by a faintly flickering oil lamp.

"Did France go with you?" she inquired sharply.

"Only part of the way," she replied, embarrassed.

"There's nothing I can say. It's a comely homestead and the boy is not too shabby. Strong, industrious and handsome. But think it over well. I don't want you to follow in my footsteps. A child without a father is a truly miserable thing."

"No, nothing happened … France says that he intends to marry me." She felt a rush of blood and knew that she was talking nonsense.

"You have no idea what it means to be a daughter-in-law, and moreover that of Mrs. Koren. She'll never accept the fact that you're a simple crofter's daughter."

Winter had come. The furious wind had filled every nook and cranny with snow. Because of its position, Koren's grandiose household felt the cold in its utmost severity; the wind crashed mercilessly into it without surcease. Sometimes the dry snow would cover all of their footpaths. Whenever the particularly harsh cold set in, fox footprints could be found in the snow the following morning, and the rabbits would have gnawed the young crops in the orchard. Hungry crows were in murders circling the courtyard and the people in the house were shelling pumpkin seeds.

Angela was with her mother at the Korens', husking the corn they had earned. They avoided leaving the house in the evening unless it was necessary, not even to go to the Korens'. Angela was at times tempted to venture out, yet to obtain work, even that as menial as the shelling of pumpkin seeds, one was required to ask especially.

And the Korens had this year not invited, let alone kindly asked, them to do any such thing.

Her mother, however much her heart had hardened, her emotions now as impervious as the tempered loam, did not fail to notice her daughter's lost expression.

"Angela, your hands and reason are your dowry. They're all you've got. No man will offer himself for this beggary, so take good care of what you do have: your wits and your health."

"But mother, I'm not looking for anybody … France is the only man I fancy."

"The Koren woman will do anything she can to ensure that you do not end up as France's wife. Surely you know her well enough by now to know that."

Much snow fell overnight.

"Angela, the way to the wall is snowbound again. Go and shovel the snow away!"

Angela got dressed at once, put on a pair of high rubber boots, tied across her chest a large old woven kerchief, took in hand a shovel and began to remove the snow. The morning was foggy and the low grey clouds still sprinkled the earth gently. The snow was soggy and clung to the shovel. Angela labored, intermittently straightening herself to look to the peak. It is precisely there that she noticed a dark figure.

"Aha, I see the Korens are shoveling too. Perhaps it's Mihol, though it could also be France," she hoped. Of course, going down a hill is faster than going up it, and the figure that was rapidly approaching Angela quickly recognized as France. He swung his shovel. By the well, the paths intersected, one leading along level ground to Angela's home, and the other upward to the Korens'.

"You're a good girl, Angela. I see you show the snow no fear." They both giggled.

"Do you have what it takes to go up against the likes of me?" France jested.

Already she had cast her shovel into the snow, made a snowball and hurled it at France. Amid laughter she said:

"Let's give it a try! Whoever will triumph?" They started with a salvo of snowballs, then each of them took a shovel and began to fling snow at the other until both were soaked.

"Enough tomfoolery," France said. "You could catch a cold. Let's stop this now!" The shovels lay in the snow. The two youths stood close to each other.

"Who's won, then?" Angela teased with a smile. France took her by the hand and looked deep into her eyes.

"You've won this time. But *then*, I was the one who'd won …"

Angela tore away her hand, her face became darker and her impeccable teeth shrank behind tightly shut lips. She seized her shovel and, without utterance or hesitation, left.

"Don't be like that, Angela! I was only joking!" She did not look back.

Slowly he was moving back up the path. He was sorry. At the same time, he was proud of his girl and knew that he could not lose her over something so trivial. He heard someone walking behind him, but he did not bother to check who. In a short while, the young mayor and the tax collector had caught up with him.

"France broke us a path," he said, baring a smile. The official, a gaunt and inamicable man of indiscernible age, did not let out a peep. The mayor stepped just behind France and carried on:

"We were at Mima Brajnik's house. She has a few dinars' worth of taxes, and she hasn't even paid that. What can we do. You couldn't find anything to seize *there* if you tried."

"I know I'd find something, and something pretty at that," finally voiced the official. His grey eyes flashed vividly as he spoke. France understood immediately and clenched his teeth.

"What, this washed-out skeleton? He'd find Angela!? I'd break his jaw!" he thought to himself angrily.

Before the Korens' house, the men went their separate ways. The Korens paid their bills regularly, so they had no need of sorting out their taxes.

France went straight to his room. He sat on the bench. His mother brought him breakfast.

"Here, eat! It's a little stale now, given how long you've been away."

She spoke in short sentences.

"I'm not hungry!" he returned curtly and fixed his stare on the window. His fingers rapped lightly on the table. Whatever for did he have to open his mouth? Angela is a resentful girl, and now there was his mother.

"I know what's going on with you. It's that crofter, she's making you lose your head. Not to say that she's not a pretty little thing with a shapely figure and who knows how to work ... But she has no place on our farm! Your father and I have worked too hard to mingle with the likes of crofters. She may be a worker here, but she'll never be a housewife!" Her voice fluttered and grew in pitch as she spoke.

"Mother, please stop! I'll choose a wife myself, and if I don't, then I have no need of one."

"If it's a crofter's daughter you want, know that it's not so much about the money, but Mimi's daughter? No, that I could not brook! Every now and again that old enmity swells ... I've been through much. You know it."

"I do not care about your enmity. That's something you ought to take care of yourselves. If Mima were had been meddling in your affairs, since you
ended up with father in the end ... And now no woman can lay claim to him anyway ... But Angela *will* be my wife."

He slammed his fist on the table and the clay bowl upon it rattled. His mother turned white. Yet she knew that she must finish her thought, that if she is already blustering, she might as well let it all out at once. She therefore played her final card:

"If you refuse to obey me, I shall sell the entire estate and move away."

"What do I care! Sell it! Father's share will be more than enough."

She now visibly trembled: "You, who so loved this earth, these vineyards, are prepared to leave everything behind for a crofter's girl?!"

The silence suffused the space between them and tore asunder the ties that had once bound them together only through wealth.

Several agonizing minutes later, his mother began again in

the timbre of a broken voice:

"France, Zefika is not so bad ... That beech forest ..."

"You've gone mad! Completely insane! You expect me to wed a woman that no winemaker likes for a damned beech forest!? So that even my grandchildren inherit a fat nose, freckled face and red hair ... Never! I'd rather live out the rest of my waking life alone!"

His words astounded her. Until today she, Madam Koren, has been the iron fist of the household, yet here is someone who would sway her power. And this someone is her very own son!

She burst into a fit of tears and made no attempt to withhold the barrage of threatening curses she now spat at her son, the likes of which he had never heard come out of her mouth.

France left home in the evening. A fresh snow fell and thickly covered the path, but this did not bother him. He knocked on Angela's door.

"It's you, and at this hour!?" she said aghast.

"Ma'am, please permit me to have a word with Angela," he said with confidence.

"All right, I'm off to bed then," she said in a tone of slight annoyance and disappeared.

"I had my first serious talk with Mother today. She became very angry. Angela, this won't be easy for us. But we have no choice but to endure it - together."

"I shall try. But I fear I'll wilt first. I know that's what befell my mother.
That's just the way we are."

She walked him to the door. There, he embraced her in his sturdy arms and kissed her.

"Angela, it's you or nobody at all! Good night!"

In the spring, everything changed. Mrs. Koren no longer had any need of Mimi or Angela. France, however, would still come by. The two youths would continue to meet and discuss plans of leaving the countryside and finding work somewhere in town.

One day, a carriage from the town arrived in the Hills. In it rode the masters of the neighboring wine storage shed. They were looking for a servant, and Angela made her decision: she would enter the service of Mr. Gruber.

"You see, France, that's a start. Later you'll follow me there, too … If, of course, it's still what you want. The choice between me and the land won't be an easy one. But it's a choice you're going to have to make yourself."

Their relationship lasted a good year longer. Angela would visit her home; the couple would also meet in the city. In the meantime there was an exchange of letters between them, though one that grew always less frequent.

One day, when Angela could already feel that France was growing colder, she received a letter from her mother. With a clumsy, heavy hand she nearly scribbled over a few words; first there was something concerning her, then, to the point: "France will be marrying. He will take as his bride Ivanka Klemenčič." She read nothing after that. She folded it in two and tucked it into her suitcase. She sat on the chair in the room and began to cry, loudly and bitterly.

After that she became acquainted with my father and ended up marrying him. She served for a while longer and soon they moved into Mother's cottage. But Father never wanted to work the land. He would go to the nearby brickyard for work. Most of what little he did earn, he squandered on drink. My mother knew that he owed people in many an inn, and slave away as she did, she could not save up everything.

On one evening in winter, my grandmother passed. Our debts increased, and not just to the inns, but also to my mother's former master in the city. It was then that Mother and Father made the decision to sell the cottage. Because Grubar's winery was now empty, that is where they moved. That's where I was born. And that's the home, now renovated, in which we live to this day.

I slowly learned about the life of the vintner in this place. Everything here tasted tart, had the flavor of bluestone, except for the harvest itself, that is. It was tough, the way loam is tough to remove from a shoe or a foot it's stuck to and has made ugly and coarse. I remember my childhood years. My mother would take me with her to the vineyards. I would toddle behind her from vine to vine. When I got hungry, I would tug on her skirt. Then she would pull from her pocket a crust of bread, most often made of corn, and slip it into my hand. I would eat it leisurely and with feeling, for I was each time aware that my mother's pockets had nothing more to offer. My snack was accompanied by cider of the exact variety that adults drink. That sour yellow liquid was never in short supply at our house. For Mother, walking through the vineyards was more difficult with each passing day and it was Father who had to work more and, in spite of his rudeness, he was good to us at the time.

I had almost reached the age of six when I got a brother. Around the house, this event was more a cause for sadness than gaiety, but Mother was smiling regardless when she said to me:

"Look, you've got a brother!"

My father looked crabbily in the direction of the bed, where the newest member of our family was wailing horribly.

"Well, it isn't exactly a blessing. I never wanted to be a real winemaker, the kind that has so many children that there's hardly room at the table for them. But because the child happens to be a son, I won't say anything of it. I just hope there won't be any more."

Father truly was no winemaker. He had no love for the vineyards. He loathed the heavy digging and weeding, but most of all he detested the days when the vineyards needed to be sprayed. He wasn't even fond of harvesting produce. Many times he would say to Mother:

"Let's leave this wretched mound. Let's go to the city. I'll work at an inn of some sort as a caretaker or procurer, and you can help in the kitchen. That's why I don't want any more children. No master likes a worker with a procession of children."

In a few days, Mother was once more in the Hills. Ivan was asleep in his bed at home. I had to run home from time to time to see if Ivan was crying. Whenever I told mother that he was screaming, sat up with her back erect and looked to the cottage, then continued to work. My concern was therefore needless.

One afternoon, a carriage was rolling along the carriageway

toward our cottage, now already half sunken in the earth.

"The master is coming!" mother said and swung her hoe even more vigorously. She now did not even have the time to wipe the sweat from her brow. Father did not seem to particularly care about the gentry. He worked on quietly and lagged far behind Mother. The black carriage turned left past our cottage and into the hill, straight toward the wine storage shed.

Mother left me in the vineyards, leaving father behind with me, while she headed with quickened step for the white solid building. Nevertheless, I followed her. The carriage driver held the two uneasy horses in his reins, while Mr. Gruber was already standing by the cart and holding out his hand to the fat lady who was barely able to blunder out onto solid ground.

The lady examined my mother from head to toe and asked in broken Slovene:

"Son or daughter?"

"A son, madam. A strong and healthy boy."

Mother turned the large key that opened the storage shed and said to me:

"Run along and get your father! We're going to need wine!"

Mother, who was familiar with Gruber's habits since her time in the town, immediately set the table and asked:

"Madam, shall I light a fire?"

"No need. I have brought a cold supper with me."

I stood on the doorstep and motionlessly peered at this rotund woman. Her fleshy fingers laden with rings, were clumsily unwrapping a white packet.

"Cut, Angela!" she commanded.

Mother, who had in the meantime washed up and had tied a white apron around her waist, was now changed. I'm not sure, perhaps she only seemed beautiful to me in that moment, or maybe she had always been so. Once the table was set, the lady handed my mother the white packet. On her ample hand something once again glittered, and her face, which to me was no more than a round lump of flesh, assumed a special kind of expression. Mother took a bow of gratitude, accepted the carton and barely audibly said:

"Thank you, thank you, madam."

When the lady and the gentleman were already seated at the large oak table, my father joined us. He had a hard demeanor. He accepted nothing, not even a handshake, as gratitude. Confidently, he asked:

"Will the sir be coming with me into the cellar, or shall I make the selection myself?"

"I will go. I shall have to see how the wine is coming along. I do hope the large barrel by the wall is no longer cloudy."

Amid the creaks that issued from the large iron door that led to the cellar, the man said to Father:

"You're fortunate to have a son. I've always wished for a sin … Such a shame, and I haven't even got a daughter."

And I, the curious child of a winemaker, followed all of this activity closely, which is why this first encounter with gentry forever stuck in my memory. The wine was then placed on the table: red wine that shimmered in the glasses like ruby. My child's eyes flitted from the glasses to the sausage, which lay partly eaten on the edge of the table. Covetously my gaze would linger, now on the sausage, now on the bread. The lady invited Mother and Father to the table. Mother stopped in her tracks. One moment she was looking to the door, where I was still leaning, the next to the lady. The lady noticed this; she took a hunk of bread, placed on it a few slices of sausage and cheese and beckoned me to her side.

I obeyed. I did not run as she might have been expecting me to. I took the offered piece, thanked the woman and walked gingerly across the flooring, scrubbed white, toward the door. Nobody had told me I was allowed to stay. Mother watched me go and said:

"Go see if Ivan is crying!"

Off I went. I sank my tiny teeth into the thick helping of bread. To my dismay, it was accompanied by the disagreeable odor of cheese and my joy died down quickly. As I walked homeward, I took the cheese from the bread and threw it to a stray cat. Being as young as I was, I had no idea that this bountiful meal was little more than a crumb, fallen from the master's table onto the floor, that we winemakers collected gratefully.

I went to school in town as my mother had, just as my peers ought to have done. They would go, but rather infrequently. In the wintertime we had no clothing or shoes to wear. I remember that the neighbors had three schoolboys who had one pair of ankle-high shoes between the three of them. The things were large enough to be donned by any one of them. Until late into the fall, when the straw had long lain on the floor of the valley, we children walked to school barefoot. The teacher turned to look at our reddened feet almost every morning as we entered the classroom; she was always inside by the time we had arrived from the Hills. Of everyone from our hill, I was the one who attended school most regularly. I find it odd that my father would constantly send me there. He would even give me money to buy a workbook or two. He carried with him until his death the hope that he'd someday live in the city. When Mother looked in the box in which we kept our savings, only to find inside little more than spare change, she said to Father:

"Either let her ask for a workbook in school or wait a little."

"No, there has to be enough for a workbook! I don't want to regret it later. You know we'll leave this muddy mound someday …"

I was in year two. My memory has always served me well, and I can still clearly see before me one episode from school. Spring was nearing and the hill children were once more in class. The teacher knew all of us. Jakec and I, who were relatively studious and attended regularly, caused her the least worry.

"And where might Jakec be today?" she asked me one morning as I put down my little rucksack.

"I don't know," I replied as I looked to Jakec's vacant seat. That day it seemed that nobody in school knew anything at all. When we returned home, we learned the awful news. That evening we went to him to sprinkle him with holy water. He lay on the bed beside his mother. He was covered from head to toe by a white sheet. I did not dare unveil it. For me, he was simply asleep, but my aunt explained otherwise:

"Yesterday evening came the master. He spoke with Nežika for a long while. There was also shouting between them. When the master left, you could see by the look on Nežika's face that she had been crying. She said the master had lied to her long enough and she would not bear another illegitimate child. She lured him out of his bed and led him to the pond. There, they drowned - both of them. Poor Nežika! But that's how it goes if the master dallies with a vintner beauty."

Once we were back in school, the teacher said to us:

"Children, we shall all bring Jakec white flowers, so gather as many snowdrops as you can find!"

Throughout the afternoon I collected these yellowy white snowdrops, or *norice,* as we liked to call them, that jutted from the moist, shady ground. When evening fell, mother wove them together into a white wreath. In this way I repaid Jakec, who would sometimes give me half of the bun he received from his father on his walk past his inn on the way to school. Gossip pervaded the hill, but nobody pronounce aloud the fate that had befallen Neža and Jakec. There were even those who condemned her; most, however, knew the whims and wants of their masters, who on occasion had no objection to reaching for a vigorous young vintner woman. Naive Nežika even believed that her master would wed her. Sometimes they would say that this made her haughty. But now, dead as she was, she was a winemaker, one of them and nothing more.

Our vineyards were being trimmed. One day, my father was at work in the barn, while I went with my mother and little brother to the vineyards. Mother was checking if the vineyard had begun to bleed. And truly, at the site of each offcutting there was a large dewdrop that shone like a pearl. Once at the very top, Mother called out to me and took Ivan by the hand, and together we walked back toward our cottage. In that moment, something unusual happened. A statuesque man, balding near the front, barred our way. Mother stopped in her tracks, then wrenched us to the side. To herself she uttered:

"He's dipping his pate in blood of the grapevine again, but it's done him no good."

"Good day, Angela! What big children you have. I only see

you so very rarely," he said quickly to get all his words out in a single breath, seeing that we were not interested in what he had to say."

"Yes, the children grow, and we grow old," she replied and suddenly turned around.

"You're still fine, Angela," he decided to add.

"Fine? What does fine mean, considering I wasn't enough for you then?" she spurned him sharply and we left.

And with the passing of that day we edged a step closer to hell, as Father would later claim.

Tired by the time evening rolled in, Mother washed up. She seemed now to perform these routine activities with greater care and thoroughness than she usually did. She hastily prepared our dinner, plain milk and *corn žganci*, put Ivan to bed, and departed, not every time, though often. Meanwhile, father drank. He was pouring himself cider, but as soon as mother left, he looked for the key to the only cupboard in the house and began tilting to his mouth, with increasing frequency, the green bottle that contained the hard liquor. When Mother eventually returned, she found him snoring in a sprawl on the bed. She switched on the light and made to doff his shoes when he abruptly awoke and bellowed in deep tones:

"Away, strumpet!" He then kicked her that she flapped her arms haphazardly and met the door with a crash. I sat up in my bed and trembling waited to see what would happen next. This was the first time my father had ever been violent. I knew full well that the neighbors would in their altercations sometimes end up bloody, but there was never violence in our home. He rarely even lost his temper with me. In the end, nothing developed. Father turned to face the wall, his foot still shoed, and snored on.

The vineyards relinquished their fruits. They called for laborious hands. Of all of us, mother was the only one who yet had them. Father managed until noontime, but by evening he was reduced to fumbling and wandering amid the grapevines. Master Gruber sometimes went so far as to scold him in the presence of the others. On one occasion he said to him:

"Tone, have you no shame? Look what a wife you have: strong, diligent and meticulous. Any man would be overjoyed to have her. But you? She does everything on her own, yes, almost entirely on her own! And she takes care of the children, as well. If this continues, I shan't have any choice but to find another vintner. She simply won't manage with all this work alone, and I already have to hire difficult people.

"Oh, sir, you can't frighten me. I'm prepared to leave at any moment. I'll be leaving you sooner and these mud-caked vineyards sooner or later. And as far as my wife is concerned, you can have her, if you fancy her so damn much, and provided she'll have you, sir. You see, she's already found herself a sweetheart." The master stared at him in disbelief. In this he remained mute.

In the evening, I told my mother that Mr. Grubar intends to fire us. This gave Mother quite a scare. Several minutes later, however, she looked at me with her beautiful, earnest eyes.

"He'll have us out on the street. We'll lose this sodding roof too!"

She covered her face with her apron and began to bawl loudly. I was standing by the table and was myself on the brink of tears. Into the room walked Ivanček in a short, dirty white shirt. The lower part of his belly was exposed. I don't know what effect this sight had on mother, but something must have clicked within her. She wiped away the tears from her face, put Ivan on her lap, clad his bare body in her apron and spoke, more to herself than to us:

"We will not die on the street! No, I shall slave away, even if it means that I am left alone in these hills! I have strong hands that can do the work of two if need be. And we won't be perishing of hunger, either. Fret not, children!"

Her words sounded like an oath. But they needn't have, for we were asking her neither for shelter nor of food. There was no wish in me, and my brother said nothing; he merely beheld, whereas I could now feel the song of the Hills become ever grimmer. Life beckons me into its turbulent waters; it no longer lets me stand by as an unaffected observer.

In the autumn, the hills came to life. Though there was one instance of hail that year, the vineyards bore ample fruit. I looked forward to the vintage; I do not know why. Perhaps there lingered in my memory the copious feast and the song and shouting of merry pickers from last year. I was even more enthused by the thought that I would not need to tend every day to the chickens, which otherwise tended to stray into the vineyards.

"There will be a vintage on Thursday and Friday," Father said. This meant that I would have to ask for two days off from school. The teachers had a special kind of understanding for this vintner's holiday of ours. The weather had been agreeable all week. The sun did seem to appear more sluggishly from behind Koren's hill, but once it did, it provided pleasant warmth to the hills and their workers.

As regards lovely days, Thursday was no exception. The frost, which had spread as far as our very own hill, was receding. The larger children among us were given pails and were made to line up like the rest of the pickers. The smaller ones, Ivanček among them, meanwhile rummaged the grass for fallen grapes with their chilled little hands. During their work, particularly as the sun fell low on the horizon, the basket-bearers would holler and sing discordantly, for my father would regularly fetch them drinks. The true meal fit for a vintage came in the evening. Mother and the neighbor had not come to the vineyards in the afternoon, because they had had enough work in the kitchen, as they had to cook the meat in addition to cheesecake.

Following a profuse supper, the men gathered in the pressing room, where large tubs had already been readied. A few women and girls who had no business in that place also showed up. I remained behind in the pressing room myself, in spite of the twilight outside. Hanging oil lamps burned dimly in the old wooden shed. Viscous must flowed in thick torrents through a sieve into a dark wooden tub. My father was first to sample the beverage, then the others tipped the jug to their own mouths. But nobody held it to his mouth longer than it takes to swallow a mouthful, for men are not particularly fond of the *must*, as viscous and sweet as it is. I was already headed home with Mother, when there was heard an odd blustering among the men.

"Hey, France, did you bring something from your cellar?" the neighbor cried.

"What is he to bring? You can see that no woman will give him *anything*. Even he is thirsty!" the second added.

"Don't let them talk to you that way, Koren! Your women take you for a fool and so do the lads!" spoke a rousing voice from the far end of the room.

I briefly turned to Koren and saw that he had something pressed against his body underneath his jacket.

"I've got some *zelenka* bottle here. Drink, lads, and do not insult our women! They are hard-working and labor like cattle," Koren talked his way out of the situation.

"And they're pretty, too. Well, yours ...'

"Mine what? Mine is the most beautiful of all! Look at her! You all know her already ... You all know! Angela is mine!"

"She was, once upon a time ... Before you mistook her for an estate; Angela the crofter. It's not as though it matters anymore. The crofter has dropped another rung. Now she's a winemaker, but she yet has her hands and her reason. Fortunately, those don't decay the way do money and that love you once swore by."

"You speak eloquently, Angela! Tell us then, since Koren has already bragged about it so, is he really such a handsome fellow?" Tone asked.

"What business is that of yours? I don't go asking you lads what your wives are like. And as for the other matter, go ahead and ask his woman ... she knows very well," Mother articulated.

"No need to fret now, Angela, you can tell us now. Your old man lies black and blue in the leaf shed. If he were here, Koren would offer offer him some of his own. Is that not right, neighbor?" Tone continued to provoke.

"I've brought you spirits, not wine for you to go barmy sooner than usual ...'

"And so that you can more easily disappear ... with her no doubt, for we know you ... If now you chase after her, then why did you once abandon her?" accused Lojze, cutting him to the quick.

Koren turned pale and lost his tongue. He was the first to

upturn the bottle and drank with long, gurgling swallows.

Suddenly, he choked. He began to cough. Mother turned to look what was the matter, but only for a shake. Shen then yanked me by the hand and said to me: "Off to sleep with you, Silva. Ivan is already in bed!"

We took the road that led to the cottage.

Someone cried out: "Angela, come back! There'll be merriment yet this night!"

"Fools!" she exclaimed as she looked back.

"Will you be going back?" I asked mousily.

"Are you afraid of being at home? You won't be alone. You know I have to be over there when the grapes are pressed. If your father were good for anything at all, I wouldn't have to drudge thus. And he, idle. He's drunk himself asleep and won't wake till dawn."

There was no uncertainty in her last words.

I snuggled next to my brother and drew the blanket over myself. Mother came to my bedside, adjusted the blanket on Ivan's side of the bed and said goodbye.

"Sleep tight. Take care not to uncover Iva; he's got the cold."

"I won't, Mother."

"Good night! I'll leave the hook on the windowsill. And you won't be going out at any rate."

"No, I'll be asleep. Good night!"

I truly did mean to sleep. I pulled the bed sheet over my head to avoid hearing the commotion coming from the pressing room. Though it must have been located some 300 yards away, that cacophony seemed to hang right above my head. The voices somehow came together and quite harmoniously sang: "*I'll buy me a little hill.*" The chorus: "*A sweet wine I'll drink*" had by now devolved into proper shouting, with no regard for melody or rhythm. Later it was the women who took their turn at song: "*All that lives be merry.*" I could precisely make out my mother's lovely alto. She always rendered that song with such feeling, for it was her song … ever since her youth. I had heard several times before that it was also Koren's …

And then, the song hushed. The only sound that I could hear from the storage shed was that of laughter - eerie, piercing laughter that did not permit sleep. Beams of moonlight were able to sneak past the flowers and through the little window. The light encroached through both windows on the house's south face. The thin rays fell directly on our bed. I recalled mother's words: "The moon should never shine on a sleeping child." These same words now lifted me and drove me to the window, the drapes of which Mother had forgotten to draw. The iron rings creaked on the rusted wire as I jerked the red piece of fabric on the first window. Then, for an instant, my heart stops. A tall figure with a white kerchief moved off and retreated behind a broad pear tree.

Subconsciously, I glued myself to the wall. There was something my mouth wanted to exclaim, but it merely shut tight. After a moment I reluctantly hid my head amid the flowers, and could soon just barely make out words heavy and slowly uttered: "Angela, it's safe down below ... The foliage is ours ...'

He went on and lost himself amongst the vineyards. Mother was still standing by the trunk. There is still time for me to say: "Mother, don't go! Mother, come to me! I'm afraid ... for you!" Yet there was nothing ... no words, no pluck ... The cold causes me to shiver, I can feel it through my thin gloves; I can feel it on my lips, which have by now become numb and incapable of speech. Then, the figure peels itself away from the pear, barrels toward the next tree, looks around again the way a timorous animal fleeing its pursuers might. One final glance at my window ... and then nothing more. The illusion that her little girl sleeps soundly in the house impelled Mother to the hills ... after him. What all was stirring in my soul? I was utterly confounded. I could feel my heart throbbing in my temples to such an extent that even the hectic singing that had been emanating from the peak could no longer be heard. I sat on the edge of the bed and wanted to cry. But not even tears would come. At that moment something possessed me.

"I'm going to get Father," I resolve in my childish mind. Already I feel my way through the dark hallway. My hand touches the cold door handle. The fingers close around it and squeeze. The door opens. I stand on the threshold in the doorway. The luxuriant moonlight spills across our courtyard and the rest of entire hill. But the rays do not reach the hollow ... It is dark in Koren's wood ... I take quiet steps beneath the overhang to the threshing floor. One half of the door is open. Immediately I detect snoring. Carefully I walk over the grass, which is scattered about on the loamy floor. I put my hand on him:

"Father, Father!"

But the words I had prepared to speak do not come. I should mention Mother, but I cannot. I am afraid, or ashamed. Once more I plead: Father, it's me … me …"

Father simply turns, contracts and sleeps on. I'm already prepared to head back to the house, but the theretofore unknown disturbance pulls me there … into the hollow. I cannot now be, I cannot now live - alone. My bare feet slide slightly across the cold grass. With each step they are heavier, less obedient. My eyes probe the partial dusk that hangs over the wood. Down there is Koren's home … and there somewhere is that foliage … What exactly is supposed to be happening in that foliage I do not know, nor do I even consider it. What matters is that that is where my mother is, and that is where he is … With the constant fading of the light in the wood, the courage in me wanes. Am I to continue? I know the way, just as I know every tree; even though mother forbade us wander Koren's world, I would go there to play anyway, to look for mushrooms. Forbade … could she not have forbidden herself? The foliage is still far away. What does she want with that place? I haven't really got to go any further … They are here … on the edge of the wood. I hear their whispers. Can they hear me too, perhaps? They surely cannot see me; I'm hidden behind a dense wall of spruces and am doing all I can to hold my breath.

"Stay a little longer, Angela!"

"No, no, let me go! I must go. Above … someone might notice."

"All right then, go. Not tomorrow, the day after."

"Here?"

"Yes, here. Maybe … I don't want to be without you. You know you're my true wife, don't you?"

She left. She slipped into the vineyards and trod quickly through them. From time to time, I could hear her clip a vine and then continue her course. I paid Koren no attention. He was not mine ... only Mother was mine. I did not see anything, but I learned much in those moments ... Once Mother was already near the house, Koren stepped through the vines. Soon after he had left, I followed along the same path. Without incident, I managed to steal into the cottage, closed the door and lay in my bed.

The old wall clock, equipped with a thick weight, indicated that it was almost ten o'clock. Unsettled though I was, I fell asleep shortly. A sudden shriek and rattle throw me out of bed. The door to the anteroom crashes to the ground with a clatter. I cry out, and Ivan follows suit promptly.

"I'll kill you, you whore!" yells my father in the anteroom.

"Don't, not here! There are children ... Help!" Mother calls out as she runs toward the bed.

"Father, no, no! Mother, run!" There are voices coming from somewhere outside, voices perchance of rescue. My father becomes confused.

"Where is she? Where has she disappeared to?" He stands with a wide stance and seems as menacing as a malevolent apparition. In the gloom, something bright glistens in his hand.

"I don't know. Here ... no ... Outside," I barely manage to spit out quiveringly. My father storms into the courtyard; in the general confusion, I have no clue about mother's whereabouts.

"So there you are, you devil! You've fallen right into my hands. And you're even decent enough to stand up for her," he now roars.

"Christ! You'll kill each other!" Mother yowls from behind the cupboard and hurtles into the courtyard.

And it might well be true. I stand in the doorway. There are people running behind the house. I can make out no face, recognize no person.

"It's over," says someone running along the side of the house. My father lies on the ground. An injured Koren is being hauled up the path by a few men. The morning dusk has enveloped our home, our peak, and has cast a shadow over our hills.

This was our natural law. Our people were impatient for justice, about everything the gentry had brought about. For that reason, they dealt with things their own way: with hoe, stake or whatever was at hand. They were well acquainted with love, hatred, narcissism and retribution.

There was no vintage on Friday. During this one night of jocundity, everything had turned into a nightmare. In the morning, a throng of people assembled in the house. The thatched cottage was filled with lamentation. Father lay on a bed, covered with a muted white sheet - dead. I wept, even though I felt ambivalent about the loss. Yet perhaps I really did feel sorry for Father. When I left the house, I heard someone say:

"They've taken Koren to the hospital. He's not going anywhere!"

The next evening, a multitude of people again gathered at our house. The entire hill had come. Some consoled my mother, others judged her in silence. That was when I first appreciated the morose voice of our hills. The Hills as well know a sad song.

The autumn wind had from the grapevines in the vineyards all but torn the leaves, which danced through the air in yellow, red and brown. For us children the leaves' falling uncovered even those grapes that clung stubbornly to the stalks. We garnered what had been left behind throughout the vineyards and were overjoyed to come across any forgotten pickings, little as it may have amounted to.

I took some grapes home to little Ivan. His classmates had dispersed across the peak, each having gone home to their homestead, for it was already getting dark.

Mother was standing on the threshold and was waiting for me. The black kerchief that hemmed her drooping cheeks almost melded with the blackened, smoke-stained wall in the background. The gloom made everything blacker still.

"Uncle has arrived, she said. "Greet him!"

"Uncle? I don't know any uncle," I replied and stopped moving.

"Your father had a brother, of course he did," she clarified and took me into the house.

"My name is Hans, your uncle from Germany," he introduced himself.

He stood before me, back straight, and looked me over. I

curiously fixed my eyes on him and in a twinkle took stock of his shabby suit, red bloated cheeks and bluish nose. His eyes were recessed deep in their sockets. The hair on his temples was grey, while that on his forehead was so scarce that one could, if so inclined, count the individual strands. Even these hung long and mussy from both sides. Judging by his appearance, he was considerably older than my father. I kept quiet. My mother had nothing to say, either. Perhaps she even feared that he would blame her for something. She prepared a holiday dinner, which began and ended with pancakes.

This was quite filling, as we did not eat eggs, save for on holidays. Following dinner, Uncle took Ivan in his lap; he even wanted to fondle him, but the boy managed to worm his way out of his arms. Uncle crossed his legs and began to tell, in a foreign accent, a tale:

"I shall stay with you for several days. You know, here there is no life for me. In Germany things are different. You complete your work in the factory and you are free. In France I was a farmhand, in Germany I was a master."

Mother was again silently scrutinizing his attire and that thoroughly oily green hat of his that now sat on the bed. So, he continued:

"There is going to be war. Hitler will come to you also. Yes, he will take the whole world! Presently we have Poland, Czechoslovakia, Austria ... Of course, he will deal with Yugoslavia in a day or two. That is power. You here on this godforsaken peak do not even know what is happening around the world.

"No, we truly don't. But we do know that a new regime is in power in Austria. And they're none too happy about it," mother returned. There was quite a bit of cynicism in her final words. It was also the first time I heard that my mother knew a thing or two about such issues.

"That they aren't happy about it, you say? During holidays, all the cities are aglow from the red flags. And the food, what food there is! We eat only white bread and even on that we spread butter and marmalade. But who am I to tell you these things, you'll see it with your own eyes."

"So that's why you're so well-fed. Of course, you sit about eating butter, doing nothing," Mother gibed again.

Ivan, as mother had known him from Father's stories, or Hans, which was the new name he had given himself, believed that he had, by redirecting the conversation to bread, struck just the right chord. But it was not so: Mother knew about more than just bread and work; she knew about love and hate.

He could not pierce her heart. To her he remained a stranger, up until the moment in which he said:

"And how they take care of the elderly there! To each is given a pension to enable him or her to live comfortably. Meanwhile, the farmers are given wheat bran and fodder, almost free of any cost."

Mother now became aroused and alert.

"Oh, they even treat their farmers well, you say?! Perhaps they wouldn't forget even poor chaps like us." Mother's icy demeanor was slowly thawing.

Hans stretched his lips to reveal a gap-toothed smile. He stood with his feet far apart and pulled his rucksack to himself. From it he pulled a red dress adorned with black flowers, surveyed Mother and said:

"Of course, you will not be wearing red now, but perhaps at a later time. It will fit you like a glove." Straight away he rose to his feet and approached mother to measure her.

"No, I'll do it myself, later," she uttered in embarrassment. Uncle then pulled out a few articles of men's clothing. At the very bottom, he had stowed a present for me.

"You see, these are white knee-highs, like the ones they wear back home," he said as he thrust into my arms a pair of oversized, roughly knitted knee-high socks, which at the hems were green.

"You will wear them when this place will already be Germany, but you can put them on before then, if you wish."

"No, she won't keep those! She still wears socks that are long and black. And no sound person wears socks, let alone white ones, in the summertime, thank you very much. Nor will I be wearing that red German dress. And I am fully aware that they wore ones like it in Austria, but even when they did and I was young, I did not like them."

"You are quite mouthy! It is no wonder that your brother ... You just wait, you'll see how your beggarly fantasies will pass once you ...'

"Stop forthwith, sir! You have no business asking for things from beggars. There is the door!"

"Are you sending me away? I shall go on my own. But I do intend to stay a few days."

"You can't. All we have is this room and that smoke-filled kitchen. There's another hole in the back with tools and other clutter. And you, sir will not sleep there, nor will you sleep in my room."

"I think we can manage to squeeze in somewhere, at least for tonight," he hinted to Mother smilingly.

I think Mother was afraid of this vagrant. That must be why she yielded him her bed by the window; I and my brother slept on the opposite side, whereas Mother ended up in the small room with the tools, where there was always a bed and covering.

Throughout the next day, my uncle sauntered about the house, and when evening neared, he vanished.

In his farewell, he said to us:

"I will come to see you again in future."

"Fine," Mother responded indifferently and thereby showed him plainly that she thought otherwise.

The gray clouds had descended low enough to obscure our view of Koren's hill, where we no longer had any wish to look. The first white specks of snow had begun their gradual descent to Earth. As evening neared, they began to cluster in large flakes, which fell gently onto the frozen loam. I was running around the house, while Ivan was permitted to only sometimes peep through the window at the courtyard, as he did not yet have a sufficiently warm shirt or trousers. Only rarely did anyone get lost and stumble by chance on our house. Once evening arrived, we bolted the doors and went to bed early to avoid pointlessly keeping the lights on. At times the neighbor would come over to tell us about the war that was certain to break out in these parts any day now. On one occasion he explained:

"It won't affect us vintners all that much - we can't have it worse than we already do. Those with sons or fathers called to live fire exercises will be doing all the worrying. Angela, yours should be going too ... as should Koren."

Thereafter it seemed as though his tongue had become knotted. Mother's facial expression now changed; something dark had swept over it.

The sunny April morning girded our hills and valleys in darkness. We learned much later that a wealthy man had lured Yugoslav officers into his cellar, where they were hosted until morning. The bridge that was meant to have been destroyed remained undamaged, open to the German army. All that fell there were the soldiers, who were unfamiliar with treacherous tactics and who thought they would repel the enemy forces.

We heard several gunshots coming from the valley. Mother dressed Ivan and together, we ran to the neighbors'. We stood by the wall and looked to the valley: soldiers, what was left of our army, were slinking in our direction and were lost in the forest. They then reappeared somewhere higher up, only to once more disappear. So that's what war is like! By our definition it really wasn't all that terrible.

In the afternoon, there was no more gunfire. Even though my mother was against it, I went with the neighbor's girl Maria, who was already an adult at eighteen, into town. There were also others who went there. They had huddled together on the pavement on either side of the road and were staring at the army, who were rolling down the road on motorized vehicles and bicycles. Some of us observed in silence this river of iron that flowed toward the south. Those in the first rows waved red flags and blared:

"Heil! Heil!"

From many a town window jutted a long red banner emblazoned with a swastika. As we continued toward the bridge, we caught sight of a triumphal arch, towering over the street, on which was engraved something in large, foreign letters. A few windows, however, remained shut. Behind the curtains idled quiet shadows that mutely witnessed this scene, of which the protagonists were the Germans, the background actors, their toadies, and we, the unimportant riffraff—the spectators.

Our peak, however, was left untouched. There were no banners here, neither joy nor sadness. Not even the Austrian masters had hung their flag in plain sight, though some now displayed a greater degree of arrogance and seemed to have forgotten what shameful little Slovene they had before been obligated to use in conversation with their vintners. Our Gruber clearly cared little for the new regime. He visited during the first days of spring to see how work in the vineyards was going. The yellow loam, heavy as rock, clung to the enormous hoes. The diggers swung their tools with such perseverance that the sweat streamed across their foreheads and down behind their dirty collars. Because we children did not go to school, I was responsible for bringing cider to the workers in the vineyards. A large clay jug travelled from the mouth of one woman or man to the next. I noticed that only my mother wiped the mouth of the jug with her hand once done with it; everyone else drank without reservation.

In the afternoon, the master departed. The workers seized this opportunity to occasionally straighten and steal a look at the hill or the valley.

Jaka Žunič fixed his gaze on the route that led upward.

My mother sounded:

"Hey, Jaka, can't you see you're falling behind? What the blazes are you gawking at?"

"There's someone down there waving with a hat!"

"I think that's just the cider talking, lad," someone gibed.

But he was right. From down by the vineyards there came a voice:

"Good evening, neighbors!" Everyone turned at once toward it.

"Well, if it isn't the fugitive! So this is how you defend your homeland!"

"What can I, a crofter, do when the generals themselves have fled?" said Tine Petko with a glum smile as he cast the black tattered hat in a large arc into the vineyards. The hat was picked up by Žunič's pup, which grappled it between its front paws and began to shred it mercilessly.

"I see they've dressed you nicely," Jaka continued, the contempt still in his voice.

"These rags were given to me by some farmer, and good thing, too, or I'd have been incarcerated with the rest of them."

After that, we children had to go to school. It was a peculiar sort of school. In the beginning all we did was listen and exchange smiles with one another. A few pupils knew German. These pupils would run toward the teachers when they were coming up the hill, while we stood separated from everything, and must certainly have been a burden on the teachers. In the morning we would begin with a march, then we exercised, learned a few songs and dances and finally went back home.

At home we talked about this very modern school, which was considerably different from what it had been before. Our mother soon realized that it would be wiser for me to work in the vineyards than that I should traipse all the way to school every day "for nothing'. The other parents shared her sentiments exactly. As a result, we only seldom made that trip. We did not know how to write a note of excuse; the teachers kept explaining things to us by fair means or foul, but to no avail.

We were still in school by the end of June. Those of us from the hill now spent time together, for it seemed to us that the town children had themselves grouped up. We were just on our way home from school and were taking the route through the town square. There were many people before the town hall. They were being driven by the soldiers to the courtyard, but they were moving sluggishly. On the other side of the pavement, we halted - I did not understand at all. What do the large bindles in the hands of the people mean and why are they crying? All of a sudden, we froze in shock. A familiar form was coming our way. It walked with a slight hunch. In one hand it held a suitcase, in the other it led a daughter who must only recently have learned how to walk. The little boy next to the suitcase carried with him in one hand a blanket, and in the other, to our amazement, a white kitten. Behind him walked two soldiers. They turned toward the courtyard. There, *she* saw us. Yes, that's when we saw her again. Her sad eyes caressed us only for a brief moment, the same eyes that had umpteen times glimpsed our half-frozen and reddened bare feet.

"Our teacher," somebody said from behind. I don't know why saying that was necessary; all of us knew her.

"Her husband has been captured. He might even have fallen," added an older man. We lost sight of them as they entered the courtyard.

A farmer holding a full basket said apprehensively:

"Where are they being taken? Do you think they'll drive them all away? My cheese ...'

"No, not us, anyway, that you can be sure of. The impoverished care not where they find themselves."

Something troublesome and unresolved was on our minds, but we could not put it into words, and the homebound road seemed as without end. Perhaps it was just this long, shared journey that invisibly linked us, children of vintners and farmers. We had found our common denominator: we were children of the vineyards.

As time flows, our vineyards awaken. The earth is still yellow, hard, impermeable and heavy. Even the people who have worked the earth have remained as they once were. The occupation has somewhat changed the lives of the winemakers. We received provision order forms; we bought sugar, marmalade, margarine. There was sugar to spare, more than we knew what to do with, for we had previously only had any during Christmastime. The people were blinded by the sweetness of this new life. Even my mother said:

"Your uncle was not lying." And nothing more. I'm not sure what was behind those words. Maybe she really did believe them, or maybe she wanted to say something to me, a child.

The first year of occupation was nearing its end. We Children went to school and felt the full brunt of lessons in a foreign language. It can be said that the teachers behaved the way teachers customarily do. They had all been tasked with proving to us how fortunate we were to have come to their great land. Some were even amiable and made an effort to help us understand their language as soon as possible. Others sniggered at our ignorance and taunted us with various epithets. This led us hill folk to keep silent during lessons. Those who were familiar with dialectal German, on account of their German birth, comprised almost half of the pupils in every classroom. We would always yield them the right to speak. The teachers devoted the bulk of their attention to them in order to do away with their accents. What did mainly belong to us were the breaks, during which we would crowd together, eat our fruit and laugh and chat.

It was just before New Year's. The snow had already days ago blanketed the hills, while the cold had showered them with twinkling crystals. Ivan and I were sitting in a room by the stove and diligently loading firewood. Ivan would now and then scamper to the window and look to see if Mother is coming. The time was already approaching midday. Ivan was growing impatient, and I with him. It was then that he began to bawl.

"Go on, then, keep crying and you won't get your boots!" I threatened him, though I was at this point aflutter myself.

"Nor will you. Nobody will get them, because mummy won't even come home ever again," he told me and howled even louder.

"Wait a minute, I'll go and have a look!" I said and proceeded to shut him in the room. I was scantily clad, so the cold chilled me to the bone once I stepped on the threshold. Yet in spite of this, I walked the length of the house to the point from which one could see, through the bare trees, all the way to the road. Far below, two black dots were in motion. I wait a little while longer and see that they have made a turn onto our path. I run toward the door, where my brother is waiting.

"Get inside the house! Mother is coming!"

"Does she have my boots?"

"I don't know, she's down by the slope already. Wait here, I'm going down to meet her!"

"No, I want to come too!"

"You git, you're barefoot!"

Without delay, he begins to stamp his feet and emit piercing squeals.

"I'm coming! I'm coming!"

I slam the door and leave him in the house, beginning my descent of the path. My mother was advancing and held in her hand a large box. So she did have the boots, albeit only one pair. No, there's a woman accompanying her and she is holding a box and a large basket. It was Maria. The slight ruddiness of her face was due to the exertion required to travel this arduous path, while the white kerchief she wore bundled her lush, black head of hair and gently punctuated her beauty. On our peak, there was much talk of pretty Maria, of Maria the crofter. I had known her ever since she took me into town on the first day of the occupation.

"Have you two been behaving?" Mother asked.

"You were away long, Mother," I replied.

"We were waiting. And for that, you've each got a new pair of boots," replies Maria in Mother's place as she thrusts into my arms a package wrapped in string. I flailed it gleefully and darted off; I could already hear my brother shouting at the top of his lungs. Mother invited Maria into the room, which was wholly untidy. Odd, I thought, had they not been able to discuss everything on their way here? I want desperate to look through mother's basket and ask her what else she'd brought. Then she simply

comes closer and sits down. Ivan paid no mind to anyone at all. Without a trace of hesitation, he snatched the box and began to try on the boots.

"It doesn't work!" he cried as he attempted to pull the right boot onto his left foot.

"Give it here, you ought to know by now that people have a left foot and a right foot!" I yelled at him and helped him don the boots.

Meanwhile, Maria and Mother were in conversation. I overheard the words:

"You know, Maria, that's the first of it, but not the last of it. You'll see. Feel better. Everything might work itself out in the end."

"Right, I'm off then," she stated resolutely, "they surely don't know about it back home yet!"

"Mummy, what's happened?" I asked after a time.

"They put Frančck Ivanek behind bars last night. He and Marija wanted to marry before Shrovetide."

"Oh, I know him. He's that carpenter who's always asking us how school's going. When we tell him, he just smiles."

"Of course, everyone knows him," Mother said.

"Why did they lock him up?" I pondered on aloud.

"Why, I can't say. And they shot the professor from the square. The people are alarmed and worried."

"How do you know that they've shot the professor?"

"It says so on the placard. There's a large red placard with a long list of names in thick white letters; his is among them. People read over the announcement with apprehension and are horrified."

"But will anything happen to us?"

"Nobody can say for certain."

Ivančck was zooming about the room, hopping joyfully to and fro in his new dark grey boots. Mine were constantly losing their shine, and with it perhaps their value to me. I find it odd even today how keenly aware of the gravity of the those times I was, even then.

Thus fell the first gloom upon our hills, one that grew continually thicker, and with it, life became more bleak. White sugar —our welfare—became ever darker, ever less sweet.

The spring would come, but it would bring with it only precious little of its sunlight and disposition. The people once again grappled with the loam of the vineyards; with their hoes they could hope to accomplish little more than to dent the half-frozen surface. There was no love left for the grapevines or for anything else in this labor. The Ivanek household, where Frančck once extended us hospitable greetings and farewells, was now marked by dourness. The window to his room remained shut the entire time, and now his family had drawn across it a black curtain. A man stepped through the door. Head hung, he walked past us and then turned right.

Once I was returned home, Mother was in the kitchen. I found it peculiar that she was not at work in the vineyards.

"Did you see the placard?" she asked in a tense manner.

"No. There are always a few in the square, but we don't pay attention to them."

"Franček Ivanek has been shot."

To be shot means to die, and death to my childish mind was a distant, foreign thing, even though I had been acquainted with the term long ago.

The next evening, Marija visited us. In her face it was visible that she was despondent. Her somber kerchief seemed to age her. Somewhat hunched, like most of the Hills people, she now appeared shrunken and somehow helpless. When she leaned against our doorframe and closed her eyes, I imagined that she could not be any paler had she been dead. But she did not weep; she merely looked in silence at my mother.

"And we thought he would make it," Mother began.

"That's what you thought, but I sensed it … I was with his parents. His mother is weeping on her bed, and his father refuses to stop cursing. You'll
see that they'll put him in jail now as well. They've searched his house a hundred times, but they'll no doubt find an excuse. And then it will be my turn, and my family's. One by one …'

She could no longer contain herself. She sat in a chair, rested her head on the table and began to loudly sob. Mother sent my brother and me out into the courtyard. When we reentered the house a short while later because we had been cold outside, Marija was thoroughly changed. Her face was still flushed, but her lips were closed, her body straightened, and there was something new and indefinable about her.

She parted. Mother said, more to herself than to me:

"She's got courage, that Marija."

"Maria, Marija," I repeated. "Mummy, we call all our Marijas Mary, and we call only her Marija. Why?"

"Because her aunt, who lives with her family, is called Mary, so they call her Marija. Understand now?"

"Of course, mother. I understand more than you think," I responded, even though I already knew that Mother spoke with me a good deal more now and clearly did not consider me an immature child. At any rate—she had to converse with someone.

Only a good two years later did the first real news of the partisans reach my ears. That was when we started going to school again. The teachers had become moody, sulky. I remember writing some girl a few lines, in Slovene, in her memory book with my classmate Danica. But because the girl was careless, she left the book on her desk. The teacher, a fervent German woman, was flipping through its pages. Once she had finished, she asked me:

"Did you write this?"

"Yes'. I nodded.

"Translate!" she snapped.

I looked at the two lines written on the page, though I by now knew them by heart; the writing was so simple and innocent, after all.

"I can't translate it."

Then came Danica's turn. Her text raised alarm in the classroom; it was a well-known poem: "*I am a young Slovene girl who loves her home ...*"

"After class you are both to report to the headmaster!" the teacher said in shrill voice and took the book.

"Francka, you cow!" someone said.

"Just you wait, you monkey, I'll give you what for. Did you have to leave that on the desk!?"

The teacher, who had at this point already begun to write something on the blackboard, turned to the class and asked:

"Who is speaking? What are you talking about now?"

Nobody made a peep, not even the Germans at the back of the classroom; they evidently did not understand.

Once the lesson was concluded, we went to the office of the headmaster, whom I knew from the hills. I met him quite often when he hiked along our trail with a full rucksack. Because he was already fully apprised of what had occurred, he said:

"Go to the classroom. We will discuss matters there."

We waited anxiously awhile and hearkened to every footstep that resounded in the corridor. Since nobody showed up, we struck up a conversation. Danica knew many things, and because it seemed our fates were linked, she told me:

"If you know how to keep quiet, I'll tell you a secret." I offered her a puzzled look, then said:

"I do if I need to."

"I'm not at all afraid. You'll see, the devil will take these Germans. The partisans are in the Pohorje Mountains. Even the English know about them. Everything will change soon."

Now it all seemed to make sense. Maria, whose boyfriend had been shot, visits us frequently, along with two men. Often they sit in our back room. Mother rarely sits with them. She tells me nothing. I was quite offended by this. Yet to ensure that Danica would not lose faith in me, I told her:

"There's something I know about, too. They're coming here ..."

In that moment, someone flung open the door. The pair of us looked together to see who it is.

"Go home. Time already three."

Amid our heated discourse, we had forgotten what we had been waiting for in the first place, and this was why the time had gone by so rapidly. We took our bags and ran home.

"How stupid it was of us to sit there and wait. I'm bloody hungry now."

"Here, take this. Home is still a ways off." Danica offered me an apple.

"Oh, thanks, but I've got apples of my own. And there are plenty on the ground there, look!"

Danica quickly reconsidered and said:

"Come with me! We've no doubt got a lunch prepared for

you! I live down in the square."

"I mustn't. What will they by now be thinking at home …?" I returned.

And I did not go. Danica and I nevertheless became friends.

The next day, it was as early as eight o'clock in the morning that we were both sent to the corner. We had been standing, Danica in front and I in the back corner, for over two hours now. There had been a change of teachers, yet nobody paid us any heed. Sometimes our eyes would meet, but we exchanged no words. Our punishment seemed also to bother the class. Most looked on with empathy, while some had on either faint or explicit smiles. While our form teacher, who was the one to have found the text, was zealously elucidating geography, everything went black before my eyes. I gathered myself, straightened myself and turned to look out the window. But it was no use. Something alien took hold of my body from head to toe and my head swam … Once I recovered consciousness, I found that my neck and the front of my dress were wet. I was perched on a stool and leaned against the wall. Nobody uttered a word.

The form teacher was standing by her desk with someone else. As though in a haze, I could make out the words:

"Italy has capitulated'. I did not quite understand that last word. All I knew was that for the Germans, this was an unpleasant notion; I could gather this from their voices and angry faces.

That autumn our harvest was miserable. I was at work in my row, picking the grapes and sometimes overhearing a word or two spoken by the adults. Yet, from them, there were conclusions I could draw. I connected these words into phrases, inserting words of my own where they were missing. The only thing I was certain of is that my ideas were too narrow, or simply did nobody any good. Quietly I wished that something would change.

In our vineyards, Maria would also pick grapes. She had long since cast off her black shawl. Her face was once more fresh and sometimes she would even let out peals of laughter. She worked adjacently to my mother and our neighbor Lizika and the three would gab about all manner of things, and the men were here or there keen on being mischievous. But it was not as jolly as it had once been. Something grim hung over the vineyards.

During the evening grape pressing, the people once more got drunk. Lojze was ambling with his large bare feet across through the pressing room and had rolled up the turn-ups of his trousers nearly past his knees.

"Wait, lads, let me hook this cat (with this, he lifted the big wooden wedge) and I shall tell you something."

"Oh, Lojz, we're tired of your scuttlebutt. We already know what you're going to say," Tone complained.

"You do not! All right then, tell me what I'm thinking!" said a now agitated Lojz, who with a crash settled the final wedge beneath the support beam. The beam slowly lowered onto the basket full of grapes, and a cloudy yellow liquid began to gush through the rings.

The must filled the entire vat and jetted through the opening in the tub.

"Do be quiet," someone whispered to Tone.

He, by this point a little tipsy, said:

"Hitler is already in Moscow or even further. It was in the Wochenschau weekly film news in the square." In his voice there was irony aplenty. The men exchanged looks.

"Quieten down, you! What do you know about politics? The Germans will win. They're a force without equal," Lojz again asserts himself.

"I'm saying that as well, but if they called us to serve in their army, they'd do it even sooner. I find it odd, Lojz, that they haven't enlisted you yet, seeing as you are a soldier, as we all know, given the way you fought so bravely for Yugoslavia. But you ran off like a dog with its tail between its legs even before the Germans had properly crossed the border!"

"Watch your mouth, or I'll introduce your noggin to this stake! What business is it of a farmhand to defend something his master doesn't give two figs about? Though I would go now. I want to see Russia."

"Ignac and Ivan already do, but I'm not sure how they feel there," Jaka shared.

"Ha ha, you believe I don't know?! Ignac is there; he's written letters from Russia. And Ivan ... what is there for me to say, you know all about it. But in the woods, the devil will take him. And let him! They send a nobody like him to do battle against the Germans? The lads must be joking. What do they expect when they've no weapons, no clothes, and no food save what they take from the fields. And they play at soldiers, so they lay mines on the railway tracks or cut the wires? They'll see yet, they will."

The men looked at one another, but none opened his mouth. When Lojz stepped behind the basket, Jaka whispered to Tone:

"It's not good that he knows." There was something else he said, but nothing I was able to make out. I made off to bed, while Mother remained behind. I began to think about Marija, Mother and all the secrecy surrounding the Germans and the partisans. Though this name for the fighters of the forest could be heard with increasing frequency, during everyday conversation, the people avoided it.

As the hills returned to their more tranquil state and the autumn rains came, Mother took the time to tidy the lumber room. More than just tidy it, she made out of it a little bedroom. She coated the craggy walls with a mixture of loam and chaff and, once the coat had dried, painted it all white. She fetched a pallet made of paper fibers and thus, on the old, rotting framework, a bed came together. The little lone window was draped in a colorful red curtain. Next to it she placed a table, which wobbled on the loamy floor as though one of its legs was an inch or two shorter than the others.

"It will be here," I told her cheerfully.

"What do you mean? What will "be here'?"

"My room."

"I don't think so! We're not royalty that each of us might have their own room."

"Well someone must sleep in it; there is a bed inside, after all," I persisted.

"Ivanček will sleep here in the summertime."

"Of course, he who's barely in second year will, and I get nothing!" I yelled, as I was a little envious of my brother. Mother was always mentioning him. If there were choice grapes in the house, she would bid me:

"That's for Ivan. Leave it!"

The two of us would have continued our bickering, had it not been for the loud footfalls in the anteroom. I looked and saw that it was Marija's mother. She walked up from behind me. She greeted me and looked around the ordered lumber room.

"You're almost like your own lords now, with the two rooms you've got here. Shame you hadn't thought of this earlier."

"Let's go inside the house," mother suggested. "Everything in here still smells of lime, and there's not a chair in sight."

A "house" was what we called then, and to this day, a larger single room.

"Have you heard the news?"

Mother shook her head. I was expecting them to send me back to again keep an eye on the chickens. And there were no more grapes now … Such was the custom we kept here, and I must admit that it made me angry. But this time, the two said nothing to me. And I certainly did not go outside of my own volition.

The neighbor said something in a particularly emphatic way:

"Koren's been released. He returned yesterday …'

Mother halted for a second, then murmured with a colorless voice:

"They're releasing criminals. It's just like them."

There was nothing else. I to this day do not know whether she hated him because he killed my father or because she had loved him.

I exited the room and left them to their own devices. Because it was already darkening, I headed in Ivan's direction. He was too afraid to walk up the slope on his own, so I always waited for him at the point where the path forked.

About a half hour later, he arrived.

"So, what did you lot learn today?" I inquired.

"*Apfel gut*," apple is good' he giggled. And that was the sum total of his knowledge on the matter. By this point even I found it ridiculous that they were forcing their language on us in this way, since it was said that none of the teachers

spoke any Slovene. Panting, we arrived back at home. I wanted to show Ivan his new room, so I ran ahead. I was about to convince him that this space belonged to me, when my mother blocked my path.

"Do not go in there!" she said sharply and shoved me away from the door.

"Oh, and why is that?"

"Because I said so and you will obey!"

My mother was not one to give orders, at least not often. But now, on account of her tenacity, she became careless and slipped up; namely, my curiosity had by this point peaked. At first I felt offended by her reproach. Then, stubbornness took hold of me and I shook off the firm grip of my mother's hands and forcibly opened the door. The scene that I witnessed was unusual. The table that Mother had placed by the window in the afternoon was now in the corner behind the bed. In the faint light, I could just distinguish three faces around my mother: two male, and one belonging to Marija. In their hands they were holding papers of some sort. That was all that I could take in in that moment, for I shut the door without speaking. I went to the bench by the oven in the house and sat on it in silence. After a time I could hear the anteroom door close. Mother entered the room. Her face was pallid, frightened. On the table she placed some multigrain porridge, with milk. Under normal circumstances, this meal would have whetted my appetite, but steam now issued from the bowl for nothing, and the warm milk failed to titillate my nostrils. Ivanček greedily snatched the spoon and drew to himself the large bowl. At the time, we all ate from a single pot.

"Won't you have dinner?" he asks me sharply.

"No!" I return in a like tone.

"Fine, you don't have to. We, on the other hand, shall, won't we, Ivan?"

"Why won't Silva eat?"

"I don't know."

"I won't either if you don't give me a little bit more sugar," he now says as he thrusts the bowl back into the center of the table.

"Here you are! And add it only to the part you intend to eat, not all over the bowl. Here, I'll do it!" Angrily, she scooped up a spoonful of sugar and poured it on the pile of *žganci* before my brother.

Not even Mother could bring herself to eat. I could see how she only half-laded her spoon and each time dragged it across the edge of the clay bowl so that it made an unpleasant scraping noise.

Shortly after supper, I withdrew to my little room. The sagging door opened yet again with a creak. In the dark, I sat onto my bed. Mother had drawn the curtain, but the darkness outside was so thick that even discerning the window was no easy task. These next few seconds seemed to last an eternity. I could have dared to ask, having known as I did that mother was hard-pressed to speak herself. But I could not call myself her daughter had I not had her persistence, so I gritted my teeth even harder.

"Silva, you witnessed nothing tonight. You may never witness anything. If you blabber about anything to anyone, it could cost us our lives. And not just us. The three of us in this unlinked chain are of no consequence; I speak of a series of other people. And that series is immeasurably long."

"No, you know me: I'm blind and deaf. I'm stark raving mad and I shall no doubt go about the entire peak screaming that I've found strange people in my room. How do you not know me better than that?! I've always known that there's something between you and Marija. And I've heard a few things at school. But you never have the time to speak with me, and I never have the time to speak with you. Well, at least now I know why you tidied up the room."

"Very well. Now you know. But you must not tell Ivan anything!"

"I know! You haven't said anything to me and I haven't asked you anything."

I'm not sure what my mother made of this. She put her hand on my shoulder and said:

"Why, you're almost grown up."

Karolina Kolmanič's birth house

The spring of nineteen hundred and forty-four had arrived. I had grown into a tall and scrawny girl. This bothered me. In school, whenever we were made to form a line, I was always fourth in it, meaning I had to stand in the front with the rest of the first quartet. I was never fond of command, but what I detested even more was marching. When we were required to turn left, I would invariably turn to the right or somehow else incorrectly. I hated myself because the height my body was such that I could not avoid the first row, but more intensely yet I hated all those who dogged us about the playground or forced us to sing. The siren seemed to more and more frequently free us from these obligations. We had heard it countless times before and knew each time we did that the Americans were transporting their bombs. They had recently bombed Maribor, and we heard with near unfailing consistency the thundering that came from Graz. Yet presently, something strange was afoot. We stood before the chestnut trees and were for once not being coerced to march. The air pulsated from the nearing aircraft. Someone exclaimed:

"*In den Keller!*" Into the basement!

Some did in fact run toward the mighty school building, while some of us became scattered in an orchard in the vicinity. We leant against the trunks of the trees and cast our gazes skyward, whence was coming a melody, for some deathly, for us sweet. Our eyes were blinded by the glistens emitted by the white planes, which clove the air on a northerly course. Once the air had stilled, little remained to be heard but the sound of hollow thundering.

"They'll be in Graz by now," said Danica, and together we made our way to the square. Our arrival in the square by descent of the hill coincided with the sound of sirens that marked the conclusion of the alarm.

"We're not stupid enough to go back now," I stated resolutely.

"Of course not, and there are others coming here after us."

Before the square, there was a line of benches. Because the sunny sides of the benches were protected from the wind, we sat on one of them. The other fleers joined us.

"Jože, you go and get the bags. You're the bravest among

us," France suggested.

"Whatever will you do with it? You've nothing of note in it," said the other dismissively.

I gathered the pluck to propose: "If you've got a proper snack in it, I'll fetch it for you."

"I may not have a snack for you, but I do have to go back and get it," he said seriously and turned to begin his journey back.

"I'm coming with you," I suddenly offered, feeling instinctively that it would please him. And that was when the first hint of love appeared, and there is something special in that feeling, one that may have arisen in me too soon.

We traipsed slowly along the path back to school.

"Take care not to turn left," cried someone from behind us.

"Or to return to your lesson. We're waiting for you!"

Some ten minutes later, we were already near the school. Once more the siren wailed. A mere moment or two later, we heard, directly above our heads, a plane; one, perhaps two. There were more. There came an unusual breeze and then, the first crash.

"Get down!" France cried before he pulled me to the ground. And then the bombs fell, one after another, and they all exploded over there, somewhere in the east.

"Don't be afraid! They're being dropped on the bridge!" France informed me.

"I'm not afraid," I responded in a trembling voice. I was, nevertheless, calmer. France knew what he was doing. He was some two years my elder and counted among the smarter boys. The airplanes vanished. France quickly rose to his feet and said:

"Get up and wait here. I'll run to get my bag. Everyone will be in the basement by now."

He returned roughly five minutes later. Under his arm he clinched a tatty briefcase.

"Good thing it's here. I was worried," he said, out of breath and looking half at her.

"I assume you haven't got a bomb of any sort in there," I said in an attempt to smile.

"Silva, I know that you're a clever girl. I spoke to Danica, after all … But for once it will be better if I keep my mouth shut.

Here are the papers, nothing but the important ones."

"How lovely! Everyone considers you, on the other hand, German sympathizer and fears you for it."

"You think there's something wrong with that? Under that sort of cover, there are things that can be achieved."

We reached the benches. They were already empty.

"The bombs must have scared them off," I deduce.

"Let's go!"

As we walked along the street, several people crawled out of hiding, all of whom were headed toward the river. That's where the two of us went as well; the siren had signaled the end of danger. The people now surged in a single direction. By the river were three large caves. Around them was scattered black earth, blent with twigs and boards. Not far away was a collapsed woodshed. And that was all of it. The bridge there still stood firm: black, outstretched between the two riverbanks.

"It's a shame the trains will still be running," France whispered to me.

I understood; I had ever more of an ear for everything that went on around me, and this perception continued to grow more refined.

Our school attendance became worse with each passing day, and when we already were in school, we could barely await the end of lessons. That was roughly when all the airplanes each day would overfly us. We would scatter about the gardens and orchards and talk. I spent more and more time with Danica and France. As we were walking to the square, France said:

"Silva, I'll be coming to your peak this evening. There's something I've got to discuss with Marija. Oh, Danica, I've got something for you."

"Come then, if you must. Otherwise, I could do it …'

"You? But would you want to ?" he said, nearly astounded.

"Very well, if you do not trust me, then go and do it yourself!" I retaliated in anger and left.

I went along the path behind the town square; at this time, the alarm was ongoing. On the tree by the path was a new, red placard: *Bekanntmachung* - Announcement. There was again a long list of names, which ended with the number forty-one. They still won't stop. Corner a dog in a dead-end street and it will turn and bite.

Around eight o'clock in the evening, Marija visited. France was with her, along with two other boys. Because it had only just gotten dark, Ivan wanted to stay up, so I was in the house with him. Mother shut the door to the anteroom and went to the little room.

Ivan had long since gone to bed when I heard the door to the anteroom close. Mother came to see me. She seemed serious, and by the light of the oil-lamp, aged.

"Silva, the boys are still in the room. They're asleep. They have been on the run for a few days. They trudged from the Pohorje to here and now they've got to cross the river. They begin their journey at three."

"Will you wake them, Mother?"

"Of course, and you as well. You'll go with them past the edge of the field as far as Koren's wood. You'll have to reach the river in darkness and wade through the river too."

I swallowed hard, watched mother with puzzlement and forced myself to say:

"Mum, I fear for myself, but I'm also worried that something might befall you if you were to go."

"Fear is a thing we must overcome. This task I've given you is not difficult, because it is your first. In due time, a greater burden will fall on your shoulders. Marija has been doing her duty for a year now, doing what she must. She never shows any fear, though she is only a woman. The truth is that she is no mere crofter. All the illegals know her."

I did not care about anyone. Something frightful took hold of me. It was not because I would have to rise earlier than usual from my sleep and go with two others, for I knew the way well, but because I had always had a fear of the dark.

"Off to bed with you, forthwith!"

I lay down half-clothed. I tossed and turned for a while, then drowsed.

We carefully and swiftly stepped past the back of the house and were lost in the wood. The blood throbbed and pulsated wildly through my veins. I could not bring myself to strike a conversation with the strangers. While we walked the wood, I felt a deep uneasiness on account of the constant cracking of branches underfoot and the mysterious rustling in the bushes. We reached a clearing. We had now made it to the edge of the field where the earth was soft. Our footsteps had become surer and securer, and our feet were fleeter. The valley was still distant. We now re-entered the wood.

"We'll be by the road in no time," I remarked, more to myself than to my two companions.

"Careful, lass! The Germans keep watch of these roads," he informed me in a dialect I did not recognize.

"I'm aware. You two wait here; just listen, I'm going to the road."

"Everything is calm," repeats the same voice. I have not even heard the other speak yet.

"It's not as terribly quiet as you say. Up in the village, in the houses, that's where the Germans are staying," I said in an attempt to inform them.

"Are you under the impression that we don't know that?" he replied again.

We successfully crossed the road and had by now disappeared within a boggy wood of willows. The susurration of the river was already audible.

"All right, lass, that'll do it. We'll continue on our own the rest of the way. You've come too far as it is."

"Good luck!" I at once whispered. I dashed back to the road. There I stopped and waited. Far off somewhere, I could hear the buzzing of a lorry, and soon thereafter, two large headlamps came into view from behind the bend. They shined into the darkness like the eyes of a giant cat. I retreated back into the wood, leaned against a tree trunk and waited. What thoughts flooded my mind in these torturous moments of waiting! When the lorry was alongside me, I convulsed with fright. Nothing happened. It simple drove on. I zipped across the road and in an instant noticed that the morning's new dawn was rising, in the east, in the form of a thin yellow-red streak. I spent another spurt running. When I found I was fully out of breath, I paused momentarily, then began my slow journey uphill.

Mother awaited me in the middle of the path that leads to our house. I only beheld her once I was virtually next to her; it was, after all, still dusk.

"You've been away long," she said worriedly.

"I had to venture almost to the river. They did have a sketch of the way, but it was useless to us in the darkness."

"You did well. As did I." She did not mention to me just what it was she had had to do. I had endured my baptism by fire with relative aplomb.

We arrived at the house. Mother put down the hoe she had been carrying with her and looked to see if anyone was nearby. We were about to enter the cottage, when we heard a gunshot in the valley, and then another, and then more that followed.

"That's a rifle," mother said, astonished. .

"You think they've caught them?" I asked in horror.

"I don't know; the guns keep firing. There's no telling who they're shooting at."

"If this is how poorly I performed my task, then …'

"Then what? You led them, as you were instructed to do. We can only hope that you pointed them in the right direction."

I settled down and went to bed.

The sun is high when mother wakes me.

"Silva, the master has come."

I get to my feet, get dressed and soon appear at the door. Mother had come straight from the vineyards to wake me. To there I now ran, where the workers were weeding. The master had been gone awhile, which must have been why he spoke at great length with Mother, who had by this point become a veritable curator of his fortune. I must admit that he never was as ill-tempered or as strict a master as were the others. Now, it seems, he had become even more lenient.

"The master also says that the devil will take the Germans

soon enough," Mother remarked.

"Does the master know anything else?"

"He knows that there are partisans in the hills who will, sooner or later, lose these vineyards, along with everything else in the world."

We were eating at noon, when one of the workers said:

"Ignac has fallen."

Another added:

"Koren and many others have been called up. They're saying that these older fellows will serve as a line of defense on the ground against the partisans."

"You needn't make such a fuss about it! We all know that that's what they call the *Wehrmannschaft defense units*."

"Many have fallen already. What do you think Koren will decide to do? You reckon he'll go?"

"Of course, indecisive as he is, he'll reach for his rifle before he even needs to," furiously interjected my mother.

I to this day find it curious that they never found us out, given the frequency of the visits the lads would pay us. Mother would sometimes treat them to wine and bread. The bread was dark brown ; the crust would crack open and peel itself away due to its soft center, but people would eat it anyway. Maria would bring us ration cards, while I would bring home bread when I returned from school.

The partisans had accustomed themselves to the use of our home. They would come alone, without Marija, and then leave. I only now realized that our cottage stood on favorable terrain. The small grove, though not expansive, could in fact be used as a temporary hideaway. Behind it were vineyards and then once more a lush beech forest. The reason that we never aroused any suspicion in the minds of the Germans was perhaps that we did not have a man around the house, or that we had an Austrian master.

The summer evening had begun its decline. I was driving the cow to pasture. Ivanček decided to tag along, since he was himself able to pasture on the lower end of the vineyards. Before I reached the path, I chanced upon Maria, who was passing through our hills en route to our cottage.

"Is your mother at home?" she queried.

"She is. I shall be there myself in a moment!"

"No, I won't pasture by myself!" my brother whined.

"Well, why ever not, then?" I asked him.

"They say they come from the forest ..."

"Who? Goblins or giants?" I said in my most derisive tone.

"I will not! You'll see, I'll leave the cow here!" he asserted defensively.

"Pasture here, by the wayside. You needn't venture into the forest, you know," I persuaded him. I was in a hurry. Marija's worried face promised nothing good.

I arrived back at home. Mother and Marija were in the room.

"Silva, our efforts were in vain. The boys did not make it. One has been killed, the other, captured," mother informed me.

I do not know quite what overcame me in those first instants, during which I could not open my mouth. Only afterward was it clear that a feeling of doubt was ramifying within me.

"And it was me ... I was the one who took them there. In truth, even further than I had been told to. I can't do anything about it," I moaned.

"We must gather all of the material at once. At night, we will move it to Kocbek's bunker. Everything has already been prepared."

She now turned to me:

"Silva, did the boys ask you anything during the foray, for example your name, or your family name? Did they perchance wish to know the name of the village?"

I had to deliberate. Fear, combined with something unknown yet strange, clouded my memory.

"No, nothing. They could not even see me clearly in the thick of night. Is any of this even important now?"

"It is important, lass. The Gestapo tortures and ... and something could happen," Marija spoke intermittently."

"Yes, I understand. You think he might give something up."

The summer night shrouded our world. The fireflies circled through the air as they always did. The silence was on occasion broken only by a dog's barking. Everything was as it had been once, when I'd been a child and had had a father. Oh, a father! What would it be like if he were still alive? And he could have been. Perhaps he would have sided with the enemy ... Or he might have been an activist ... Who knows? If he had been killed, we would at least know the reason for it. But in this way he died for nothing, or for nothing important. Perhaps it once was important ... Mother does not speak of this anymore. In the early days, he would take us to the cemetery on Sundays. There, the two of us would recite the Lord's Prayer while Ivan stood by the wooden cross, observing, comprehending nothing. We go there only rarely these days. My mother once said to me:

"Now it is time to mind the living, and there is no more time for prayer."

My puzzling thoughts drifted as I sat in the vineyards and kept watch over any might-be visitors. At the other boundary at the wood's limit, a pair of boys with rifles stood guard. Whatever could I do if someone were indeed to come? My thoughts were now of France. Because I no longer attended school with any regularity, I saw him rather seldom, which was a thing that I, at the core of my awakening childish soul, wanted intensely. To me he was a grown-up young man, and now even more so since I better understood the meaning of his work.

I did not know what time it was. We would sometimes in the quietude of the night hear the ticking of the clock tower in the square. I recall how I many times sat on the threshold and counted the clock's ticks. There are no bells now; they've been taken away. Someone mentioned that they'd be melted down and recast as cannons. I last saw them by the church when they had been removed. It was the first time I had ever seen such an enormous, brown-green bell when they dropped it through the opening in the tower and it fell to make a huge crater in the ground. Thus had fallen the largest bell, while the smaller ones id with less force, in accordance with their softer and more modest voices.

The women had cherished these colossal friends of theirs and wept for them. They had been accompaniers of the fates of men, they had signaled weddings and marked deaths ... But now, nevermore. Only one remained—the smallest. While the others were being loaded onto lorries, that one merely jingled. The larger three shall henceforth ring only if they perish, even if they make it all the way to the end.

My sentimental pondering of neatly arranged thoughts was cut short by the barking of a dog down by the neighbor's house. The faint moonlight outlined a figure that drew nearer to our cottage. I was angry with myself for having not been more attentive, and it was clear that the stranger had not taken the woodside way on the other side so that the watchers might have spotted him. But now is no time to occupy oneself with thought. I run through the vineyards parallel to the way that leads straight to the house. The stranger on foot was far behind.

"Someone is headed here! Straight for the house ...'

"Alone?" inquires Mother.

"Alone," I reply and move quickly to the corner, from where the entire length of the path is visible.

Mother follows me.

"Return inside this very instant. We'll lock the house and pretend that we are sleeping. The boys have put out the candle, though not all of our work is yet done. They shove off around ten minutes from now."

Everything fell silent. Mother sat on the bench, I on the edge of the bed, while Ivan slept.

A knock at the window: once, then again and again. Neither of us moved. It was dead quiet in the room on the opposite side of the corridor, too. Immediately thereafter, we heard a series of light taps at the door.

Mother got up and tiptoed to the anteroom. The visitor made himself heard by the window:

"Angela, open up!"

I walked to Mother in the anteroom.

"Your uncle is here."

"Oh, Lord, why now?"

"We must let him in. He won't cease otherwise. Banging on the door might make matters even worse."

I returned to my room and whispered a question through the window:

"Uncle, is it you?"

"Open up already! Is your mother not home?" he snarled.

Mother opened the door.

"Good evening! Are you already fast asleep, or what?"

"No, we heard you, but one must first get dressed here, for nobody expects visitors at this hour," mother explained impolitely.

"Get inside!" I said in a similar tone.

He left his knapsack and cane in the anteroom and then made straight for the room.

"Quiet, Ivan is asleep!" I chided him.

In the pale glow of the oil lamp, his face reminded me of a haggard man from a fairytale. He was unshaven and thin, and in these past four years he had lost the final tufts of hair that he had once had. A truly sorry image! From the moment of his arrival I apprehended that he might stay with us. The tension increased.

"We've got milk, but we're a little short on bread, I'm afraid," Mother said as she went into the kitchen. I could hear her enter the little room first, probably to explain to the others what was going on. Following this, she returned right away. She brought a pint of milk in a pot, then fetched a slice of black bread from the cupboard in the room.

"This is what we have. You no doubt eat white bread in Germany," she goaded him.

"No, not any more. You know, the Germans are a patient folk and do not complain one bit. Well, perhaps some do, but they get rid of that sort quickly there ...'

"Is that so? Now that they've devoured everything they could get their hands on abroad, they've run out, and, of course, so have we."

"You're incorrigible, Angela! And besides, what good is bread to you? You never had enough of it in Yugoslavia anyway. Sugar, on the other hand, you've not seen as much of as you can now get in your whole life!"

"What good will the damn sugar do me!? We're all swimming in sugary things of one sort or another ..." she hissed. She held her tongue at the correct moment.

"I'll be going to sleep, if you're willing to make my bed. I'd be satisfied in the lumber room in the back too ... I mean to stay a few days, after all … Do you know, there's bombing each and every day back up north and …"

"Scared, are you? Someone as clever as you has nothing to fear from the likes of bombs, nothing at all! You can sleep right here, and I'll move to the back room."

Mother must have been hardly awaiting this opportunity. Even though she knew that Uncle would not settle for the back room, she was quite impatient. When it was dark, I squeezed into my brother's bed. Uncle fell asleep soon afterward. His even breathing soon turned into insufferable snoring. Now and then he wheezed repugnantly. I found everything about the situation revolting. I would have liked to get up and pull his nose. But in addition to everything else, there was in me the trepidation that he might see me in that short, sleeveless shirt I had on. I was just of the age during which I was maturing from a girl into a young woman, and the very thought that it might be an unpleasant old man who would be first to catch sight of me half-clothed disgusted me.

I listened intently for when mother would swing shut the anteroom door. Some time later, this is precisely what happened. I sat up in my bed. Shadows flitted past the windows. They had gone.

Indeed, they left and took with them anything that might appear suspicious in an investigation. My uncle, however, stayed. The next morning he heated up some water for himself and shaved. He wasn't as ugly anymore, but he was pale, his likeness most like that of a skeleton. Mother had even washed his shirt. He would amble about idly and argue with Mother and Ivan. He made an effort to be kind to me, but I spoke to him sparingly.

From time to time, I watched him. He seemed ever more resolute to establish a rapport with Mother. From a distance he surveilled her, as she climbed the hill holding her hoe, and smiled frailly. I could not tell what was going through his mind, but it stimulated my curiosity. Lately he had several times taken a hoe and gone off to the vineyards, in spite of the fact that there was nothing for him to do there. Mother was weeding the carrots and cabbages planted among the grapevines. He was standing there and watching her work. I was by the barn. Then, as though possessed by the devil himself, he stepped to my stooping mother and attempted to take hold of her leg or waist. He no doubt said something to her. I could only hear her reaction:

"Bugger off, you damn scoundrel, or I'll give you what for with this hoe!" This frightened him. The garden hoe had been the source of many a killing blow to people in the vineyards. Relieved, I sighed:

"You're fearsome, Mother. And I, I had already thought that … Children can be rash in our suspicions and harsh in our judgments."

I did not hear whether she said anything else. At any rate, Uncle made his way down the hill.

In the evening, Marija came.

"There's going to be a storm. It's turning awfully cloudy," she remarked.

"I can see, it's coming this way from the south . If the hail comes and brings ruin to everything, so be it. It never seems to find the guilty," mother fumed.

"Are you alone, Angela?"

"Of course, Ivan is still outside, and Silva already …"

"Knows everything," Marija completed her sentence.

"I don't mean her, I mean Hans, or whatever it is he is called."

"Hans? Lucifer is what he's called; a burden on our shoulders who pilfers what little bread we have left. I should tell you, Marija, that even though I never had much use for my husband, if he were alive today, I'd gladly be rid of that parasite. Now, as you can plainly see, he's remained where he is and shows no signs of scurrying off any time soon."

Mother's words opened my eyes to a sudden and strange possibility. Not all of them, mind you, but in particular those about my father … He would move his hard hand hesitantly across my face at times … to dry my tears. I cannot count how many times I would need it then and later … It's a shame that that hand had been nothing but a burden on mother. And now, all of a sudden, the image of my beautiful mother in my mind faded … A minute misgiving stirred within me … Koren … It was unfortunately impossible for anyone to quell it. I had to redirect my thoughts elsewhere, so I again listened in on the discourse.

"Angela, yesterday evening at precisely eleven --'

"I understand, but Uncle is here. He is dangeros."

"He cannot and must not be an obstacle. Let him drink himself into a deep sleep, or whatever else it is you wish. This mission must go through. You have to help. We are in danger. We suspect Dragan."

It was not clear to me what this was about, but I had already discovered that one of the partisan guerillas whom I had led was named Dragan. He was the one the Germans had captured alive.

Uncle did not return before nine o'clock. Mother was jittery and could no longer hide it. Reluctantly, she thrust the stale potatoes before him together with the words:

"We do not dine so late."

Uncle grimaced, ate the roasted potatoes and said nothing, whereas Mother's expression soon turned into a feigned smile, which she offered him.

"I have a little drink. The master has provided it." She slid before him a pint-jug of wine that had about it the faint stench of spirits. An hour or so later, Uncle already lay on his back, sprawled across the width and length of the bed. Wheezingly he snored through open lips. The whole room was filled with the reek of alcohol. Outstretched on the bed, he reminded me of my father. Only I had loved my father, and I loathed this man so much, I was surely capable of smothering him. I shivered at the thought of it; neither then nor at any point in the future could I bring myself to do anyone any form of harm."

Silva looked Rick over. He was still awake, but he had not once broken his silence. Only his occasional making a fist signified that he had not been asleep the entire time. The dawn that heralded the morning suffused the room and sharply brought out his features. She now became aware of it: Rick was old; much older than he had looked yesterday and the way he would look in the morning when he would return from the bathroom.

"We ought to sleep," Silva said after a while and shut her eyes.

"I'd love to listen a little longer. Your story's fascinating, that world of yours. And you sure are one heck of a storyteller."

"Not good enough for either of us to not need sleep, I'm afraid," she said with a tired smile.

The waiter had just cleared the table. The pair are waiting for coffee. Several Italian guests sit on the opposite side of the platform, while everything else is empty. The guests have eaten and left the inn.

"What a wonderful, sunny day! Far down below us the sea … A ship, from here a barely noticeable white speck, rocks on its surface. And here behind us, mountains, and before those a forest from which winnows a soothing breeze. Pure beauty. Isn't it lovely, our little slice of homeland, which on a map is no more than an insignificant dot."

"I know it's beautiful, which is why I've come to see it again. And to see you … Silva, you are part of this beautiful Earth, of this wonderful nature, and you belong in it … But I would rather pluck you from it … No, not pluck! Gently I would conduct you to my own homeland and wish to plant you in my own milieu; I know you'd meld with it quickly. You breathe warmth, harbor happiness; where you stop, the sun shines, and all must prosper …"

"Rick, I've never heard you speak this way. Did you think of all this now, or did you come here intending to say it?"

"I didn't come here to take you away. I didn't even know if I'd find you. You could have been married, after all … But on the day I met you and learned so much about you, something new and unprecedented grew inside me. I desire you, Silva. I want us to spend the rest of our life together."

"There probably isn't much of it left …"

"Be it a day or a decade that I have left, it makes no difference, so long as I spend it with you."

They drained their cups and got in the car.

The road continues to steepen. The sea, a transparent line on a dark background, fades in and out of view before finally disappearing.

As they stop on a hill covered with low grass, the sun continues to beat down. Rocks protrude from the dry earth. Silva steps out and
looks about her. A wood lies several feet away and behind it cliffs.

"Let's drive to the top", she says and sits back down.

"My dear, I think the road ends over there. We'd have to walk the rest of the way."

"Let's go until there then!"

"It's enough. I can't be bothered anymore." Silva turns and goes to sit.

Holding hands, they walk slowly along the narrow path.

"Wait, I'll get us a blanket so we can wait here for sundown."

"That's still so far away! The Sun almost never tires at sea; it seems to shine forever here."

"As it has for me, ever since I've been with you. Would you care to return with me to your vineyard?" he asks tenderly.

"Perhaps, if you would accompany me. But what more is there to say about this? You already know everything. October fifteenth is your day."

"What isn't there to say? Together we'll relive this odyssey, fateful as it was for us both. I couldn't tell you anything at the time. Everything played out so rapidly and unexpectedly. We took off from the base in Italy like we always did. We were no more worried than we usually were. It was a sunny morning, although summer was slowly giving way to fall. I was young and I liked to live, but not so much that I would spend every conscious second worrying. John - he was our pilot - had always been my idol. He was intrepid, though he had a wife and a daughter no older than a few months waiting for him at home. Only when he received a letter would he crawl back into his shell and to nobody in particular say: "Damn war, why do you have to kill instead to love? Good thing I have a daughter who'll never need to go to war. Though I guess it is the women who suffer by bearing more children for us to kill. Someday, we'll have no more of that, either. I'm not hopeless or anything, or I couldn't stand these flights, or pilot a plane, or sow death everywhere."

The squadron thunders northward. There's no time for thinking or for talking on the way. The equipment works just like it's supposed to. The heavy bombers slowly glide through the air. There may be no roads in the sky, but they stay right on course. Our destination is Wiener Neustadt. It seems odd that we aren't being hunted today; there's no anti-air forces anywhere in sight. The pilot lowers the plane, its payload falls and explodes, whether it hits its target or misses. Clouds of dust and smoke rise all the time. The thundering drowns out the hum of our engines. We make our return trip, relieved, unburdened.

"This bit I remember, as well. The Germans had already closed their schools, and even had they not, they were no longer our concern. Since our vineyards had already been harvested, Mother and Ivan were picking on another peak. I was in charge of pasturing and doing the evening chores. Uncle would still be gone for a few days.

Twilight was falling. I had already tied the cow inside the barn. Suddenly, I hear a horrendous roaring. I run before the house and look to the north. The plane is low and, with a muffled growling, races straight for us. I cover my ears and stand there as if frozen in place. I then spot white parachutes careening in the valley. They sway to and fro like butterflies and slowly descend on the meadow. In an instant I count six. Everything happens
too suddenly for me to follow. Two more fluttering parachutes come into view. The wind carries them toward the forest. Then, there is a frightful crackling in the forest canopy. I hear a "crash'! and make a run for the cottage. The door that had been open now lies on the floor, and the windows are shattered. I turn and proceed into the forest.

I'm still certain I shouted something as I went. Maybe I wanted to reach the plane, but I doubt it—I was afraid of everything that had and might yet happen. That's when I saw you. You were wrapped in ropes from which you couldn't wrest free. I tried helping you, but didn't know how. You rolled and wriggled to get out of those knots and loops with your good hand and both feet. Your left hand didn't move. Your forehead and the left half of your face were uncovered. Blood dripped from your mouth when you asked:

"Austria, partisans?"

With that you stood up and bolted.

"Yugoslavia," I responded once I had caught up with you in the forest.

You smiled. I grabbed your hand and led you towards the cottage. You held in your hands the rolled-up parachute as you dusted yourself off. You looked at me and asked:

"Frank?"

I understood. I looked around. I could see no sign of him, but I did see people, running from every direction. Fortunately, the twilight had thickened, so we were harder to spot. I managed to get you into the room in the back. I shivered with fright, even if I at first hadn't thought they'd search our house to find you.

I ran to the courtyard. Ivan came running from somewhere.

"They've captured five parachutists. They're watching them. They're with Vogrin on the threshing floor."

"Quiet, Vanček! One of them is at our house," I spat to entrust
a child with such knowledge against my better judgement.

"Where?" he asked and started for the cottage. I pushed him into the living room and myself ran to the back. You were lying on my uncle's bed and breathing heavily. I couldn't see you in the dark.

From underneath the overhang, I could hear footsteps, accompanied by a voice:

"Silva, where are you?"

I dashed out. "Mother, I'm here with Ivan."

"The plane is lodged in the ground. Nothing but wreckage ... two are dead," my mother said glumly.

"Mother, here ... there's one here!" I whispered and tugged at mother's sleeve.

"Oh Lord, he must leave forthwith. This is the first place they'll look for him, because we're the nearest."

"Where, mother? Vanček knows', I uttered.

'Have you lost your mind!? The child must be put to bed right away. He must sleep or feign sleep lest he blurt something out.'

"I won't, mother. I'm not stupid." He from somewhere inserted himself between us.

"Marija's gone. We must find a connection. Once they flood in from the town, it will be lost. Where do we take him? We hadn't counted on this …'

"What's more - he's wounded, mother," I added.

It had grown dark. We got Vanček into bed. I looked to the ruins; there were still some locals in the forest. Someone was shining a torch on them and waving them away for the possibility of another explosion. What else could possibly exploded I did not know, since anything that could be torn apart was already in smithereens. I could not see Marija anywhere. No one of the German army was there yet. The people were looking for something among the debris, perhaps chocolate or something else.

I set out for home.

"There's still nobody here," I consoled mother.

In the meanwhile, Marija had arrived.

"Let's get him into the leaf shed and wrap him in a blanket. He is to be covered and his wounds seen to. In the night, we'll take him to Kocbek in his bunker until he heals."

"You stand guard in the courtyard, Silva!" she commanded.

"Angela, bring me some liquor, and bandages!"

"I've got none of those, I'll fetch a bedsheet instead."

"Just hurry! It might be a while before they crawl over here. And there's the question of whether they even know how many have jumped."

I ran into the room.

"He's unconscious," Marija said. "We'll have to carry him."

"I've dug a hole in the leaf shed; right by the opening. All right, he'll make it."

They got up. I made sure myself that nobody else was nearby.

"Carry him, quickly!"

"It's done," Mother said, relieved. "Go into the room and turn on the light!" she commanded me.

"Where are our boys now? I'll have a look in the valley. Maybe the captives can be saved. Maybe someone's hidden them already."

"If the Germans aren't here yet, they can be. They just had

the rotten luck of landing on the meadow. Who's guarding them, I wonder?

Marija set herself on the path, and I with her. On the main road here lights could already be seen searching.

"They're coming. It'll be too late," Marija told me.

We managed to take cover before the truck's arrival. The prisoners were being guarded. One look at their captors was enough to take our breath away.

"Koren, you!?" exclaims Marija, once she sees him with rifle in hand.

"Me, and there's more of us!" he brags. A dim light reveals dispirited faces and bodies shriveled with sadness.
There in the corner by the wall is our uncle Hans. I swallow and in my intense hatred say nothing. The truck and its lights already approach the slope. A few more minutes. Each moment is more intense than the last. We all know that they're uncatchable. The truck stopped, its wheels dug deep into the mud. Maria was shaking. She walked to Koren's side. Nobody knew what she whispered him, but something unexpected occurred.

Somebody cried from the darkness: "*Laufen!*" Run!

In a heartbeat, the despondent figures came alive and began to run towards the forest. Koren did not raise his weapon, nor did the other three. Uncle Hans roared:
"*Halt! Halt!*"

In the darkness, someone walloped him on the mouth and he quietened. Meanwhile, the truck continued to huff and puff along its path. They must already have run to the forest, when a barrage of gunfire pierced the air. The bursting went on and on. Soldiers charged across the field and fired their rounds. There came no reply from the forest. Harsh searchlights would occasionally flash in the darkness. Marija and Koren had also disappeared. Two farmers serving as watchmen, both of whom had been, like Koren, armed by the Germans a year ago, stood confused before the threshing floor, rifles hanging loosely in their hands. The gunfire ceased. A voice from the distance:

"*Hier sind zwei Tote.*""Two are dead," someone approaching the house spoke.

"Three merely escaped. Damned fools, why couldn't you think of someplace to hide them sooner!" someone cursed in the blackness.

"It was still light," stammered one of the watchmen.

"You old ass, what the blazes compelled you to come here?"

"I had to come. They made me," he objected.

"You'll hang for this!"

Four soldiers now showed up. They shone their batteries on the watchman's face. We had already removed ourselves and were watching from a distance.

"*Du alter Esel!*" You old fool!, fumed the German as he struck the farmer's shoulder with his rifle. The old man collapsed. I don't know what happened afterward. I hurried home. Mother had already replaced the door on its hinges, so I now banged upon it.

"Mother, two parachutists appear to be dead. They're looking for the rest. They've scattered throughout the forest."

"And Marija?"

"Gone. They were being guarded by Koren and two others, whom I didn't know. They didn't shoot when the boys fled. But it's too late now."

"Why did they even come in for guard duty? Old Vogrin is supposed to be part of the *Wehrmannschaft*.

Suddenly, there was a loud knock on the window.

"They're here," mother said and went to open up.

A German aiming his rifle stepped through the door, and behind him another. Mother was calm, but I could hardly hold my breath. I stood by the stove next to her, looking to see what was going on. The German rummaged through the cupboard, then darted for Ivan's bed. Ivan let out a cry. By this point, the other soldier had returned from the room in the back. Mother had turned pale now. What if we had left a trace there? The soldiers then hurried to the courtyard. Mother stepped to the door holding an oil lamp. The soldiers were discussing something, when my uncle appeared from somewhere.

"Who are you looking for?" he asks in German.

"What's it to you, geezer? Besides, you already know!" he scoffed and made his way to the barn.

"There's nobody here. I know there isn't. No one would come here because of me. Me, I'm ...'

"You're what? Nothing!" the soldier yelled contemptuously.

The soldiers nevertheless calmed down somewhat. They stopped to have a word with Uncle. Perhaps it suited them that they had encountered a civilian who spoke German, or perhaps they even feared for their own lives.

"I'll report anything I learn," murmured my uncle as he and the Hun shook hands.

"We need to get rid of this old viper," my mother swore once we were alone. This is just what I thought to myself, since Uncle was a danger to us all, and to you most of all.

I lay down. Mother was cold and simply threw herself on the bed.

"Won't you go to sleep?"

"It has to be done tonight!"

"What? With what? With whom?"

I wasn't sure whether she meant my uncle or someone else. Uncle had gone to his room. He was either asleep or pretending to be. Mother went to have a look at him. She returned and said:

"At midnight they'll be coming for the airman." Time seemed to pass slowly, as though charmed. At eleven, mother lit a match and raised it against the shuttered window.

"Whatfor this, mother?"

"To signal that the old man is asleep."

While we waited in vain, I napped and mother snoozed on her bed. The wind blew all night and everything in the house creaked unsettlingly. The very first signs of dawn portended an agreeable day. Mother got up, took her pail and left the house. Soon after, I rose as well. Quietly, I crept into the leaf shed.

"What are you following me for? Don't you know someone might be watching!" she scolded me.

"I only want to see him."

"That's not enough. Look, the man's all sweaty and swollen, and his arm is surely broken. He'll die in this den."

I heated you some milk in the house and brought it to you. Your eyes were so swollen that you could barely tell night from day. You quaffed the milk and pointed to your injured hand.

"Hilfe! Hilfe!" Help, help! you pleaded.

I understood German, but I didn't know how to help you. Mother fetched a wet towel and placed it on your face. We both used our hands to sweep away leaves that had been rotting there since the year before. We made a larger hole by the wooden wall and made you a bed of straw. Onto it we unfurled a thick blanket. With difficulty, we rolled you over onto a more comfortable bed and covered you with a blanket and father's old coat. Occasionally, you'd let out a sigh. We worried that you'd begin to yell as soon as you regained consciousness. So I said, whether you'd understand or not:

"*Still, ganz still sein.*" Quiet, be perfectly quiet!

With that I placed a finger on your lips. You understood and kept silent. Then, mother and I left. We covered the entire part of the shed with straw. It occurred to mother then that Uncle might suspect something, and so I had to ensure that my mother took take care not to inadvertently bury you. Your hiding place was quite cosy and secure, but Mother and I knew you needed medical attention."

"How do you remember those days?"

"I don't remember every detail, but I know they hit us somewhere around Graz. The plane managed to stay airborne for some more minutes. That sound grew eerier every moment; it echoed in the plane horrendously. From somewhere I heard a cry:

"Jump!"

The first crew members began to plummet. There was no time to think about life or death. We began to feel enveloped by an entirely new kind of numbness. The tension grows by the second. We give one another our final look. We're young ... We don't want to die, but war doesn't give you what you ask for ... There's a green hill below us. We're just about to crash into it, but we manage to overfly it. Any moment could be decisive. Our farewells fade as there is no time to say them. It's my turn. White butterflies zigzag beneath me, and before me the engine emits its tragic death rattle. Another man plunges. And then nobody else. A massive explosion shakes the air. And with it dies our good old silvery-grey bird … Yet we live on, swimming between the earth and sky, teetering between life and death.

The hours spent in your care were unbearably long. I was sick. My arm pained me the most. It was also cold, since the cracks let the wind in. It was all I could do not to scream. But I had no clue where I was, or how I had wandered into that hole. The leaves were suffocating and I had to turn to the fissures to breathe. I thought I'd freeze or die, hidden from the world in some rotten den. And then, out of nowhere, a soothing heat. I was no longer afraid. The smell of mold was gone, and my thoughts sank into an endless relief. And so I slept, wandered in my dreams and finally returned to reality.

"It was a sunny autumn morning. My brother and I were driving our cow to pasture. I took a basket to collect chestnuts in the forest on the way. Curiosity, however, drew me to the wreckage of the airplane. Quite a crowd had gathered there. Looking for Marija proved fruitless; she was nowhere to be found. I saw only a few familiar faces. People were stooping to better inspect the shiny shards scattered far around the scene. The front of the plane was embedded deep in the earth. We children looked on only from afar, because the adults were persistent in keeping us from the site. The dead pilots had already been taken away.

"Only a single one lay in the forest. The rest were nowhere in sight," said a man.

"What do you reckon, that they won't find them?" inquired the neighbor.

"I don't know. The question is, whose hands did they fall into," he said plainly, so that nobody would know whose side he is on.

I came home.

"Is Uncle still asleep?" I asked first.

"I suppose. I haven't seen him yet," Mother returned.

"I couldn't find Marija. Only she knows about the connection. Lizika and Julka must also know the terrain, but they're even harder to reach."

"We can't guess about what to do. We must help the American and get him to safety and to medical care. Silva, we cannot get to Marija. You will go to the square and find France."

"France?" A warmth surged through me. Somewhere from my inner deeps swelled a barely recognizable emotion, one that would later burgeon into love.

"And get the bicycle from the neighbors," she added.

"Mother, I've only just learned how to ride, and Marija's bicycle at that. The Kavčič family only have men's bicycles," I made my excuse.

"Men's or women's, that doesn't matter now. Get the bike or run to the square! But you must be quick!"

I walked my bicycle briskly down the steep to the path. Then I made my attempt. Though I could barely keep my balance, I managed with all my strength to propel the bicycle up the slope all the way to the main road. Things went more smoothly from there on.

About half an hour later, the square lay before me. But where to now? Home to France? I knew where he lived, but I had never been there. Anxiously, I knocked on the door. His mother opened up for me.

"Pardon me, is France home?" I asked waveringly.

"He's not, no. How can I help you?"

"I'd like to speak with him about something."

"He's gone somewhere in the square. I don't know when he'll be back."

"Thank you, goodbye!"

I stood by the fence before the road and pondered. Where to now? I can't just return home without first completing this task. I couldn't figure out what to do. I stood by the rusted old bicycle, when suddenly I thought of Danica.

"Danica, you've got to help me. Where is France?"

"What's so urgent?"

"There's an American in our house. A wounded one. He needs medical attention and we've got to get him somewhere. He can't stay with us."

"France left for the castle with our Milica. They're doing

some typing for the Germans.

"For the Germans?" I was surprised.

"Yes, they have need of a machine. Then they'll do it themselves.

From the main road I made a turn for the castle. It still stands on the hill there today, amid the greenery, removed from the road and the people. The manor was still well preserved. By the entrance to the courtyard, its monstrous cellar door was wide open. Thereabout, a few cellarmen wearing shabby leather aprons weaved. I turned onto the staircase beyond them, which winded in rectangular fashion into an open corridor. In it were many doors, all locked.

I finally reached a door in the final wing of the castle from behind which I could hear the clacking of typewriter keys. I knocked, again with some apprehension.

"Come in!" sounded a man's voice.

I entered. France was hunched before the Milica and was making an effort to finish his sentence. I resented the fact that he immediately paid me no heed.

"France, it's me ...', I muttered.

"I know. Marija and her group are responsible for taking care of him."

"Wait, you know?"

"Of course, they should already have done so last night, but everything was being watched. They'll get him to safety today. If not, you know the drill ... he needs to be looked after."

His last words rang decisively and I knew he had meant them to. I made my way toward the door. France accompanied me through the corridor all the way to the stairs.

"And take the shortcut. It turns left behind the castle, here!"

I obeyed him, though I soon regretted it. The path north of the castle was narrow and all damp. I would constantly brush up against the bushes. Down below, there really was a road that on that wonderful, sunny day stretched across the mountaintops to our homestead. But before I ever reached the road, I had to traverse a loamy slope wedged narrowly between two wooded embankments. I felt somewhat afraid in all that solitude. My shoes were sinking ever deeper into the light brown slush. It clung to the wheels as well, and soon they would no longer turn. Pushing the bicycle was hard work. Every so often I'd have to clean the wheels with a stick, or they wouldn't move an inch. I felt about ready to cry, not just because of this horrid path I was on, but because France was the one who had recommended it. Did he not know about the slope, or had he done it on purpose? All of this tormented me until I made it to the road, just passably cleaned the bicycle of mud and rode into the valley. I had to walk uphill again. On the way up, a man whom I knew only fleetingly joined me.

"You're Angela's girl, aren't you?" he asked me.

"I am."

"How are things with those Americans? Did they catch the rest of them?"

"I don't know. I don't know anything about that."

"They treated them poorly. They didn't need to kill them, after all. People today are such beasts; like I said."

Seeing that I had nothing to say, he continued:

"What about the hail, did that cause you any trouble?"

Now he had begun to annoy me.

"Of course. On that evening in August the hail damaged everything on our peak. What can you do?"

"You know what I carry around with me? Wait, let me see if I've got a summons for you, too! I carry summonses; there are trenches to dig. I have one for almost every house. Look, I find it odd that they've let you off scot-free. Ah, here's one for Maria and one for Lizika. Do you want to give them these?"

"Well, if you offered me something good, I'd take it to them. This, you can go ahead and take them yourself. I might even lose something if I do it. Bye!"

I rode off. And now this, as well? Trenches by the river— and Maria will be digging them!?

I was nearing home. The thought of you put some spring in my step, so that I continued apace as I pushed my bicycle. Just as I never was afterward, I was now not entirely hopeless. Even though it was late in the day, from somewhere in my subconscious came encouragement:

"What if they've already carried him to safety? Someone might have come to examine him." But as soon as I thought of my uncle, such futile consolations lost their meaning. He could have discovered, reported, or even killed you. My not-so-encouraging thoughts were further substantiated by Mother, who was standing by the woodshed and waiting for me.

"Nothing?" she asked dejectedly.

"In the evening, the night ... or not even so soon as that. Where is Uncle?"

You couldn't have possibly had any idea how we fought to keep you alive, even though the state you were in in that hideaway no longer very much resembled living.

"Uncle is home. He's holed up in that snuggery of his and says he's ill."

"And the one in the hideaway?"

"The fever hasn't let up yet. I gave him vinegar compresses. They ought to be changed regularly, but I can't visit him so regularly. Fortunately, there's enough foliage along the bushes that he's out of sight of the neighbors. And anyway, they're far."

"You think the neighbors would ...?"

"You can't be sure of anything; such are the times that father fears son and daughter fears brother."

I brought my uncle some potato soup. He sat up in his bed and looked me over with a lost expression on his face.

"What's wrong, Uncle?"

"I'm ill. I can't breathe and something hurts here'. He pointed to his chest.

I already had a bitter comment prepared:

"You were fine last night when you ...'

"When I what!? These bastards all need to be killed! You know how many *they've* already murdered. Entire German cities lie in ruins!"

His watery little eyes glinted furiously. I might have taken a risk, but it was sooner or later good that I had learned the truth. In silence I went to Mother.

"Mother, Uncle would turn him in in a heartbeat. Us, too. He doesn't care one bit. This I know now, even though I was once actually convinced

that he could see the absurdity of his vain hopes for victory."

I took a bowl of homemade vinegar, placed it in a pail and made my way to you. Do you recall?"

"Yes; 'Rick', I said to you. You smiled and told me your name. I ran my fingers over my face and wished I could be well. Perhaps it was you who ignited this silent wish in me. You were so adorable, a wholesome girl with rosy cheeks. You took your hand and stroked my forehead and put a wet cloth on it, and I knew my eye was still bruised and swollen because I couldn't open it. Then you put that wet, unpleasant-smelling compress on my chest. It helped, but I knew that it wouldn't be enough for my pain and injured hand. Your good intentions would not have cured me. As you were leaving, you asked if I wanted food or drink. I shook my head. I wasn't hungry; not afraid, either, because I knew that you wouldn't turn me over. Still, the pain of losing John added to my physical suffering; it was obvious to me that he couldn't jump from the plane in time. I was also worried about all the others who had been forced to land. You put the straw back in place and went away. The only ray of light left in that place was thin and golden and crept through that slit in the wall and only died down in the evening. That's when I a few pleasant thoughts finally came ..."

"Yes, we had renewed hope in the evening as well.

"Mother," said Ivan as he came running from pasture, "they asked me if I knew where they are ..."

"Who asked you?"

"I dunno, some men in brown uniforms. I dunno what they're called. They talk in Slovenian," he said in one breath.

"And what did you tell them?"

"That I didn't know anything. I only saw a broken plane and that's it."

"You said the right thing. Where are those people now?"

"They went in the forest again ... to the airplane."

"And the cow? You say it's waiting in the vineyards. You must go and get it right away!" she yelled at him.

"Mother, it's a good thing he told them what he did and came here right away."

"What good will that do us? If they start sweeping the area, they'll find him."

"And then they'll kill him …"

"Yes, and us as well … But if we don't get him out of the den, he'll die all the same. His hand is all black and blue, he's got the fever …"

"I know mother, I was with him … He speaks, I don't understand him, but still …"

"Perhaps another night or two …"

All at once, something new came to mind. I hastened to Uncle's room. He was lying on his back, groaning." Once he saw me, the expression on his face eased.

"It hurts. Here, you see." He found my hand and pulled it towards his chest. I had never touched a man's chest covered with sparse grey hairs before. My fingers therefore contracted and resisted on their own. My body shivered at the sense of something obscene, perhaps it was repulsion. I stepped to the door. I turned to look at the man for another brief moment, and then was gone.

"Mother, uncle is ill. What if we were to call the doctor and …"

"You can't your mind off the American. I see."

"There's only one doctor in the square and he's German. He'd do for Uncle, but for him … no."

 She went to see Uncle, and I accompanied her.

"We're sending for the doctor," she told him.

"What doctor now?! I'm hardly so ill as to need one. I have a fever, that is true, but it will pass," he said, his voice verging on anger.

It could be gathered from the look on mother's face that she was also disgusted by the odor of his sweat, the sight of Uncle and of everything that was happening around her. It is true that we tended not to see the doctor over minor ailments. We had never had a physician in our house, nor had any of the other locals. People believed in using homemade remedies, and if those didn't help, the patient would be taken into town, if he hadn't died by then.

The thought of the doctor now began to hound mother and me. It was ridiculous. Everyone in town knew that uncle was a thorn in our side, that we'd rather be rid of him sooner than later. He had social insurance, after all … Somewhere deep within me burned a thought—not of him, but of you.

We lit a paraffin lamp. Mother said to me:

"Go and fetch a small light, light it and take it to your uncle!

I obeyed. I groped the surface of the table, and realized the lamp hung on the wall. When I wanted to draw back the curtain to see a little better, the lamp slipped from the wall. It glanced the edge of the table and shattered. The unpleasant smell of petroleum filled the space. My uncle muttered:

"Well, now I'll be in the dark!"

Mother heard the clattering and came running.

"You silly cow! You'll be holding a splint all night long, will you?"

"I didn't mean to, mother," I apologized and went into the courtyard.

A thick gloom hovered over the hill, and the valley below was just as dark. The wind had ceased and it seemed the night would be cold. Sullen, I entered the leaf shed. I slowly crawled across the straw and descended toward you.

There was something I wanted to say to you, but I knew you couldn't make sense of it. My hand felt your forehead. It was hot. There was no sweat, only enormous warmth. You pulled your good hand out from beneath the cover and with it gripped my own. You squeezed my hand, and from your chapped lips issued indiscernible sounds. I forgot about uncle and suppressed my fear. At a loss, I sat beside you, the way a helmsman sits aboard a ship, in the middle of a raging sea - with no sign of a lighthouse to lead him to safety. I went to mother. Normally I would have sulked at her for what she had said, but there was no time now.

"Mother, he has the fever. He'll be cold in the night. Please, find him another cover while I make him limeflower tea."

"You aren't possibly implying he'll stay another night? It'll drive me mad. They promised you."

"Of course they did, mother. But anything can happen."

"Ivan." She turned to the corner, where my brother was removing his boots. "You shall go to Maria's house and ask her family to lend us a light. Say your uncle has taken ill. Tell Marija she is to come stay here with us tonight."

I took mother's blanket, while mother took a kettle of tea and a light and we went to the barn. Mother hung the lamp inside and followed me as I crept toward you. You lay on your good side. Mouth agape, you gasped at the nearby opening for air. Mother palpated you and said:

"The boy's got pneumonia or worse. He's hot enough to catch fire. Help me move this foliage. He needs more room."

I covered the entirety of your face and body with mother's blanket so that the dust would not suffocate you. We used our hands to tear apart the litter and throw it towards the exit. This caused dust to rise and make breathing difficult, but we managed anyway. We made roughly a yard of room alongside your body so that we could better settle you in.

"Uncover him. I'll raise him up. You give him some tea," whispered Mother. Fortunately, the tea kettle had its lid on. Mother, whose legs now had enough room to properly support her, lifted you somewhat. I set the tea kettle to your lips and immediately felt a liquid flowing over my hand.

"Mother, he isn't drinking. What if he's dead already!?"

"You twit, he's too warm to be dead. Come now, you hold him up and I'll give the spoon a try."

Gradually, you sipped the tea, until I felt the full weight of your upper body on my arms.

"That's enough tea. He can't have any more. Let him lie now," I told Mother.

I lowered you to the pillow deliberately and covered you. Mother and I then piled Father's old clothing against the wooden wall, leaving only a narrow crack visible. Finally, we piled on you everything warm that we had at our disposal.

"The uniform keeps him warm as well," I assured myself.

"It's all too little for someone with a temperature like that.

The night will be cold. There might already be frost in the morning."

We wanted to give no thought to the morning or to anything to do with the coming day. It was, after all, so very far away … Besides, something would have to happen between that day and the next. They have to get you away from here. If they don't, you'll either be discovered or death will be the only thing left for you.

"You know, Mother, it would have been better for him to die in the air or in the forest, just as the others, not here in this damned hole …"

I know that mother thought the same, yet she dared not speak.

"At the end of the day … why on Earth are you sighing?! It's you who brought him here."

My voice trembled. Her unspoken words conveyed to me her every thought. She wanted to say to me that I should do what I wanted. She must have been sick of all the burdens life had given her to bear from the day of her birth until then that she had been unable to shake off.

We loosened the straw behind us and pulled ourselves out into the courtyard. Mother tarried in the barn, while I went to my room and waited in the dark. I pulled and the rusted stove door opened with a pleasant flash, threw wood on the fire and sat. Yet I could not bear to stay in the room. Ivan had been gone for far too long. Before, mother and I had passed the time by your side; now she did this in the barn, and I in my room. I got up, tied mother's kerchief around my head and headed in Ivan's direction.

I had only taken a few steps on the path from the house, when he came running uphill.

"Is that you, Silva?" he asked, panting..

"It's me. Did you get what I asked for?"

"I got the light," he replied briefly and walked on ahead of me. Not until he was indoors did he say:

"Marija wasn't home. Her aunt will tell her when she gets back."

A faint hope sprang out of something not fully understood. What if she went to bring people here to take you away from this place? From out of the darkness rose an even darker thought: What if they've caught her, locked her up? Her and the others? They'll come for us and strike us down - everyone from Ivan to you. Though we were certain Marija would not betray us, such thoughts were never far away in our minds.

Mother returned from Uncle's room and spoke:

"He's fallen asleep. It seems we should bring in the doctor in the morning after all. A fever is a fever. Perhaps we'll receive medicine for your uncle that will do *him* good, too …'

"Mother, do you really think he'll still be here tomorrow?" I asked fearfully.

"If neither Marija nor anybody else comes … Nobody knows …' she answered calmly, as though she had accepted the notion that she must sacrifice another night for a stranger.

"Mother, do you think he will heal?" Ivan butted in.

"He must heal! And that's no business of yours. You know nothing! You cannot know, understood!?"

"Understood, Mother. I know how to lie, you know. I already lied today. It's not a sin anymore; I haven't been to church in a long time."

"Lying is dishonest, but now it's what you must do!" she proclaimed, trampling on the principles she had once striven to ingrain in us.

"Let's go to bed!" I urged.

"You two go! I shall wait."

Mother left with the light, while I, now feeling cold, got myself into bed. Ivan soon fell asleep, but my attempts to do the same were in vain. I might have lain an hour or more when mother entered my room. She was surprised that I still woke.

"I went to see him. The fever has him trembling. His teeth are chattering. I'm afraid. I cannot take your uncle's covering, nor Ivan's, which means that our bed is almost empty."

"Mother, take this too, and give us a tablecloth. There are two more in the closet."

"Yes, now I remember. Those two were a gift from Mrs. Gruber."

She sat awhile on the bench. It was dark, yet I knew she was leaning on the wood-fired oven and staring at nothing.

Suddenly, she got up and felt her way past the table, chair and bed to the window. Even though I had begun sinking into a drowse, I was now alert.

"Mother, do you hear something?" I asked in a subdued voice.

"Maybe. It sounds as though someone is walking," she says as she ducks by the window, while I sit and hold my breath. Minutes pass. Nothing anywhere stirs.

"It's nothing," she remarks disappointedly.

"Better nothing than a search party," I reply.

Mother, seeming only now to realize that the thing that might come to the house quietly might not come to save us, assents to my thought.

"You're right. The Germans would likely also come here in silence."

Yet nobody comes. The time is already past midnight. Mother is again seated, whereas I am in bed, waiting for sleep. With a start, Mother says:

"I'm going to go to see him. It must be difficult for him. He's so alone … He's got it worse than if he were dying on the battlefield."

She might have been carrying this thought around with her all evening long and had only just decided to act on it, or maybe it had only now occurred to her.

"Go, mother. And lock the door. I'm a little bit afraid," came my reply to her as I turned to face the wall.

I wake up. Morning already peeks through drawn curtains. Mother is already up and is straining milk on her bench by the stove.

"Mother, did they …?"

"No, nobody was here. The fever shook him almost throughout the night. I lay close beside him and warmed him. Near morning I began to shiver as well, but then he had somehow warmed up and stilled, as though he had absorbed my own warmth. He now sleeps, absent fever, or so I think."

Her words consoled and excited me all at once. That she spent all night snuggling you … warming you; that was the last thing I wanted to contemplate. I could not imagine anything definitive, and you were sick besides. And yet, perhaps a suspicion like the one I had had about Uncle had surfaced. It had been unjustified then, and it was even more so now.

We didn't bother with Uncle much. Neither of us said anything, but within the depths of either of our souls was buried the wish for Uncle to be seriously ill. Soon, mother came to my bed with the words:

"Your Uncle is also free from fever. He even has an appetite. He wants to hear no more about the doctor. It is true that a temperature drops with the approach of morning, but we shall see later."

"We won't give *him* any compresses. Maybe ... well, we shall see."

Uncle had finished his milk and had succumbed to sleep. Around midday he began yell:

"I'm going to die; you'll all let me croak like a rat in this hovel!"

I ran to his side. He stood in the middle of the room with feet wide apart and a puffed up face, staring at me with bloodshot eyes.

"But I won't expire here, no! Not before someone else does. You think I don't know, ha-ha!" he guffawed in his malevolent voice. He raised his arms and marched toward me. I'm not sure where mother came from.

"Back in bed!" she cried and shoved him backward.

"You think you can tell me what to do, you bloody-' he wheezed, attempting to rise.

He could not. He merely thrashed and flailed his arms stupidly about the air.

"Yes, *I* can! If I tend to you, then I can as well have my say. Don't play the hero while you're still ill. Lie down, you've got the time and space for it!"

"You call this space? This is a stinking rattrap. Yuck!" He spat forcefully at the wall.

"Ah, so! Then out of this rattrap with you. I'll drag you out into the open. Thither where it's fresh and everything smells agreeable." She charged him.

"Mother, leave him be! He doesn't know what he's saying."

"Don't hit him!" implored Ivan, who had rushed in from somewhere. She turned to me, calmed herself to a degree and told me:

"Go to the Kočevar's house. Tell them to yoke the cattle and fetch the doctor. Or, if they wish, they can just as well drag him to the hospital. I shall waste no more nerves on this old nuisance! I can pull my own weight without issue; tell them that."

"Not to the hospital, I'll be good. Just not there!" began to plead Uncle, now even redder than before. He seemed completely helpless to me then, shriveled and pathetic. Even though I had thought a minute ago that we'd be rid of him and that you'd take the place on his bed, I pitied him now. As I went hastily across the hills, with the leaves shed on the ground, , I knew all I wanted was that they seek the doctor's help.

Mother was cooking chicken when I returned from the Kočevar house.

"Will he leave?" she asked impatiently.

"They've already yoked the animals," I replied.

Meanwhile, Ivan had arrived. Straw clung to his back. He said:

"The American ... he's gone all grey ... he isn't breathing at all."

"Shoo, shoo! I was there an hour ago and he was still asleep. Who gave you permission to go there, eh?" Mother grabbed his ear and angrily jerked him toward her.

"Ow! Let me go! I always go there. And he likes me. He always smiled at me. But not this time, because he's dead!"

"Little rascal, don't you start now too!" she mouthed angrily and headed for the door.

"No, mother, I'll go!" I said. With difficulty, I wormed my way toward you. I climbed down the straw directly to your feet. You did move an inch. Your face was motionless. The light fell upon it, which made it appear even paler. Only your untrimmed beard was dark.

"He *is* dead! Ivan isn't an idiot after all!" I said to myself. At first I kept my fingers from reaching for your face, but after a time they did so as with a will of their own. Your cheeks were cold, your eyes closed. I stooped over you and whispered:

"Rick!"

Nothing. I spoke your name again, louder this time. Your eyes began to slowly open. Even the injured eye peeked through its swollen lid in the shape of a thin, light line. In that moment we were both resurrected: you as well as I. I smiled and you smiled back. You could not, however, speak. For that reason, the sword of Damocles, suspended above our heads, could not be lifted … Stilly it loomed ominously over us, the entire peak and all of the valleys among our hills … Mother spent the morning cooking and cleaning the house. The clock had already struck three when we heard Kočar's voice in the courtyard.

"The doctor is here," I ran to tell my Uncle.

Mother stepped in the doorway. Kočar explained:

"The doctor's not here, but I have brought this lady."

Into the room walked a woman roughly forty-five years of age. She had an unusually round face and fair hair combed across her forehead. She tried to say something in our language, but did so with a comical stutter.

She then went to see Uncle in his little room. Mother and I stood stiffly before the door and exchanged glances.

"Mother, will you tell her? She's a woman. And she's certainly not German. Perhaps …'

"That doesn't change anything. I don't know what it is we should do. Should I try? It would be better if the doctor were here instead; we wouldn't be at all tempted then. But now … I simply don't know. Tell me, what!"

"Mother, I don't know. We stand to gain or lose everything."

Time was inevitably running out. Any moment now she would come out of the room and soon after, leave the house. And he would die of pain or poisoning, it didn't matter which … He would simply perish. We wouldn't even know where to bury him.

We were terrified. At times I would act as a pillar of support for my mother, but on that day I could not see the glass as half-full. Mother's outlook was even bleaker, for she knew life better and was more aware of its very real consequences.

The door creaked open. The woman came into our room and

washed her hands in a small wooden trough in which we too would wash our hands. Who knows, perhaps the object reminded her of something, for she smiled amicably, took the trough in her hands and examined it. She said something unintelligible. My mouth was so dry that I could scarcely move my tongue. Mother, however, collected herself and asked:

"How is it?"

"Sickly ....badly. He is clearly sick."

With that she pointed to his chest.

"Pneumonia," Mother affirmed.

At that moment, Kočar joined us and began to converse with the woman in Serbian. They seemed to understand each other. To my mother he said:

"He's spent several nights outside. It's no wonder - he must have caught something."

"Well why did he? I didn't force him to," mother answered rawly.

I knew that Kočar had now thwarted all of her plans, yet she made the best of it and sent him to uncle.

"Go ask him if he wants to go to the hospital."

The doctor ruined everything with the words:

"All full of soldiers."

Hence Kočar stayed. The doctor wrote a prescription for some medication that would counter the fever and another to dull the pain. She bade farewell and climbed into her carriage. We later learned that she was Russian and had fled the advancing Russian army. The Germans did not like her, but they did need her.

"Will you bring the medicine?" mother asked Kočar as she waved him the prescription.

"I cannot leave the horse alone on the road. Have Ivan accompany me; he's got time."

Ivan seemed quite joyous at the occasion of riding to town, and in a carriage at that.

"Remember, for the fever and for the pain." Mother was rubbing her hands together.

"What about his hand? It's still completely bowed out and swollen. It may not be broken after all," I mentioned in an attempt to comfort Mother and myself.

"You know, your father once sprained his arm and I remember what we did. He asked that I place it between two boards and tie it all together. Shortly thereafter, everything was in order again."

"Yes, Mother. If the bone isn't broken, that might help. We can surely try. Is the soup ready?"

"Go and look, and add some sliced meat to it for me, would you? Something warm and filling will restore the man's strength. It's a shame we've only got three chickens. I had intended to keep those for Christmas."

"By then the war might be over and we'll be able to buy something."

"Perhaps. We'd have more chickens if Gruber weren't so petty. They ate some of his berries and would only get in his way. And now that the hail has battered most everything this year, everything's just peachy."

"Thank goodness, too. If we had had a normal harvest, we'd still be picking grapes and pressing them into must. What a headache that would be. This way, we finished with everything in a single day. There's only one barrel of must in the cellar this year, but what do we care?"

From the grape press, wherein the smell of grape skins still abounded, I took with me two slats. Mother prepared a grey flaxen towel. I came to you first, and mother followed some time thereafter. She placed the pot of soup in a tub, which she left in front of the barn. First, we fed you the thinly sliced meat and soup."

"Yes, I remember this. You pushed spoonful after spoonful into my mouth, so fast I could barely swallow. But it meant a lot to me …

The worst part was when the two of you took on the role of doctor. Your mother stretched my arm and tried straightening it. You were ready to compress it with those boards, but you noticed I was getting all sweaty. I was literally sick from the pain. So you threw away the boards; your mother rolled up my shirt sleeve. She looked in disbelief when she felt my forearm and saw that the bone was almost sticking through my skin."

"She said: "Let's leave it, it's broken. He must be in great pain. It's just as I thought, because of how bad the swelling is.""

We wrapped your arm, tucked you in and left.

We waited impatiently for Ivan. Mother did her chores in the barn while I took care of Uncle.

He had no interest in eating and seemed to be doing worse than you, at least as concerned his condition.

Every so often I looked at the big old clock, which was running slow at the time.

"Uncle, you'll get your medication soon," I joyed to say.

"I don't care for any medication! You'll poison me!" he barked.

"Mother, Uncle says he won't take his medication!", I said to her when she had entered the room.

"What have you got to fear? This is your medication, German medication, and German means sweet and good, does it not?" she said bitingly.

Ivan returned by dark. He set the bottles and boxes on the table and said:

"Everything is written here. One bottle and box for that man …"

"I suppose they didn't tell you that," mother smiled warmly.

Oh, in how long we had not seen her this way! And how in need we were of her lighthearted words!

"They didn't say anything, they only wrote this: twice two and thrice one—what? spoonful …" my brother sluggishly read the German word.

"That's good news. If they knew we're harboring an American they'd have given us poison."

"Or a whole mountain of medicine, considering we don't know what type runs the pharmacy," I added to what mother had said.

"If they were our people, they wouldn't have written

"*Löffel*", but spoon, the honest way, in our language," she added.

Ivan opened the bottle of tablets and emptied its contents onto the table. Several rolled over the edge and onto the floor. The cat lept from its basket and tried to catch one of the tiny white objects.

"Hold on a moment, that isn't for you. As for the mice ..."

"Look at this! Now you've rolled them on the floor!" Mother swung and her hand grazed his head.

"I've picked them up, haven't I? And I only dropped three," pouted my brother. He collected the tablets, wiped them on his jacket and laid them on the table.

"Put those away. We might not need them!" ordered mother as she removed the tablets that had been on the ground.

"Fine, I'll take them to Uncle first, to see whether it does any good," I suggested.

"You think it's some miracle tablet that will take effect immediately? Waiting is required with every medication. At least that's what I think, although we used homemade remedies if someone fell ill. When could a vintner ever afford to see the doctor? Once, there was not enough money in all the house to buy a candle for the dying. Now then, give me the spoon and tea and let's be off."

We went to see Uncle. He was thrashing and flailing as if to express an aversion to everything. This angered Mother, who said:

"Do you think we sent the driver to town to fetch you your medicine for nothing? I certainly have no need of it. It's for you!"

"Give it to me, Mother, I'll give it to him!". I took the spoon, scooped up some of the disagreeable liquid and slowly carried it before uncle's mouth. He was too slow to fend me off."

"Ugh, that's bitter. And the smell!"

With that he screwed up his face and I became afraid that he would spit it all out. I knew then that he was nothing more than our guinea pig. I'm ashamed of it today; mother may be too. He was a stupid, misguided soul, but he was nonetheless a human being, and we at the time had so little time for people, particularly those of Uncle's sort.

I left the room with mixed feelings: what effect will the medicine have? If it helps Uncle, there's no certainty that it will help you in your shed as well. In these times I, the child of a winemaker, was pulled into the tides of life far too soon.

I was too young for love, if I should even call it that, for it might as well have been a foreign word in our parts. It was altogether too noble for our ears and sounded too mild to exist amid a flood of rough vernacular expressions. It was known to our people through poetry and song. It held a special place in the melodies the singing in our hills was so replete with. Yet this premature emotion that I felt did somewhat resemble love, or at least a deep affection, for a foreign soldier. I was concerned about your health, and as well as I knew that to help you meant to let you go, so much did it pain me to know that we would lose you. My daily trip across swirling leaves was accompanied by fear, yet also by joy.

As I sat helpless at the table trying to organize my thoughts and feelings, into the room walked Mother and Ivan.

"What do you think, Silva, would it not be a good idea if the boy went down to Marija's?" she asked uncertainly.

"I'm not going now! It's getting dark . You should have said earlier. I'm not going!" Ivan protested decisively.

"Ivan, you're a big boy now and you understand what's at stake. Now, go and ask when they're coming!"

He put on his patched jacket while mother wrapped Uncle's scarf around his neck. As he donned the hat on his head, his light hair peeped through the tattered crown. Before he had even entered the anteroom, Mother held him back for a moment and demanded of him:

"Be back immediately! You know we'll be waiting. We won't give him any medicine, and they might take away this very night."

I now remembered Uncle.

"Let's take a look at Uncle, see how he is."

He was asleep and snoring as usual. Mother felt his forehead. I could see how she wiped her hand in her apron afterward. She was disgusted by everything about him.

"He's still hot," she said eventually, "but he's already begun to sweat."

In the room, we measured out his dose of medication.

"Let's give it to him. It's almost a fever now."

"No, if they come to get him tonight and he's sweating, it won't be good."

"Very well, we'll wait then. Ivan ought to be back soon."

Mother set the *žganci* on the table and poured hot milk over them. I had the taste and put down my spoon.

"Mother, the flour is bitter; it's old. They taste awful."

"Add some sugar, then. Be happy they taste the way they do … That was the last of our flour. Tomorrow they won't have any taste at all. You'll be eating potatoes with your milk. There won't be fresh flour anytime soon; the maize hasn't dried yet! And we've only got five baskets of *that*."

Along the loamy path beneath the overhang, the stamping of feet, joined by Ivan's voice, is heard. We shoot each other glances.

"They're coming. Marija is here," I hear mother cheer up.

"Come in! Don't be afraid!" we hear from the anteroom as the door into the living room opens.

"Mummy, I brought a dog," he says gleefully. But once he sees the look of anger on mother's face, the spark leaves his eyes.

"I didn't go because it was dark … And this dog … He came, he barked and I was scared. I turned around and ran home. And he followed me."

"So that's how it is! One sends you on an important errand, and you go looking for mutts! You beautiful, intelligent child, you! Make sure you get out of my sight this instant with that beast!"

"Mother, let him be. The dog isn't ugly at all; in fact it looks like a pup."

The child's big eyes lit up like tiny stars that brighten the night sky.

"We're keeping him!" he exclaimed.

I gave him a nod.

"I've got some dinner for him!" I encouraged him.

"You know, first I was scared of him. But when I saw that he was only sniffing me I grabbed his collar and we walked together. He didn't even make a fuss. I only wanted to see what color he was. And now you're saying ... We're going to have a dog. I've always wanted one," he lied.

"Look at what you've done now; you're putting silly thoughts into the child's head! We haven't got food for ourselves, and now we're to raise a dog as well? And anyhow, it has an owner who'll want it back. If we wanted a dog we'd take our pick from the Kocbeks' litter: they have so many in the spring that they have to drown them all in the pond."

"And the Korens have such lovely ones. Tinek showed me three of them. And one was like this one ... brown and white."

Mother blushed. There was something youthful about her cheeks, something painful long buried. This I saw, though Ivan did not ... All he could see was the pup, the pup that belonged to Koren. In a flash, Mother's cheeks lost their redness, and with that, the past was engorged by the present. Mother's mouth hid the row of white teeth and through ajar lips she fumed the words:

"You don't say? You've been going to the Korens'? I wonder if you haven't blurted out something about our leaf shed to them!"

"I haven't, mother. I only go there to see the dogs; and they've got rabbits, and ...'

"And horses, and cows, and a large estate!" she hissed.

Ivan paid no more attention to Mother. He sat at the table, drew a spoon from the table drawer and began to eat. The dog, a smooth animal with brown spots, sat on the floor and watched him.

There was no need to guess whether he knew Ivan; the dog clearly behaved as though right at home. In her huff, Mother had forgotten about dinner.

"Nobody is coming. This idiot won't be of any use. Maybe I should go there myself."

"You know what, Mother, I think it would be best if we gave the medication a try anyhow," I suggested.

Ivan had already put down his spoon and was petting the dog's head.

"Good boy, Miki!"

"Now you even know its name. Perhaps it wasn't a chance meeting on the road today then, but ...'

"Let's not discuss this now. I've already prepared the tablets, and I've measured out the liquid into a cup."

We brought you the medicine. Mother once again placed the whole thing into a tub while I held a lamp that provided the necessary light. I covered the flame with my right hand, so the wind would not extinguish it, but more importantly so that nobody would take notice of us. Do you recall that evening?"

"I do. You came with that tiny flame in your hands. But to me, it shone like the most brilliant light of happiness. The fever was oppressive and I could have drunk an entire bucket. First you gave me the pills. I swallowed them without thinking twice and I grabbed the cup of tea so hard you couldn't pry it from my hands. Your mother held my head up. Then you forced me to drink that liquid. It came up a moment later. I thought I was about ready to choke."

"Mother ran to fetch a rag and cleaned you up nicely. You used your good hand to signal that your nape was still wet.

"Go and bring another dry rag that we may put on his neck. The medication won't do him any good now, anyway."

I entered my room. I stood there, not knowing whether to laugh or fume. A large bowl of *žganci* had been placed beneath the table; from it the dog was quaffing milk.

Ivan sat next to the animal, so distracted by it that he did not notice me. I smiled, for in that moment he seemed the happiest among us.

"Here, eat, have this, it's sweet!" he said to the dog as he got very close to it.

"Ivan, what are you doing? If mother sees you!"

"We're eating. The *žganci* aren't that great, I mean, Miki doesn't even like them so much. He's almost done. I'll put the bowl on the stove."

I strained some linden tree tea, sweetened it a tad, took Ivan's scarf and returned to you.

I find my way to you by touch; I hear the abrupt rustle of straw and leaves behind me and become alarmed. I mean to say something, but the dog barks first and heads down to you. The barking is furious now. Mother is disoriented at first, then manages to say:

"Give me that pot! Grab the dog and drag it out! It can't just bark here when it pleases! Someone will be here before you know it! It will get us all killed."

I take hold of the dog with my left hand and use my right to help crawl out of the hole. The dog races about, barking and jerking in the process. I step out of the leaf shed. Ivan is waiting for me by the entrance.

"Here, keep your eye on him! Shut him in your room!" I whisper as I bear back toward you. As soon as I prostrate myself on the foliage, Ivan stops me.

"Silva, someone's coming. You two turn off the light and hide! I'll wait with the dog by the door."

Once we had returned to my room, Marija and France were already waiting for us. Mother gave them a questioning look. Marija understood immediately and said:

"Nothing tonight. Tomorrow evening. If you've been patient this long, you'll have to be until tomorrow afternoon as well."

"Afternoon?" Her mouth was agape.

"Yes, Kocbek has raked together the foliage in the valley. He'll load it up and drive here."

"Now? Won't that seem odd? Nobody rakes leaves this early when it isn't dry," Mother remarks waveringly.

"Don't worry, the leaves don't matter at this point. You do understand," interjects France.

"So at the first sign of dusk … The leaf nets with the hay will be on the cart. Store the leaves. The hay must stay. Cover him with it … Kocbek already knows … We have to be off now. We're in a hurry. France has a long week ahead of him."

"Good night!" they both whisper simultaneously in the doorway and vanish into the darkness. Just as Mother intends to bolt the door, the dog slips past her and runs straight for the leaf shed. Ivan races off after it and hauls it back.

"Mother, we'll keep him in the room so he doesn't bark," he tells her convincingly.

"Of course, he'll sleep with you! And where will you put

him so that he won't bark?"

"Only for today, Mother! Tomorrow I'll take him back, if you want."

"I do! Of course I do!"

With those final words she unloaded all the ire she had for the dog, for Koren and for everything else that had made her life difficult. In truth, the dog had only been the cause of her outburst of sadness and anger, but it was Koren who had put her off her stride. The wrong he had done her had never been satisfied. This stung her. The war, which had brought others misfortune, had been his salvation. He had donned his brown uniform and frightened people with it. It is true that he had permitted American parachutists to escape, and there was no crime of which anyone could accuse him, yet he never showed his true colors.

The people could loathe him, but the hills would not ostracize him.

He may have tried to get to Mother; perhaps he wanted a third time to revive what had once been left to perish. Maybe he succeeded.

Their secret agreement remained a secret to us. Maybe they had made the most of a situation that fate had offered them. Fate had truly showed Mother no magnanimity, but Koren had no right to complain, except because of a guilty conscience. My Mother he owed a twofold debt that remained unsettled.

Mother did not have much time to think. She was harried by her work, by her worry for the two of us and as well for you. It was besides not possible to sink into deep contemplation while performing household tasks. That last forenoon, the one on which you were still with us, she spent outside by the house. I'm not sure why. Perhaps it was because the trees had already shed their leaves and one could see all the way down to the valley and to the neighbors' peak. Her eyes, which with each passing day sank a little deeper into her yellowish and ever more wrinkled face, wandered into the distance - to Koren's place - to her own. Only seldom did those eyes carry that look. To us children, it was alien. A fire burned in those eyes, the fire of youth, as it once had, when that comely girl had woven bright dreams of a grand homestead and of him … Of him, for I think she loved him more than her possessions. What leads me to this conclusion? She never seemed to mind living in poverty. It is true that she did not speak to me of love. How things can change in one's life! Later I came to accept the fact that it is possible to lose everything we have in this world. She had Koren, and that's why she lost him.

I watched her through a little window. She was still standing outside beneath the overhang and shielded her eyes from the sun with her right hand, all the while gazing *thither* … In vain. I left her to her trance, knowing that as a vintner, she could only rarely open her heart to inner motivations, since they were now outnumbered by those without. When she came into the room, she seemed ordinary in every way again. The tiny creases around her eyes deepened and gave her a stern and sullen countenance.

The ache that lingered in her heart had again hardened. Perhaps it had never arisen on its own, but simply as the companion of jealousy - of "that", as she called it. I was curious how long she would tolerate their dog. We ended up keeping it for quite a while.

The time had never flown so quickly as now. Our farewell lasted from the moment we learned that you were bound to leave to the point of your actual departure. In the morning I brought you your tablets, yet gave you no more fluids. Your eyelid had lost its blue tinge and was now instead the color of a lime. Your lips twitched when I explained to you that you would remain for another seven hours before finally leaving."

"I was gathering my thoughts and forming them into words. I should have told you about the feelings you get when you're about to die. They coursed through me in those very dramatic moments when the damaged plane dived headlong towards the ground. When it was close enough to almost graze the tops of the trees, all I could see was blackness, and blackness was all I could see when I parachuted and my feet looked for solid ground. And when I left you, all I could do was thank you. My conscience couldn't register the meaning of "goodbye' at the time."

"And I wanted to tell you to come visit us. But not when the hills lose their fruits, not when the bare trees stand in melancholy solitude and the last few leaves are carried away on the breeze. No, come when the peaches blossom in the vineyards, and wait for the apple trees' blooming. And then spend all summer long with me until the hills are flooded with the songs of the grape-pickers and those meld with the song of the wind rattles and then fade in the pressing room. Then you shall see that our world is wide and vast, and despite its paucity, rich. Do not judge us by this little hole we live in, for we are good. Our coarse words hold the truth, and we wear our hearts on our sleeves. My mother is part of this world: she's as rough and hard as the earth, but like the earth, within herself she hides treasures; the earth gives birth and proffers up its sublime grapes, just as mother comports herself nobly in the grave and earnest moments such as the ones the war brought. Had the war never occurred, I might never have known the wealth of her spirit.

We said nothing then. Your lips had hushed, tightened, so that your eyes were all that moved and occasionally stopped on me. Our last, silent moments together became etched in my heart and captured your image. I took your hand, did my best to smile. Then I rose; you turned after me and said something … Your sick eye shuddered, but in the other I saw the glint of wetness.

I did not go to you the rest of the day. Mother took care of everything. We bade each other a farewell that endured in our childhood memories …

"Ivan, go and see if Kocbek is already in the forest. I'll go help him, so people will think we're putting away the litter," commanded Mother.

"I'm going. I'll go right away. Mother, the American is well. He laughed when I showed him … the dog. He didn't even bark at him any more. He licked his hand."

"Is that so?! You've still got it then, have you?"

"I shut him in the empty barn, Mother. He's inside and he's whining, but he won't bark anymore."

"Return that animal! Take it back to where you dragged it from!"

"I can't, mother. I already begged him in the summer. They killed the other ones, they only kept three. I only got to take mine now. The others got theirs ages ago, because they were too big. But I was afraid ... Now that that man will leave, we can keep him ..."

"Mother, I like him too. He's such a beautiful animal," I did my best to help my brother.

"Enough of this now! What did I tell you? Go down and look!"

Ivan obeyed, as he had already been given partial assurance that he'd be allowed to keep the dog. He took it in his arms and carried it with him like a child. He ran with it through the hills, no, not ran; flew. How little a child needs to be happy ...

Some ten minutes later, Ivan was already back. Mother was just with
you. She seemed oddly pleased when she returned and said:

"The boy will make it out alive if the right people take care of him. I don't think the medication is so terrible after all. He's eaten, and I washed his face and hands today. He can't leave us all filthy."

"Mother, take the pitchfork. Kocbek is already in the forest," reported Ivan.

Mother departed. Ivan scampered off after her. I grappled over whether to go to you once more or not. What would I say to you? Nothing, I didn't know how. In my mind still lingered the reflection of your gloomy eyes.

Kocbek had nearly loaded all the leaves himself, so it wasn't long before mother was back.

"Where is Ivan?" I asked to break the silence.

"He's sitting on the cart, cuddling that mutt." She waved her hand. "And Kocbek is riding up the hill toward us."

I stood at the lower end of the house and stared down the path. The wagon stopped in the middle of the incline. It was a steep slope; the wheels had lodged themselves in the viscid mud. I heard

Kocbek goading his horse, and I couldn't keep from hearing the cracking of the whip. One more turn was all that was left of the path, and one that was gentle, and not as mired in mud. Then he'll be here and he'll steal you away, from us, but most of all, from me …

The seconds fly as they bring they bring that final moment of farewell constantly closer. I could have still come to your side, tucked you in your blanket, stroked your forehead. Yet I didn't. Kocbek now appeared together with Mother—yes, Mother, who always plays her part to perfection.

They are here already. Ivan jumps from the cart, the pup with him. I retreat to my room to calm my nerves as much as I can, but Kocbek's yelling serves to do anything but calm.

He turned into the courtyard. The cottage shook when the horse by the drawbar jumped.

"Damn creature, have you not tired yet?" cursed the driver.

"How will he tire from hauling a handful of foliage?!" Mother chimed in.

"Foliage, no. Mud, aye. This treacherous slope should be all covered in gravel, or the livestock might bloody well drown in it," Kocbek grumbled on.

"I have no need of any. If you farmers want a better path, you'll have to make it yourselves. I'll make my way just splendidly up the grassy path with my wheelbarrow and basket," Mother countered.

"Let's go, let's to it! It'll be dark soon!" impelled Kocbek as he grabbed the wheelbarrow that had been tipped up to almost vertical, and threw it onto the meadow.

We hurriedly emptied the leaves out of thecart. . We worked carefully, making sure to not dump any on your hideaway, even though Mother had covered your face. Kocbek pushed the cart backward to the very entrance of the shed, so that you wouldn't at all need to be carried out. I stood beside the horse. Ivan was pacing about somewhere near the back of the cart, while Kocbek and Mother went in to get you. In the half-darkness all I could see was how they laid you on the hay and placed next to you a few leaf nets full of hay. The horse should have drawn the cart by now.

Suddenly, from out of the barn sounds, like thunder from a

clear sky, a hoarse voice:

"Haha! I was right in the end. I've got you know, my little darlings ... I always suspected as much ... That's why I had to stay in bed. But now, just you wait ...!"

"What do you want, old man?" Kocbek made to approach him.

"Go, he doesn't know you!" commanded Mother and shoved Kocbek against the cart.

"What do you want, you vixen?" Uncle asked Mother once she had moved right next to him.

"Nothing. Go to bed, you're ill!" she placated him.

"To bed, you say? I'm going down to tell them ... to stop wasting their time looking for him," he hissed through clenched teeth.

"Have some of this, scoundrel!" She walloped him on the head with the pitchfork. He wheezed and slowly sank to the floor beneath the doorway to the barn.

"Go, drive," mother urged nervously, "let's be done with him already!"

Kocbek hesitated for a moment longer, whereafter the horse finally drew. Instead of stepping to your side and stroking your cheek, I was obligated to tightly take hold of my unconscious uncle by the hand and drag him indoors.

Ivan escorted the cart a part of the way. Once Mother and I had moved the old man inside, he did not stir.

"Mother, you've slain him!" I said in horror.

"I have not. I've merely silenced him," she reassured herself, though I could see the unease she herself felt. I ran to fetch water.

"Oh, it's all bloody in here," I sighed when I had returned.

"Curse it ... I didn't think that ... The pitchfork is sharp I've cut his scalp. It's not too bad. It'll be fine for today. We'll manage with it tomorrow."

She wrung out the sponge and washed out his wound. The water became redder.

"Mother, what if it doesn't stop?" I asked timidly.

"It will. It must; if not, we'll think of something to say. It's not as though he can speak anyhow."

"I'm sure the doctor can revive him," I prattled on.

"Who'll go looking for a doctor now, then?" she snapped, agitated now.

By the time Ivan reappeared, the wound was no longer bleeding.

"Out with you. There's nothing for a child to see here!"

I walked up to my brother and asked him:

"How far did you go? Did anyone see you?"

"Well, it's dark. The Kovačes were on their barn and asked us why were out so late."

Ivan began to nibble and sip his supper of black bread and milk, while I returned to Mother and Uncle.

"It looks better. He'll be himself again soon."

"What if he finds himself wanting back into the valley once more?" I asked.

"This one isn't going anywhere tonight. He's feeble and would collapse on the way."

"Mother, I suppose that wouldn't be a bad thing," I mouthed a thought that had suddenly surfaced.

"Perhaps, but before anything would befall him, he would make his proclamation as loudly as he could. Someone would surely hear him. He must not leave this house, do you understand!? If there's anything more he demands, we shall convince him that he's lost his wits and that none of it has any truth to it. Or, or … I'll …'

Her eyes shimmered menacingly. I had only seen her so bothered once before: when she had met with Koren.

"Mother, you mustn't, he's a living, breathing man. You'd only bring woe upon us. On yourself, most of all. I'm frightened enough as it is," I sighed.

"Quiet down and get yourself in bed. I'll take care of the geezer; don't fret for him."

How everything changed in a heartbeat. First I was trembling for your life, and then I wanted them to take you away. Once they had, there was no time to think of our parting, or of anything else. This uncle of mine made a mess of everything. And now I feared that mother might lose her temper … I do not love him, I may even hate him, yet not so much that he should die for it; at least not like a dog at the hand of my own mother. No, my Mother, crude with me and others though she has been, must not become a murderer!

I toss and turn on my bed. Ivan has squeezed himself against the wall and sleeps tranquilly. The two of us are clad and covered more warmly tonight so that we have no need to huddle together closely. I wrap my arm around his neck. I need something, someone warm by my side presently; otherwise this disorder is sure to undo me. I listen for the creaking of the door and with it, mother's appearance. I hold my breath, hark so intently to discover what goes on behind that door that I hear the pulsing of my veins in my temples. And then, footsteps … redemptive footsteps.

"How is it, Mother?" I ask impatiently.

"What are you afraid of!? That you feared for the other, I understand, but for this one … He will be all right. Sleep."

I forced upon myself this idea and slept a little more easily. The following morning was dreary and cold. I could feel my soul chill as well. Your hiding place was dead. A lightless void now yawns where yesterday you had lain and subsisted on warmth and light. For a minute or two I rested on your bed and stared blankly. I rose and sealed tight the hole with leaves. Do you remember how it felt in the bunker?"

"Only vaguely. All I know is they had a lot of work with my hand, because it probably wasn't healing right. The nurse, she might have been a doctor, was experienced and worked with skill.

Under her care I gradually got better. A few days of rest in the warmth of the cellar did me good, but later I began to feel caged. I was sick of walking around that same few square feet, sick of sitting and lying down. I listened to the radio, but the reception was so bad I could barely make anything out. It lifted my spirits all the same. As cramped as it felt, I wanted to live for something, to do something, to savor the air itself. Maybe somebody else would be content to pass the time waiting for the war to end like that, but I wasn't. I got chills when I heard the buzzing of our planes from that damp cellar.

I was mad at myself, and I cursed the guns that hit us, that plunged me from the clear skies into the rotten depths. Now and then I'd see one of those activists come by, but not one spoke a word of English. Luckily they had taught us basic German back home so we could at least communicate some.

It was the middle of November. I looked at the bleak weather through the window of the big house that I now called home. It was as though the earth and sky had fused, the way the low clouds lay across the barren trellises in the vineyards and bare trees in the orchard. I would only occasionally wander up to the upper level, when my hosts were busy in the courtyard, to see in time if anyone happened to be approaching the house. As soon as I saw anyone doing so, I'd move the bed and drop back into my bunker.

Then, one day Marija came. I had seen her a few times before. She never paid much attention to me, I mean she did have more important things to worry about. But then, one time she sat next to me. She laid out a sketch of some paths and began to explain something in broken German. Her effort was in vain, though, because I didn't catch the most important details.

In truth I didn't need to because I was counting on not being sent anywhere by myself. Marija—I called her Black Marija, since I never memorized her last name - reminded me of someone back home. Once, when I was younger, I was in Mexico, and that's where I must have seen her … Wait, no! That girl *did* have thick black braids, soft skin and a row of strong white teeth, but her eyes were different. And aside from all that, Marija's eyes were dark blue, and her eyelashes were long and dark. Her actions and her form melded into a single harmonious being, and I believe that's what you call *beauty*. It wasn't you that made me shiver, girl, it was her. Anything she told me to do, I'd do it. And tell me what to do is all she would do. I know she didn't catch my telling looks, and my poorly expressed thoughts didn't make any sense to her. It's not that I wanted anything from her - only to call her "beautiful Maria'. That same night, she shook my hand and handed me over to two of her comrades and off we went into the night.

I joined the partisans and spent the remaining days of the war, for better or for worse, with them. I still came across pretty girls and women, but I never saw eyes like hers again. I'm sorry, but that's the truth."

"I understand. You're not the first to say she was beautiful, and many wanted to tell her but never got the chance.

As for that uncle of ours, from then on he refused to ever leave the house. I don't know why, he just lay in bed and accepted his condition. He began to fear for his miserable little life, or perhaps he simply enjoyed being holed up there. Snow fell overnight. The white flakes danced through the air, and one morning Marija knocked on our door.

"We've managed to get the American into the partisan unit. They're already headed for Koroška. He's completely healthy now. He'll be fine. It's no small matter that we kept him alive.

The Germans buried the pilot and two other Americans on the border and covered the grave so no one would know about them. But people knew. Almost every day a few youths would sneak there and shower the grave with flowers. Sometimes the Germans would post guards, but the youths would remain vigilant. Then Mother Nature showered the grave with her own soft white blossoms and there was enough of them for everyone.

"Is there any other news?" came the interruption from Mother, who had no interest in the realm of Marija's daydreams, thought it was a place to which Marija only occasionally drifted.

"There is. I've brought pork sausages. We slaughtered a pig the other day, a registered one. The mayor was crawling about the sty measuring the pig and it made me want to lock him in. We managed to fool him all the same. Mother said that if one pig around the house is squealing that it's best to slaughter the unregistered one in the basement as well. We've got enough of everything in the house now. Once upon a time we were allowed to slaughter a single pig, but now it's got to be two. Everything is measured and weighed so strictly now."

I joyed at the thought of the sausages. The animal we had in our barn couldn't even be fattened up by Christmas with the turnips and carrots we were feeding it.

Mother was emptying her basket and saying:

"We'll be sure to repay you at Christmas, provided these bones collect any fat. There has been no feed this year. I was unable to earn any corn, with all the work to be done at home all year round. Uncle still had his health and might have been of service. Instead all he did was go for walks through the hills and be in everyone's way in the house trampling the earth for nothing. Now he's even more of a nuisance. He squats in that closet of a room and keeps himself warm."

"It's a good thing he's indoors and doesn't know anything. The Kocbeks have a bunker full of people. Even their attic is fully occupied. The family is taking care of everything. The boys will stay another day or two to collect all
the brown uniforms in the village and around the peak. There's to be a big operation in the night."

"This night?" asked Mother.

"Yes, it has to happen tonight. We already have the lists," Marija explained. Another unusual thing happened that afternoon. The Germans moved their troops into the valley; they were posted at nearly every house, if they hadn't already been there before. There weren't as many at the houses of the winemakers near the peak, because the cottages were not spacious enough. At around midnight, there came a loud knock at our door. Mother became frightened and first asked who it was. "*Aufmachen!*", Open the door, came the gruff reply. Mother mumbled something and went to wake uncle. Uncle awoke and leapt to his feet immediately, apparently gleeful at the occasion to once again meet a German soldier, and turned to Mother:

"They want the key to the storage shed. They say they're going to sleep inside."

Mother, who had gotten dressed in the meanwhile, rooted

herself before Uncle and said loudly:

"Tell them that I haven't got the key and even if I did … Gruber is their man, let him give them the key. I am nothing more than his vintner."

"What do you mean you haven't got it?! Even I know where it is … And I'm going to give it to them. You ought to know that people need a roof over their heads and some warmth to sleep. I know there's a great big oven in the storage shed," he bragged, and from the corners of his mouth, an evil grin spread over his pale visage.

I stood in the middle of my room and peered through the murky light trying to guess what would happen next. It soon made sense: they'd make their residence in the shed, and then Uncle would wander there and tell them … If not today, then another day.

Suddenly, Mother spots me and exclaims:

"To bed with you! What are you doing here …?" Her eyes light up, and a moment later, hint at something. I understand.

I leave the door ajar, allowing me to take the key from the closet and climb under the bed without arousing notice.

"Will you give it to me or not?" I hear Uncle say.

"Take it yourself; I shall not give it to you!"

Uncle hobbles in the direction of the closet, Mother shoots me a glance, I close my eyes and we understand each other. The soldiers still stand at the door and wait.

"It's not here!" says Uncle as he continues to search the closet.

"Where do you have it, eh?" he sniggers and steps right next to Mother. The soldiers are now at his back.

"Don't know," Mother shrugs, with less conviction than before.

"Here, this is for - well, you know what it's for!" He slaps her cheek, clearly not with much force, as she sidesteps and spits in his face.

"And that's for having treated you, you pig!" she erupts.

I do not understand why the soldier jumps in and strikes her once, twice, a few more times, every time on the head. I jump from underneath the bed and scream so loudly that the soldier pauses his assault and glares at me with furious eyes.

"Here, it's here!" I shriek and take the key before Uncle. The German freezes, then launches himself straight at me. In that instant, something inexplicable happens. My Uncle cries out:

"No, she's only a child!"

The soldier's hand, in position to strike, finds only the air. Mother was leaning against the closet. Her eyes were shut, her face blotched red, and her hair mussed and hanging over one shoulder. Ivan, whom the commotion had woken, was now at Mother's side, clinging to her tightly and wiping his face with her apron. Indignation and hatred shined in Mother's bruised eyes, yet there were no tears - not one. At a slow pace, she made her way to the bench and set herself on it stiffly.

She placed her head on the oven top and surveyed us indifferently, as though she no longer knew what was going on.

"Mother!" I called out.

She did not react, except by fixing her eyes on me in a peculiar gaze. Looks like this frightened me, just like everything that had happened and might yet happen. The other soldier held the key in his hand. He twirled the large rusted piece of iron in his fingers and would occasionally take a gander at me. There seemed to be no enmity in his gaze, nothing warranting fear. Only the one who had beaten Mother still seemed agitated as he spat through his teeth:

"*Banditen, nur Banditen!*" Bandits, only bandits!

He looked Uncle over. I did the same. In that moment he needed do nothing more than simply nod, and he would have affirmed everything that had happened with Rick ... so, with you. The little space was suffused with suspense, yet Uncle did not make a sound.

"Let's go," placidly stated the soldier holding the key and made for the door.

From outside, we heard another voice, foreign and incomprehensible. Uncle translated, perhaps for Mother's sake, perhaps for mine; the Germans had no need of it:

"They're already in the storage shed. They opened the door."

"Broke in," spoke Mother now for the first time, "which they could have done in the first place."

She said nothing more. Yet I felt relieved, because I knew that her thoughts had again become engaged in what was going on around her.

The silence, totaling no more than a minute, was nevertheless oppressive, perhaps even to the soldier who had no business striking Mother, perhaps to Uncle. Uncle broke the silence:

"Is there a light upstairs?"

Mother gave no answer. As though she had again distanced herself from us, she was looking in front of her. She wasn't holding Ivan's hand anymore, either.

"I think there is," I took it on myself to reply in her stead, "otherwise give them ours."

In these torturous moments, my brain served me well. I understood that if Uncle went with them to find a light, he might blurt something out. He must stay in the house.

When the old man extended his quivering hand to offer the soldier a lamp, the latter shook his head and showed a large pocket torch of his own that flickered redly. Normally, Ivan would have quickly grabbed the thing and taken note of its every detail by touch and by sight. Now, however, he was utterly uninterested. I could have switched off every light in the world, for it felt as all the lights within us had been snuffed out.

Since that night, which all of us but Ivan obvious spent waking, Mother did not speak a word to Uncle. She wouldn't even look at him.

' "Go ahead and give him that slop if you want to. I don't care. And let him wash it himself if he wants, and if he does not, let the lice chew him clean." she told me when I asked what to give him to eat. Fortunately, the ancient felt unwell and could not leave the house. He limped to the barn with his walking stick and, panting, crawled back into his bed.

His resting place was completely neglected. His unkempt appearance was capable of scaring the casual passerby. But visitors to our house were rare, and those intended for him rarer still.

It snowed without a break. The heft of the fallen snow caused our house to tilt, and the beams in the attic to creak at night. Mother came to wake us, though I was still awake.

"Silva, get dressed! The roof could cave in on us and bury us alive."

She got dressed herself, put on her high rubber boots and went into the courtyard.

"Shine it here!" she ordered.

She was already carrying a long pole to which was attached a ring that we always used to shovel snow. She stepped out from under the roof, used her eyes and foot to fathom the snow and told me:

"I must start in the back. It's leaning that way."

Holding my oil lamp, I followed her. Pluckily, she trudged through the thick snow and carefully cleared the roof. I spent a good hour attending her with my light along the edge of the house and listening to the sound of the snow crashing onto the ground. The house was now surrounded by piles of snow that could nearly reach its straw roof.

"The barn requires my attention as well," she moaned, distancing herself from me.

"Here, mother, let me give it a try," I offered to help.

"Go ahead! You'll see how hard it is."

I raised the pole and set it against the roof. I slowly pulled downward. Then again and again. The heavy pile of snow collapsed and caved in the thin sheet of snow below. From somewhere we could hear voices; they were foreign, and they were drawing closer. From the darkness appeared two soldiers. One of them took the pole from my hands and began with all his force to pound the roof. This gave Mother a scare and she said to me:

"Tell him that if he continues raking in this manner, there will be nothing left of the roof but the rafters."

"I don't know how," I replied. The soldier, as though having gleancd something from what was said, tugged with more feeling. Once the work was done, the pair went down the narrow snow trail back toward the storage shed. Mother removed her drenched socks and threw them on the firewood by the stove. She poured the snow out of her boots straight onto the loam floor. Her face was red, she was out of breath and sweaty.

"That well-rested villain could have pulled out from the shed earlier instead of waiting for me to exhaust myself," she seethed.

"That is true. But they were not even obligated to come. Do you think the other soldiers went to help the winemakers? They care nothing about the shelter offered to them by foreigners, when the roof of their own country is coming down."

The next day I broke a trail to the neighbors' house. Marija was doing the same from her house on the hill. We could barely make each other out in the weather, yet waved a greeting with our shovels all the same. The snow clung to my shovel and the work was strenuous. With difficulty, I shoveled it as far as the neighboring house. The housewife invited me inside and offered me some pork cracklings.

"You've not had your slaughter yet, have you?"

"No, but we shall. I'm not hungry yet," I resisted, even though the inviting scent of the hot cracklings tempted me.

"Please, sit. Marija will be coming as well; she's earned herself a meal too, after all. Our bread is so brown you'd think it were made of chestnuts, and it's as heavy as a rock."

"Ours isn't any better. Mother just mixes in more corn flour," I said.

Once Marija had arrived and had thrust her spoon deep into the steaming rinds, I gave in and followed her example.

"The soldiers have made a mess of everything. They've slithered into our sheds like vipers," Marija fulminated.

"And in the spring they'll surface from their holes and that's when things will get truly awful," complained the neighbor.

"In the spring, ma'am, are you joking?! Belgrade was liberated long ago and so much other territory with it, and you think we'd wait until the springtime? These soldiers will be gone before the snow has melted. And then, ma'am, the hills will come alive again. The wind rattles will sing, every grapevine will fill a whole pail with wine, and not for some master to then take."

"When that happens I won't even deny my old man a drink. Let him get hammered then, even if he ends up snoring the whole week away in his chamber," jested the neighbor.

Marija continued, partly scornfully:

"We're only about to drink, while some have already

indulged in their feast this evening."

"I have no trouble believing that. Did somebody smother a pig under the counter again?"

"No, no! The mayor's stuffed himself full of cardboard."

"I didn't know he was so hungry so soon. He's got his ration cards, hasn't he?"

"The partisans came and told him to remove the picture he had of Hitler from his wall, given how many of his goods he'd already gorged himself on. The picture was big, taped to some cardboard and colored nicely, but he seemed not to have much of an appetite for it; especially because the geezer only had a single tooth left on his upper jaw. When his wife arrived and began to complain that her husband has no teeth, somebody quickly tore away for her a good quarter of the picture so that she could help him. They say that the two of them finished with impressive speed. They've probably had all the Hitler they can stomach now."

"Well that's a joy to hear! Once, around the start of the war, our children brought home one such picture. Right away, I hid it in the oven. I went into town to buy a large red flag, which was the only fabric in the store available without an order form, and it wasn't half bad. Everyone who came to the town square on that last day in April bought one. I dipped it in black dye in sewed the children some violet undergarments. Good thing they ripped, too, or I'd have to fold them away now and again."

"You can't be serious. The mayor *is* the mayor, after all," Marija giggled.

When I returned home, I told the whole story to Mother. Ivan, who was shoveling snow from the wall, entered the room and said timorously:

"Uncle is up. He is going to the storage shed."

"How on Earth did I not see him!?" Mother said with a start.

"Mother, he must not reach it. They'll lure it out of him!" I rapidly concluded.

"Then again, why would he betray us? He has no concern for this cottage; nor does he wish to work. What does he stand to gain if he double-crosses Rick? He's no longer here anyway. He doesn't know about anything else, and he doesn't know Kocbek ...," Mother assured herself, though her words were not so full of certitude.

Ivan went to the door and watched him. Mother also stared at him, through the window, crawling uphill through the vast snow. The black shadow began to disappear among the leafless trees, stumbling away from us into the distance.

"Thank goodness there's no footpath. He'll never make it to the peak," I said, turning to Mother.

"True enough. He's weak, but the soldiers might come across him. After everything that's happened tonight, any sight's a welcome one their eyes."

We exchanged several hard looks and turned to the storage shed, which stood supreme atop our peak, covered by a thick blanket of soft snow from which protruded a dark, domed tower that the snow had failed to encrust.

As time passed, the struggle for my uncle became ever more troublesome.

"Ivan, run after him and tell him … Oh, what? I can't think of anything. He's almost vanished already. He's halfway there now. They'll spot him from behind that turn," Mother grumbled.

Ivan ran along the path. A while later he returned. Alone.

"Uncle is walking all over. I can't," he excused himself. Then was off again.

"Silva, go see Marija. There's a path leading to her house. You'll get there quickly. What if he *does* know Kocbek? Then everything is lost,
if they're still there. It's crawling with army personnel here … Tell her to intercept him, invite him inside, offer him a drink, to lock him in or kill him … it's all the same to me."

I took mother's brown shawl, wrapped it around myself and quickly shut the door behind me. I caught sight of Ivan. His lips beamed widely, his usually pale face now aglow with joy.

"Uncle took a tumble! He's lying in the snow there … Let's go …"

We climbed the hill, endeavoring to overcome the collapsing snow, and nonetheless reached our Uncle. He lay prostrate, his face buried in the snow. His hands struggled to be free of the frigid surface and left deep imprints in it. I lifted him and turned him on his back. He gaped at me stupidly, as though they were seeing me for the first time.

"Uncle, you must come home," I said in an attempt to restore his wits.

Nothing from him. Not even a blink.

"He's loony!" Ivan grinned.

"Be quiet! Help me with him!" I scolded him.

I pushed his hands under his underarms and bound them firmly in the front. His chin was in contact with my hands and for the first time, I did not feel abjectly disgusted by this pitiful and deformed creature.

"Take him, by the legs. And go forward, he isn't heavy," I instructed my brother.

"He *isn't* heavy. Too bad he didn't fall over before so we wouldn't have to carry him so far."

And thus he became bedridden. When Mother realized that his illness would be long-lasting, if not fatal, she even washed that scanty bed of his and attended him.

"Dear, shouldn't we take a break? It's getting dark," Rick said, intent on getting up.

"No, not now! We've got plenty of time. I must tell you how fatally bleak everything became at home. A peculiar silence loitered for a few days and nights, and in the air hung something horrifying. The soldiers would infrequently leave their dwellings in the daytime. When they did, they travelled in groups. Then, one night they simply uprooted. Most of them departed. Even our shed was left empty. In their wake they left desolation. They had indulged in drink in the cellar, so that every barrel had been opened.

A few days later came Mister Gruber. He leant against the doorframe and surveyed the disrepair that had been allowed to pass throughout the house. He displayed no disappointment; his apathy suggested that he had long anticipated this. He then took a pitcher, filled it with wine and thrust it into Mother's hands.

"If they had a drink, you can have one too," he said calmly.

Mother gave her thanks and left the gentleman to his affairs.

We were sitting at the table and dining, when he entered the room. Mother leapt to her feet, wiped her chair with her apron and bashfully offered it, saying:

"Would you like a seat?"

"I would, Angela. And there's something else … only I don't know … the children are here," he said with no regard for us.

"Go to your Uncle in his room," she told us reluctantly.

Then he turned to me and said:

"Silva can stay."

Ivan shot me an angry look, took his food in its clay bowl and exited the room.

"You see, Angela, now they're going to account for the rest of the wine. I don't care much about it, the money is worthless, and I don't drink it much myself. But it seems a shame to let everyone else guzzle it."

"I understand, but what can I do to stop it?"

"I'll hide it, and I'll at least leave one barrel here with you in your back room.

"Mister, our Uncle is in the back room. He's ill."

"Mother, what about the leaf shed?" the thought occurred to me.

"That would work, you're right. But he'll be cold there," she added.

"We'll bury him deep in leaves and put a thick blanket over him," Gruber explained. I looked him over more closely. Time had left its mark on him as well. His hair had greyed, completely at the temples, though a darker patch was still rooted above his forehead. The creases at the corners of his eyes extended along the side of his face. The cracks had also lined his cheeks and terminated beneath his chin. His back had become slightly hunched.

"This we can do; but I cannot do any of it alone. The snow is deep, and the cottage very distant from the storage shed. If you decide to stay the night here, we might attempt it tomorrow. I'll warm your chamber on the upper level of the house."

"Then stay I shall. Perhaps we'll manage to salvage something …'

"How? Why?"

"There are Cossacks in the square. They drink and destroy anything they come across. They say they've brought them here to undermine peripheral support for the front."

"Cossacks, I've heard of them, but I've never seen them," pondered Mother.

They really were here, they came that very night and strewed the hills. We could hear commotion and wild cries in the valley through the night. Approaching morning, Gruber knocked on our window.

"Angela, they're here. We shan't conceal anything; what will be, will be. I'll drain the barrel. Better that it should waste than that they should swill it and cause an even greater stir."

"Remain here for now! They surely won't be here at the storage shed before morning," Mother told him in the anteroom.

"No, I am returning to my house to watch over it and my possessions. I have no desire for anything, but I shan't let them have their way with it!"

"No, stay … Sir, you've been drinking, and …'

"How dare you imply that I am intoxicated! You!" he frothed.

"All it will do is hurt you. These days we speak our minds, and I am not I afraid to do so myself."

"I have drunk and drunk I have my own drink. And now I return to break the kegs. Let it flow …'

He careened off into the cold, dark morning.

Mother slammed shut the door, dressed herself and sat down by the oven. Ivan awoke while I kept astir with Mother. When the day had dawned, she stepped into the courtyard and set to her tasks. She came back with some milk and said to me:

"Cook the milk so that I might take it to the gentleman in the shed."

I readied a bucket and poured into it the warm liquid.

"You take it to him instead; I'll take the geezer his breakfast," Mother reconsidered.

I pulled on my boots and stepped into a clear wintry morning. I could feel the frozen snow biting my toes through the rubbery soles as though I were barefoot. The dormant grapevines had been caked in a glimmering sheath of ice. Frost dangled from the trees. A red sun rose from the horizon, but it could not dispel the

cold. The path to the storage came to an abrupt halt. I had to take big, high steps to continue on the trail Gruber had made two hours ago. I recognized the dents already down by the orchard; I was
not a child of the hills for nothing; I could make them out clearly: gashes on filled barrels. I walked straight to the cellar. In the doorway I detected the familiar sourish smell of alcohol and earth. The blows, which rang with the occasional metallic clink, did not cease.

"Mister, mister;' I called into the murk.

No one replied. I stepped onto the loamy pavement and walked slowly toward the man. The first few barrels were empty - this I knew. Inside, there by the wall - a liquid, red as a ruby, was in thick torrents soaking the ground. Gruber stood in the corner. In one hand, the sleeve of which was rolled up, he held a cooper's hammer. Once he espied me, he momentarily halted his destructive work, whereupon he no longer let himself be distracted. He placed his feet wide apart, took in his left hand the wooden bung and used his right to hammer it once, then over and over again, even though he did not need to. I recoiled as I was sprayed by a golden-yellow liquid. He, meanwhile, stooped and opened his mouth to drink. Our eyes met: his were half-shut, so that their grizzle could barely be distinguished from his puffed eyelids.

"You'll have a taste, no? It's choice. How nice smells and how pleasingly swishes my wine ... no, *our* wine," he roared as he lifted the glass toward the light and peered through it. He maintained his gaze for a while, looking now at me, now back at the glass. And then, something incredible happened. The glass slipped through his fingers and landed with a splash in the liquid on the ground, and Mr. Gruber collapsed immediately afterward.   At first he was hunched against the barrel rack; then he straightened and lay with his eyes shut. And the wine flowed ... there was nobody to stem it, nobody to speed it along. I ran out into the courtyard and cried:

"Help! Someone help me! Mister Gruber ...!"

Nobody heard me, not until I ran to the neighbors. One of them
headed directly for the cellar, while I went home to tell mother. Before I could catch my breath, she said to me:

"Your Uncle has vanished. He's gone."

I was so confused by everything that had happened in the cellar that her words nearly flew completely past me.

I followed my mother to the storage shed. I lit a fire in the main room. Mother and the neighbor hoisted Gruber into bed.

"He's fine. He's just drunk," the neighbor established.

"I could have suffocated. How much wine do you think was spilled while he was all the while inside?"

"He caused such a waste, the fool! He could have shared it with us," the neighbor said angrily.

The night kept Gruber confined to his bed. He slept and no longer had the stomach for wine or for anything else. At night, Mother locked the cellar and returned home.

"The operation that should already have taken place is instead happening tonight ...' Mother informed me.

"Oh, right, they'll be collecting the uniforms ... Who told you?"

"I found out. Marija's brother Janez is back ...'

"Her *brother*? I had almost forgotten she has a brother," I said, surprised.

"He's her half-brother, actually. He's with the partisans, but he's most familiar with matters around here."

She stopped to think and continued:

"Where on Earth to has the old one gone? What does he know and how much?"

The night is boisterous. Rockets glare from the valley, and the occasional rifle cracks. Still dressed up, we lie in wait in our cottage. The night drags on forever. Ivan dozes off every now and then, while mother and I walk about the room, which now seems to us so cramped that we can barely breathe.

"Lie down awhile," Mother suggests to me. "The fire has died and we haven't anymore logs in the house."

I bury myself in my bed sheets and hope for sleep. Yet at this moment, what I want has no bearing on what is real. I am young, yes, but, being at the end of my tether, can no longer follow orders. The world now starts to spin and my head with it spins and swims and my thoughts drown within ... Until Mother grabs my shoulders:

"Silva, get up!"

I need only a short time to regain alertness, for in Mother's voice I detect an especial excitement. She rests against the window and looks through it. I step to the other window. I occasionally close my eyes, and my ears correctly recognize the approach of thundering hooves and shouting. A dejected procession approaches the cart track. It is beset on all sides by Cossacks smiling broadly atop their mounts. They ride, first this way, then that. The horses intermittently whinny, turn in place, then again break into a gallop onward. I strain my eyes and mean to let out a cry, but instead stifle it. They're close now. There are nothing but strange faces, twenty, perhaps more, in shackles, battered and bruised shadows of human beings ... And then I see, mounted on a horse there in the distance next to one of the Cossacks: Marija. The Cossack spurs the horse, and Marija's black hair flutters in the cold morning; she scans the horizon, perhaps in search of our faces; us or anyone who might free her from murderous clutches, and glimpses our cottage. But we are shut in our houses, our hands are empty, our feet falter and our reason fails at the notion of bayonet muskets, black rampaging horses and their even more violent masters. The people simply go. Some are barefoot, tattered. Marija tries to free herself from the grip of the Cossack on his horse. Her feet now touch the ground; this is her forest, here, it all belongs to her. And this world of hers would conceal her in it, for there is not an inch of ground that her feet have not traversed. But no longer ... A strike quells any thought of escape. The rider has taken Marija and has blended with the hills, while the column marches on down the slope.

I slowly opened the door to the house. An hour or so later, when Mother and I were awake enough to move about, we ventured toward the storage shed. The traveled snow across which the captives had been moving had been pocked with footprints and spattered with blood.

The storage shed's cellar door was open. Mother entered first, and I followed her.

"Jesus!" she exclaimed. I jerked myself away, then asked what was the matter.

"He's dead ... Mister Gruber has been laid low." She turned

and ran for the exit.

We dashed next door. The neighbor buried her face in her hands and sobbed:

"They got him in the night; we heard it happen. They killed Kocbek's mother and little Janez too. There in the bunker they also found all the partisans they had taken away before. They resisted, but it all happened so suddenly. It was one ambush after another. I believe Kocbek alone managed to get away, as he was not among the prisoners. There were around twenty partisans. They came for Marija right in her home. Lord, they're going to kill us all! Somebody must have said something. Nothing else explains it … Why did they go straight to Kocbek's place?"

Both Mother and I fell silent. The neighbor looked at us askance. She was no longer crying.

"It must be. How else would they have known about Marija!" mother added.

We went home downcast from everything that had occurred, but even more so on account of our neighbor's words.

"What do you think, who did she suspect?" Mother asked me impatiently.

"Uncle, and I do to."

"Of course, his illness could have been feigned, his frailty a well-masked pretense. And how convenient that he has just now disappeared. Everyone will think … If anything befalls Marija and her family,
they'll never be able to reveal the truth and on our family will forever be a stain - if we survive the war at all, that is."

The dour day sank into uncertainty. The next was even drearier. Spring was already due to appear from somewhere, yet it did not want to, as though it too had been swallowed by the war, and the sun refused to shine. The fog lingered nearly until midday. People walked around aimlessly and waited for the night to come again.

And nothing at all happened on that day, or on any of the following days. The vintners and farmers alike walked the hills, but nobody trimmed the vines, and the vines therefore did not bleed.

When everyone had already grown weary of the evil there, having had to endure the barrage of Soviet grenades from the river's left embankment, we began to feel the weight of guilt on our consciences. The Germans had executed the captured partisans at Kocbek's house, and Marija with them, and the battered corpses had been left in the forest by the filthy grey river. Was not everything in those days filthy, grey, black? Even the snow was black and trodden, having been desecrated by foreign boots. Only the dreams of the young hostages had remained white ... White dreams of freedom.

Later, people set to pruning the grapevines. They shed their blood for all those who had once lovingly grown them. The sugar that the foreigners had once scattered across the vineyards had now been drowned in acidity.

Two days later, in the pond below, they found our Uncle. His hands were bound; his face disfigured. I dared behold this sad grotesque only from a distance. Not even the water could wash away suspicion of his treason, for it was yellow-brown, as cloudy as Uncle's past. Stupid as he had been, he could have been a traitor or he could have not been a traitor. Nobody ever found out.

Yet again we found ourselves at a funeral. Uncle lay in his snuggery, covered in a sheet that had once been white, but was now as grizzly as his face. Everything in the little room was muted, grey. Even the candles, which were said to have once shone for Father in Heaven, were now a dirty grey and shone sallow and pale. Monstrous shadows were cast on the support beams on the ceiling. Uncle was now shaven and spruced up as he had been only seldom before. The women in the living room had made two wreaths and decorated them with violet roses made of rough crepe paper. Uncle was alone in his snuggery with an older fellow whom he might once have known. Other than this man, Uncle is all alone during these his final hours on Earth, just as he was in life. Who knows, perhaps he once loved another, and perhaps another loved him. We certainly didn't, least of all our Mother. If ever he meant anything to anyone in life to us or to our neighbors, he was of no import to anyone dead. There were far more significant things afoot then: a dead Marija, a dead Kocbek's mother and her children, the fate of twenty partisans - this hung over us in the air like lead and weighed heavy on the local inhabitants.

They buried Uncle next to Father. The few mourners who came were not truly there for him; one in the back said:

"He's dead, but he died far too late."

Mother understood what he meant by that, and I did too. He could not have continued to live life this way.

The night, a clear February night, gave birth an all-encompassing horror. From parts deep within, the Cossacks were unleashing all their demonic energy. The valley was burning. Crimson hellfire rose to the cloudless heavens and dyed them orange. The last-quarter moon, suspended as by a thread above the hills, paled before the torch the people had lit. The moon knows no evil, but nor can it show compassion …

I walked with Mother next door. In times of crisis, Mother always tended to seek company. Though the neighbors were around a three minute walk away or more, they were still the nearest.

We sat in their room when the master of the household entered and announced:

"Someone is coming; I heard a girl crying."

Our neighbor stepped to the door, and Mother and I followed her.

"Who is it?" she inquired into the moonlight.

The crying hushed, and the girl continued her approach. We pressed ourselves against the wall and kept silent. Once this person had reached the house, our neighbor sounded again:

"What's happened? Where are you going?"

No answer. She means to circumvent us, but decides to stop in the snow.

"Come then, dear! What's the matter?" my Mother says mildly.

Perhaps this softens the stranger, or perhaps she merely seeks the company of another person. Some inner force draws her to us. She steps to the wall and blubbers:

"Mummy, Papa … in the fire. I ran away … Mummy said to run, run to uncle … No, I won't tell you that!"

She wipes her face in her hand and runs along.

"Whose is she? She sounds highbred, perhaps, and she's wearing a coat. And she's young, a child," I say as I look after her, until she is lost in the moonlight.

"That such a girl is not afraid!" scoffs the neighbor.

"What does she have left to be afraid of? She's got no parents, nothing left to rescue but her own empty life that she can't have much to expect from," his wife rebuts.

The time had already slipped past two when Mother says:

"Silva, we're going home. You shall likely be going to bed as well."

"We shall have to. You can leave Ivan here. He'll skitter on home in the morning," says the neighbor and straightens my brother's blanket.

Mother and I hardly take a few steps before I sight on the other peak the florid glow.

"Mother, there's a fire's there!"

"Yes, there truly is. Let's run back to the neighbors'. They won't be abed yet."

I'm not quite sure what drew us to the fire. One of our neighbors was a firefighter, but his adherence to this profession certainly now held no meaning. All the same, we set off. He walked in front, I and Mother behind him on the path.

The neighbor looked, said: "It's Kocbek's," and sped his step.

"Kocbek's," repeated Mother.

"Let us go only as far as the orchard; we don't know for certain what has happened," the neighbor suggested.

The orange flame, engulfed by the thick black smoke, betrayed that the house had been doused in gasoline. Nobody was extinguishing it, nobody was calling for help. The dead home was quietly flagging. The occasional splitting sound signaled that a beam had hollowly collapsed onto the ground or into a flame and begun to burn even more intensely. We stood at the edge of the forest and watched. The neighbor knew what it would be his duty to do—to put out the fire, even though the water was deep in the ground. Even Mother and I looked on with a hard-to-bear helplessness at the ruination of a mighty home - your home, Rick, a sanctuary to many partisans and their supporters. We were already intending on going through the forest, when a gruff voice made itself heard in the vicinity of the burning house:

"Ah, little bird, you flew to this place, not knowing that the nest here crashes down just the same!"

Two uniforms, of indistinguishable color and ownership in the fiery blaze, stand with a girl, whose hands cover her face.

"You will speak, brat!" the first patronizes the girl and yanks her by the sleeve to himself.

"What are we waiting for? We drag her away or we let her burn!" the other added.

"Mother, let's go!" I utter out of fear for the little girl and myself.

"She's the one who passed in front of our house before. We should not leave her ... Of course, now it makes sense. Kocbek had a married sister in the valley," the neighbor remembered too late.

Mother chided him:

"My dear, you should have recalled this sooner. What will they do with her?"

"Who knows; none of us, for a certainty, and neither of those two, or they would not hesitate so. If one could be sure that it's the two of them ...' he says with temptation in his voice as he clenches his fists.

"They are armed. You are not ...' Mother reminds him, having realized right away what her neighbor intends.

Nervously, we shift our weight and wait. The city girl is standing and her hands no longer hide her face; the soldier harshly pulled them asunder. Her arms hang limply at her sides, her head slumps between her shoulders. She may be giving soft answers, or she may be silent. Her voice does not reach us, yet the fire crackles as though it must needs warm the entire world, for in the hearts of the people there is only ice.

The air of the still night is shattered by an explosion.

Splinters of flaming wood, intermixed with metal, sprinkle the air. We protected ourselves by taking cover behind the trees. Only now did I become aware of how cowardly a folk we were. We stood gaping into the flames; just as the average person would be limited to doing. And we *were* merely average people: we guarded our humble lives, if they even resembled lives any longer. Then there came a series of bursts. The guards ran downhill and straight for us as they sought cover. The little girl, the only one among us with any real measure of courage, raced across the snow in the direction of the gunfire. The guard, whether to protect the girl or the flaming house, I even today do not know, turned around and fired a few rounds after her. We were later relieved to learn that she had eventually saved herself. Deep inside, we felt ashamed.

When we on the other side of the river heard the booming of Russian cannons and therefore the end of all these terrors, the vineyards once more shed their natural tears. The spring had deposited on the vines large, pearly drops. They adorned every pruned grapevine, bobbed in the wind and shimmered in the first rising sun ... Eventually they slid off and seeped into the loam upon which people and horses alike had once walked and trodden ... The hills teared and bled for all twenty-five of the hostages tied to a stake in the valley by the mill; they wept for all the partisans being held in Kocbek's home; but most of all they sorrowed for Marija. The river had swallowed up and obscured its final victims in its muddy waters. In their pained grief, the hills died down; even the gloomy songs were no more ... Our stockpiles of sugar had long since been depleted."

"It's nighttime, dear. Don't you feel it?" Rick said with the intention of interrupting her story as his hand found hers.

"I do, I know. The sun withdrew a long time ago. The earth is cooling. I know you probably want to go home. You must be hungry. I, however, am not. When I'm having a good time I forget all about hunger and my other common worries. I think about the people, haranguing each other with their problems, nervously gasping for money the way I do for air, turning green with envy whenever they peer into their neighbor's yard, and they seem silly. They hoard it and pursue it and want more and more. In these people there is no longer a place for their fellow man, no more room for love. Their love is a tin box, their happiness is a villa and a summer house. No great love can live in these people."

"I have a small correction to make. What you say is true. But in general only of older people; and I already count myself among them. Look, if I had no money, I wouldn't be able to fly across the ocean to see you. The older we get, the more we become afraid of uncertainty. So we become stingy, selfish, ambitious."

"So far I've been doing all the talking. Is there no, let's say, humorous encounter that you remember from your time with the partisans?"

"You're asking for a lot! Do you really think things are as fresh in my memory as they are in yours? I think you could tell your story forever and a man could just listen. My thoughts aren't quite so organized, but there are a few memories left of those bittersweet days.

In our unit we had this little Englishman. His name was Tom. He wasn't terribly fond of sharing his life's story, but when he met me, his kindred spirit, he decided to confide in me:

"I came with my parents to a village on the outskirts of Zagreb. We stayed at my uncle's place. I'm not quite sure why we never returned to England. My mother and father hesitated and for a while and then some, until they had no money for a return trip. So we ended up staying. The two of them were quite happy with things at first, but later they began to feel that we were in my uncle's way in that little house of his. And then the war broke out. My uncle told us:

"Stay, you can't possible go anywhere now."

And we worked and lived; my father and uncle would go to work in Zagreb, whereas my mother, aunt, cousin Marica and I would work at home. I worked the field there, tending the cows in the pasture and playing with our pup. Everything was grand until that one morning ..."

He looked past me into the distance and I was worried he might begin to cry at any moment. But he didn't. His lips simply began to quiver and turned into a frown. He closed his big, blue eyes beneath that high, child's forehead of his for a second, then opened them again. He then began, with difficulty, to recount his tale:

"It was raining. I don't know why my father and uncle decided to stay home that day. The Ustashe came ... They were only looking for my uncle, who immediately escaped through the back door. My father tried to make a run for it as well, but he didn't make it. He was left lying in the field. My aunt, upon witnessing this, froze in place, while my mother ran to him. Before she could reach him, she flailed her arms and collapsed into a wet ditch. Everything was black: the field, my mother, my father. I screamed and ran and ran and reached the forest. I leaned on the tree and bawled. Then, I heard more shots. I knew they must have hit my aunt or Marica, probably both ... I ran deep into the forest to outrun the truth and the pain, no, that isn't true - I ran so that I could die. And right by the river, hugging the ground, my uncle was waiting for me. So we both went to the partisans and right until this spring, he was my father, my mother, my everything . He took care of me, kept me safe and would give up his last slice of bread so that I would have something to eat.

An assault. The sky vibrates. In front of us, a forest is on fire, behind us are enemies. Shrill shouting pierces the tense atmosphere. Even though I'm not afraid, I sometimes close my eyes.

"Here, to me!" yells my uncle as he throws himself on me to shield me. The booming and crashing deafens our ears to the gasps that come from the trenches. I crawl out from under my uncle's body, which suddenly feels heavy as a pile of bricks and pins me to the ground. Something warm gushes over my hand, but I feel even colder than before.

Victory! The enemy has been driven away. Many comrades are dead, and more still are wounded and living. But I am alone. I now spy my uncle's
wide-open eyes, his cold hands, but what good is any of that. I'm alone with a wounded face and completely lost.

When we buried my uncle, I became a part of our company. Everyone began to look after me, a fourteen year-old English lad, maybe because my uncle had protected me too jealously.

"And you want me to take your uncle's place now, is that it?" I asked him jokingly.

"I'd gladly accept, but permit me to remain our company's Tom, 'our Tom', as they call me."

"Of course. If I'm already fighting for freedom in general, I can't take a man's personal freedom," I told him.

Once, during that great spring, as a matter of fact, we were situated somewhere on the Austrian border. Tom and I were tasked with goading the cow. Personally, I'd rather carry a wounded man than pull a heifer along, but it was exactly what Tom wanted.

"We shall get her to safety, we will. Well *you* won't even have to do anything at all; give "er the occasional lash if she refuses to move," he explained when I told him that I'd never seen a cow with my own eyes before, let alone known what to do with her.

The animal was hungry and was already poking its maw at the barely ripe meadow. Now and again I cracked my whip to make her pick up her pace, but she seemed to barely notice my painful caresses. We were all tired by now. The men could barely shuffle along. I was fortunate enough to be wearing comfortable brown shoes, albeit worn, when everyone else's were too big, too small or tattered.

"Come now, cowboy, step a little faster or we have dinner in the morning," the one called Henrik, who knew a little English, joked.

"What do I have to do with dinner?" I asked, a little offended.

"You no, but this cow is our dinner," he answered.

"We've been driving her since yesterday, she could have been our lunch or breakfast instead of dinner," Tom butted in.

"No, she must be for dinner, asked commander. He know what he says. We must come to valley, there we meet comrades and.."

"Eat the cow," I added.

"Rick, I'm sorry, but ... She's been so good. She even gave us our fill of milk. I thought that ..." the boy began to stutter.

"Just what kind of a soldier are you!?" I scolded him, affecting heroism, even though I was fond of the animal myself.

"Faster, come on, let's go!" came the word from behind.

"No can do, the cow's over the hill. It's a senior citizen," I said like a professional.

"Oh you know about this!? It is not quarter of your age. Since when you are cow expert?" Henrik provoked me.

Sluggishly, we climbed the inclination. There was a valley on the other side, and it was already fading into twilight. We got to a forest that was almost dark, because the treetops, which weren't yet thick with foliage, were densely packed above us. From behind we heard a clatter.

"Get to shelter!" was the order.

The warriors jumped behind the nearest trees and prepared for an attack. In that moment we heard a long, drawn-out croaking sound. The cow lifted her tail and started trotting toward the incline across brushwood that snapped underfoot; Tom followed her.

"Tom, get back here!" I commanded.

He came back and took his rifle. It was no big deal. When the situation calmed down, we sat down together in the valley and stared hungry into the darkness.

"Where did your dinner run off to?" Tone asked us.

"You two are cowboys head and shoulders over the rest of the herd: both of you had you hands on the leash, you were armed, and yet it got away anyway."

"We thought it was old and tired," Tom murmured.

"It was a German cow, and it ran directly to the Germans," Henrik cracked up.

"Quiet, all of you! I'll send you a real cow from Texas, one with discipline that was raised by cowboys and that doesn't run away at the first loud noise," I told them."

"Rick, what happened to Tom? Did he survive the war?"

"He did. Right before it was over he was given a nice dark brown uniform that fit him perfectly. We stood on one of the first tanks to drive through Ljubljana. He was a nice kid; I was proud of him."

"But he wasn't yours."

"That he wasn't. He was one of us and we were a unit."

"Yes, Rick, all of us were as one. Our meadows, our vineyards, the canopies of our trees all pulsed to the rhythm of the humming of your airplanes …

These days your squadrons ravage the Vietnamese countryside. Do you think that the forest there would hide you in its bosom? Does the grass green in your honor there? Is a welcoming hand extended there for your pilot?"

"No, Silva. Few wars are just, but the one that we and you were in was. That's the reason your hearts were open, your forests mighty and your knolls welcoming blankets that offered us foreigners soft shelter."

The night had long since ignited myriad stars on the celestial arch. The two were driving to the hotel. The road was now rising and then once more descending at a gentle grade, until it at last turned slightly to join the sea.

"There, do you see the ship?" Silva asks eagerly

"That ship? Of course I see it; look how lavish the lighting on it is. It wanders the sea, probably in search of a port."

"It will find one. There are no on the water, and if there are, they all lead to the shore."

"And the two of us were like a ship. We cruised the blind greyness, spotted an island, stepped onto it, then shoved off again. It took us twenty years or more to find our harbor. Yet we knew from the moment fate threw me on foreign land among foreign people that we'd dock at the same lighthouse. It's just down there, and it shines for us the way you shone for me when there wasn't a single light in the sky and the ones inside me had already died out. After every night of torment there rose a morning in which you appeared before me in my delusions and suffering. And every time you appeared from my dreams, you were more beautiful and better. You, my savior at the time, my girl. At night you would lie with me in my bed instead of her ... my wife ... cold, stiff beauty that she was."

"I know you had a wife, but you've still told me nothing about her."

"I had to tell you things in chronological order. Now comes what might be the hardest chapter ...

I met her the same way most young people end up meeting. Well, that's not true, it was *a little* different ... She was with a friend of mine, but not exactly. She belonged to anyone who would pay - she was an exotic dancer, you see. I married her. I did my best to ignore the nasty comments my friends made and we tried to live a normal life. It didn't work out. There was something bigger than me - her dancing. She would always gravitate back to that bar and when she heard that music, her whole body would shake and she'd run around the room like a bird in a cage. She couldn't last around me, even though I wanted to tame her. She had no interest in family life; she always thought that she was born to spend her time doing something more ... which is why she was always cold as ice towards me. One day, fed up of that life, I went out on the town with the boys. I came back around dawn to find the bed empty. She disappeared without a trace. I looked for here everywhere, but even with the police's help, she was nowhere to be found."

"And now?"

"Now I have you by my side. You didn't replace her, no, you were a part of me long before her, and you existed in me ... The world has gotten smaller, it's shrunk so much that we're the only people left in it. I know that our wishes can't unite the religions and perspectives of the world, but if everyone shared our thinking, lush glades would overgrow our human boundaries and we'd all walk barefoot on that soft, dewy carpet. Everyone would be rejuvenated on it, then would rise—fresh, magnificent, joined in an endless human circle that wouldn't know the booming of cannon fire, but only the hymn of love."

"I'm afraid you'll have to trade in your poetry for prose now, Rick. We have to sleep, or the dawn will find us still waking."

"Let's sleep, then. We'll have plenty of time for conversation. We'll spend the rest of our lives together, until it runs out ... Our ship has arrived, and it's firmly anchored in the harbor, and the lighthouse is no longer blinking, but shines with immeasurable strength."

"So, will you being staying here then, Rick?"

"No, my dear, you'll come with me! My home is there, my house, my city and my parents. I won't spin you tales of wealth and riches. I can only promise you a calm and decent life. And any illusions you might have about glittering gold or a special kind of happiness in my country will be shattered when you see the old and decaying and poor districts ... The contrast there is night and day, and we will be somewhere in the middle, which is where most of our people find themselves."

"But Rick, you know … you know that I'm not alone."

"I know, I'm not a child to forget about something like that. Your son will be my son too. I've wanted a son my whole life."

"And it will never, ever bother you, you know … It wasn't some misstep I made … the wish, the endless to desire to have children …"

"I love you, darling. I want to make you happy. And you'll only be happy with those dear to you by your side. Your heart is so big that it can hold the three of us."

"How do you know there will only be three of us?" she said in jest.

"I really don't. I want there to be more of us. Really, Silva, if you could have my kids, it would make me happy."

His hands tenderly ran across her warm and willing body. Silva felt them on her; she loved it when those elegantly long and shapely hands caressed her face. But they now felt cold on her body. She did not resist; though tonight she could not even feign to play the game that had become so familiar to her. This made Rick realize, for the first time that evening, that she was completely absent.

"Should I turn the light on, dear?" he asked.

She lay quietly and looked at him with large, bewildered eyes. In them there was neither the plea to leave her alone, nor any enthusiasm.

"Silva, what's with you tonight?"

"Nothing, nothing. It's not just tonight. I'm always like this," she could barely utter.

"Is there someone else?" he continued calmly, aware that the passion in him had abated.

"There was. But not any more. Rick, I have to confess something to you … He's with us every time we're together. I can't get rid of him. Perhaps
because he reminds me of you a little, or because of something words cannot express."

"God, who is he?" He became upset and shuddered on the bed.

"You don't know him. You shall never see him. He's a married man, and over fifty by now … Yes, I'm telling you the truth. It was he who discovered the woman in me. Nobody before him or since ever has. Even France was only half a lover."

"And from the moment we met until today you've been pretending the whole time?" he asked indignantly.

"It was all but a game with a more or less unhappy ending."

"No, I can't and won't believe that, Silva! You'll never convince me that I'm worth less to you than that paramour of yours. If that's how it is then why didn't you tell me right away?"

"I was waiting for that moment of complete bliss to arrive."

"Then tell me, did you not feel complete relaxation when you were with me? Did I never manage to satisfy you?"

"Rick, this is something you can't understand. If it weren't for my memories of that youthful passion, which from the first time he and I touched excited every nerve in my body, I would think that our shared experience now is perfect," she explained in a voice that meant to appease.

Rick came to his senses. He no longer felt scorned. He remembered the love he had shared back home, one with a cold blonde beauty. Even with her he had had to strum a different tune, and this was the same selfsame tune he was now trying to play for Silva. He loved her and would not for the world want to lose her. His lips latched onto her white flesh and made her moan. His powerful body conquered her forcibly. He observed her face, which had suddenly become flush; her partly open eyes and her lips. He felt with each passing moment that she was his. She responded to his light thrusts, until she relaxed and lay still on the bed.

"And now?" he asked after a time.

"There is no third person between us now. Now we've connected."

"I'll remember that," Rick muttered with satisfaction.

Bliss did not return to them during their time together, even though their souls had been liberated from their physical shackles.

NEVER

Silva sits at the table. Her head rests on her left hand, while her right hand slowly glides across the page. Her eyes scan its contents, upon which her hand flinches, and she crumples up the paper and throws it away. She looks with deliberation around the barren room, where no life, no single, solitary flower can any longer be seen. She had stuffed anything that could be picked up into a suitcase, and she had consigned any unnecessary junk to the landfill. A coworker, who had long waited for this opportunity, would be living in her home now. All she had left to do was the thing that she dreaded most. Since Rick had left until today, she had wavered between yes and no. She sought an inner support, a fortitude, but there was nothing. She again looks within to find the right words, words that will sound neither like a plea nor like a command. Of the few meagre words that inhabit her thoughts, she finally pours several into a new and final letter:

Dear France,

I am letting you know that my son and I are leaving for America. Even though there have until today been no ties between us, at least not visible ones, I would like to invite you on the forenoon of October 15th to Brnik airport so

that you can say goodbye to us. I know how far away
Belgrade is, but I remember a time when we would bridge
even greater distances ...

Silva

She folds the paper and on the envelope writes the address.

Who knows whether he's still there. Many years have passed since that address belonged to him. "But anyway, it doesn't matter now ... I've
completed one of my final duties, if it was even mine to begin with," Silva ponders.

She then gets up from the table, stows the letter in her handbag, wherein are concealed a blue envelope with two airplane tickets, takes her last two suitcases and sets them before the door. She comes back to ensure that the windows are shut tight and that no light has been left on, locks the door and hurries down the stairs.

There was no time to bid farewell to the room, wither to the furniture or the memories that remained here. It was in fact unnecessary; since she had decided to leave, she was constantly saying goodbye to everything and everyone. Even parting with her colleagues was not easy. She placed her luggage into the boot of the car, sat behind the wheel and drove off toward the post office.

"I must, I must, even if it's not my duty to do it."

She quickly reached into her handbag for the letter, which she then dropped in the mailbox, and then drove off ... home, into the hills.

There, everything begins anew. Tonček returns from school in the afternoon and hands his mother a present, wrapped in white paper, tied with red ribbon.

"My classmates and the teacher gave me this."

Silva carefully undoes the large red bow, removes the wrapping and reads: *Little Luke and His Starling.* One of the pupils had scribbled on the first page of the book, in handwriting that was plainly juvenile: "*In memory of Tonček, pupils of class 2.a*

"Curious book," she says more to herself than to the child, "they already know why they bought you this book in particular. Let's have a look at the other one!"

"Teacher gave me this one, and she wrote in it too, you know," Tonček says boastfully.

"Ivan Cankar, *Na Klancu ("On the Hill")*. It's a nice book, and you'll read it once you're grown."

Near the front of the book, the teacher had, in a gentle feminine script, written: "*May familiar words warm you in a distant, foreign land.*"

Silva closes the books, rewraps them in the paper and says to herself:

"She probably meant to write: *In a cold land*, because that's the only place where you need someone and something to warm you. But we've got Rick, anyway, big, old, sweet Rick. He'll keep us warm and take care of us and we will live a life. *Will* live? Have we not so far? And I took care of my son on my own and needed not ask anyone for help. Away with these foolish thoughts! The tickets are waiting, via Frankfurt to … America."

Ivan, who had worked diligently enough at the factory to be able to build himself a new house, waits for his bride.

"Silva, you really could wait three weeks for the wedding to be over and leave afterward," Ivan began.

"If indeed you must go at all," Mother finished.

"I must, oh yes, I must, and now! Besides, you never told me to stay before. And you know who I'm going to be with; we all know Rick."

"Know him indeed we do. But don't you know how sorely I'll miss your brother? I can't even imagine not having him around anymore." Mother had already begun to cry.

"Mother, you'll be getting little grandchildren, a house full of them, there is after all room for everything," Silva consoled her.

"Well, what was it I wanted to say … The Kocbeks are pressing grapes this evening and wanted you to come. They've saved the best grapes for you."

"Really? How is old Kocbek doing these days?

"He's old and sickly now. He's given his entire estate together with the house to the young ones. Lojzka is an industrious housewife and a good
woman who will serve him well. Do you remember the night there

was a fire and Lojzka ran to get to Uncle?"

"Ah, Mother, if I recall everything else then that's not something I'm likely to forget. Who would conceive that such a lovely home would spring from those cinders."

"Lojzka helped a great deal. Kocbek had been left alone in this world, and she, only a child, had been as well. It is true that our entire locality lent a hand in rebuilding Kocbek's homestead after the war. You won't even be able to properly remember that. It was when you had left for Maribor, and later for Ljubljana. It's a shame you ever went at all … If you hadn't spoken any English, perhaps you wouldn't be leaving presently …'

"Please, don't worry! Everything will be all right. When we say our goodbyes, the first few days will be difficult, but then we will each accept our destiny. Some of us forge it ourselves, while others have it forced upon them, but the fact remains that you cannot be constantly at odds with it."

The sun is setting. The sky is stained reddish there in the west, and a few of the dawn's golden hues still reach across the vineyards here. A warm October wind; a gentle breeze pulls apart a cobweb stretched between the vineyards. On every peak, the wind rattles sing. Their harmony is perturbed by the hollering of the lively crowd, who occasionally sing a domestic tune.

Silva treads the narrow path, confined on both sides by a dense mess of vines, sagging almost to the ground under the weight of ripe grapes. Tonček walks before her. Without asking, he makes a turn into the vineyards, picks several small, yellowish peaches and brings them to his mother:

"Here, Mother, they're ripe and they're good even though they have black spots. Grandmother says they're sick, but I eat them and I haven't gotten sick."

"Thank you, they're good. We also ate ones that were spotted like these, and we were healthy."

"Mother, will I really vomit on the airplane?"

"You won't. I've bought some tablets for the both of us. And don't think about the flight today; not tomorrow, or the day after …"

There is gaiety at the Kocbek home. A young, comely housewife offers a large oval plate with slices of flat cake, while her husband circulates with a pitcher and pours old wine. Silva stands in the doorway and observes this bustle.

"Come on then, pour me some, neighbor! You'll press so much this year you won't have anywhere to put it!"

"Quite so! He's a miserly master. He brought back five empty barrels and nothing more," the other added tauntingly.

"What else would he bring? I found everything at Kocbek's: earth, livestock, vineyards, a good master and a dutiful wife. I knew the only thing they lacked was a few hard-workers and a container for a few hundred gallons of wine."

The old neighbor sets the little cup under the current that issues from the grape press.

"You'll have plenty of wine, but it won't be as sweet as it used to be," notes the old man, as he licks his lips and deposits his cup.

"I'll sweeten it. You can get sugar, and it doesn't cost very much," the young master responds.

It dawned on Silva: there had been sugar in the past, too, but it drowned in sorrow. The times had changed for everyone: the sugar would now dissolve in wine.

"Shall we sing one then, lads?" Miha suggests.

"If it's only the lads who are allowed, then you shall have to sing all by yourself," retorts the master.

"Well then, I suppose I can assist him," Silva intervenes, "I *am* still a girl."

"Well, seven hells, Silva, we shall sing another today, but then you're through. They say you too are to tie the knot," Miha replies.

"Fret not, Miha. The groom is far away, he couldn't see us here in this pressing room if he were gazing from the Moon itself. It is however a great sadness that we have to marry off our greatest beauty there, to that place. Weren't you local boys born with a pair of eyes?", the neighbor laughs.

"She would always hide from us. She was always a highflier. Always on a plane, I mean," he recovered.

"Well come on in, Silva! We're all familiar, don't you be afraid of us now! We're a little rounder and merrier than you may be accustomed to, but you'll recognize us all the same. Only a fool would decline a drink like this! Bottoms up, lads!"

A few more men and women appeared from somewhere. They were young and Silva did not know them. They were well dressed and neat. The girls wore their hair short, while the boys' hair was longer. The older ones among them began to sing, and their song encouraged Silva and Lojzka to join in: "A girl stands on the hill', followed by "Where are those little paths."

One of the young men made a snarky remark:

"So, father, won't you sing the one about the twelve girls?"

"Oh, be quiet, you! You don't know a single one! You'd like the one the English sing, eh? But you haven't got a clue how it goes, not that or any other. There were times we'd belt it so loud the doors would rattle near off their hinges."

"You see how it is with young people, Silva. They go to the cinema on Sunday, and then home to watch their televisions. Once there, who knows what they watch and what they want. The first one says he'll be a singer, the second an actor, and God only knows what the third one wants to be. As long as work isn't involved. Young folks only want to work a factory job or to go abroad. They don't even fancy these fine-smelling vineyards anymore. What has it come to ..." old Potisk groaned through laughter.

"Let them, father. There was a time when we also wanted something more than work in the vineyards, but it was a different time. Youths will figure out how to live; we shouldn't worry about them too much," Silva comforted the man.

"Mother, let's go home!" Tonček came running into the pressing room.

"It really is quite late already, we must be going. Goodbye, everyone! Have a good time and sing another pretty song or two. When there's singing in the hills, it rings out for an age and a half."

"A safe trip to you both! And think of us from time to time," several voices at once replied.

"And these grapes are for your journey. They're nice and ripe. Lojzka and I looked for the very best. And do say hello to our Rick for us! Tell him I've got enough of his tobacco left for a year. When you come visit us, he can bring me some more." The old man quivered as he handed her a basket containing the fragrant grapes.

"Thank you, father Kocbek. I'll be sure to tell him."

Her feet sank into the soft ground as she walked toward the homestead, while her mind retreated to thoughts of the past and how it compared to the future. The past fanned out before her clearly, yet the future remained wrapped in mist, fantasy, illusions.

She had once walked barefoot along these paths. Loam had clung to her feet so that the skin beneath it had become hard, like the bark of an oak. In the summer the paths were desiccated and cracked from thirst, and the loam was unforgivingly hard and matted into clods. During the spring, one's soles would still feel the ground's keen prick, but by the fall they would have hardened to such a degree that they could skip across thorns. Yet these paths were no harder than the asphalt roads abroad might be …

A spider web glistens in the morning sun. The frost oppresses the autumn flora as silvery grey crystals rustle underfoot. A car waits ready down on the road. All there is now left to say is "farewell and thank you, Mother'. Yet those words are immeasurably difficult to utter. Through
barely open lips they can only be spoken bitterly. Even tears well only briefly in the corners of the eyes, caught promptly by soft, white tissues.

"Mother, goodbye! Do keep your health, now," Silva says as she tears away from her mother and runs to the car.

"Tonček, obey your mother, and don't forget to write me!" his grandmother hardly managed to say with tears in her eyes.

"Hey, we're going to be late! That's enough, we aren't going to a funeral!" Ivan calls from the road below.

Before she sits into the already running car, she looks around one more time. Mother is standing at above, crestfallenly shrunken and hunched. An apron hides her face as it did once upon a time, when she was a woman with virtually no equal on her peak.

"This is so difficult for me. What if she needs me the most right now?" Silva asks her brother, who is behind the wheel.

Another view of her Mother, her homestead, the trees and— farewell. The car now bobs along the cart track until it arrives at the road.

And then there are no more vineyards or hills, no more of her world. The road, the houses and their gardens: they are now all so common, so provincial, and hers no longer. These things no longer bring tears to her eyes or give rise to sentimental thoughts.

She and her son sit calmly in the backseat of a white Prinz.

"Mum, will I really see Indians there?"

"You will, son."

"And real cowboys on horses too?"

"Maybe you'll see them as well. I don't know for certain. I've never been there."

"Matjaž said I have to take a picture with a real horse and a cowboy hat and send them the picture or they won't believe me."

"We'll sort it out," came her automated response.

"Why am I not more excited about this trip? I'm almost afraid," Ivan says quietly.

"We're afraid of things that are new to us. I, for example, avoid marriage, even though I know that's not the same thing as what you're talking about."

The automobile has no such human concerns. It willfully racks up the miles, obeys the driver's hands and carries them toward their destination.

Their destination is very close now. The world here stretches out into a wondrous valley, white houses sprinkled among its verdant gardens. The entirety of this barely-discernible garden is surrounded by a wreath of hilltops guarded in the background by mighty mountains.

"What's all this? I've driven through this valley a hundred times, looked around me the way I am today, but I did not see it. Is it only today that my eyes are open to all this beauty and my soul is receptive of life's finest experiences? It's too late now, Silva! How will you reconcile that foreign world with your own little one? How alluring this tiny world of yours is: vineyards bathing in the October sun, grape pickers competing in song with the wind rattles from one peak to the next … In the evening the pickers gather in the pressing room, bow a little, have a few drinks and then again break into song to drown out the rattles, which in the breathless eve have either fallen silent or sing a barely audible tune … And then the hills fall asleep. In the cottages, lights come on that coyly pierce the small curtained windows. This is how it once was ... and almost how it still is. That *once* has, in these last few minutes of my living at home, merged with *today*. In my heart has resonated in full force a melody begun long ago, which never faded. It now resurged together with the image of my Mother, yet not of the gloomy one from this morning whose cheeks were moist and who waved away hand sadly, but rather of an endlessly great, fair and strong Mother, the way I knew her in my early years when she toiled just to keep her family alive, when life had stranded her with my indifferent Father, Uncle and Rick ... Yes, Rick ... And given this heavy burden she, Mother, did not buckle a single time. She dragged him about heroically, sometimes silently, sometimes with imprecations under her breath; the situation did not change at any rate. That's why Mother is what she is today: hard as the earth she lives on. Only today did she weep like a vine pruned in the springtime. Maybe the same thoughts were passing through her weary head: why leave now, when the skies above the vineyards, above our homeland are clear, if we had nowhere else to go and did not abandon these hills and valleys when they were being smothered by a blanket of suffering; when people were dying for this land; when the fires were swallowing up homes whole; when Lojzka Kocbek could unearth nothing but her parents' wedding rings from the ashes ...

Oh, disappear, all you thoughts! Direct yourselves elsewhere! Petoskey by Lake Michigan is your tomorrow. The hills and vineyards and your homeland are yesterday or the distant past. Does not the sky above Lake Michigan have a blue reflection? Is not the sun there red-yellow when it rises? It's all splendid, Silva. And a *new* home awaits you there! The strong hands of a man will keep you safe from evil. A futile consolation! You can lie to everyone else, but not to yourself! I even told my colleagues when we parted that I was happy. They might even have believed me. Yes, if I were twenty, perhaps I would be. There'd be no memories of my experiences at home. But then there would be no Rick either, and no two tickets in the bag ... one-way tickets. You take those tickets and ride in one direction and stay there ... And in the sky, you'll look for a star whose glow will point homeward, and on the surface of the lake you'll look for the reflection of the blue eyes you once loved … Nevermind! Rick also has blue eyes … yet only Tonček's are of the truest blue … his blue … Nonsense, my wits must be leaving me! I must get back to reality. Once I was tempted by the sky, so I flew through the air; then I was drawn to the sea and Rick and I rode upon it; and with the other one, too - Tonček's father. That's when he was born … But now I'm on dry land, hard though it may be, yet also secure and firm. Hide your tears, grit your teeth and say that you're fine. Oftentimes that's what everyone else does. Do so for the sake of Ivan and for the sake of Tonček. I'll have to wake him now; it's almost time to go …

"Ivan, drive a little faster. I'd prefer to be in the air already, I don't feel all too well."

"I thought so, given how quiet you've been."

"Oh, not at all, that's not why. You know, I've just spanned the long path connecting my earliest memories to the present day. It's a good thing you left me alone."

"Well I can't drive any faster; you can see there's a speed limit. And we've still got a good hour besides."

She lightly slides her hand across Tonček's forehead. She stoops down to him.

"Tonček, wake up!"

"Are we there yet?"

"Yes, son. The airport is there, just behind that bend."

"Look, mummy, is that snow?"

"It is snow, yes."

"Will there be snow in America too?"

"I don't see why not. You already know how to ski."

"Mother, how will I talk to father, if he doesn't know Slovenian?"

"The two of you shall find a way to communicate; we did as well, after all."

"Is my papa big? And why didn't I see him when he was here?"

"You were at camp. We once truly wanted to visit you, but something came up. Don't worry, you'll see him soon."

"Mum, what about the white Prinz? Will Uncle sell it?"

"No, he'll drive about in it. And when we come here on vacation, we'll drive about it in ourselves."

"And I will sit in front with Papa, you know."

"We've arrived. Park right over here," Silva says anxiously.

The fear and homesickness are joined by something else:

"Will he be here? What's he like? What will he say?"

"Look, Uncle, that's our airplane over there!" Tonček says as pulls Ivan toward the fence.

"Please look after the child while I go have a look at something," Silva says to Ivan and heads to the cafe.

Cars are arriving, some are departing. Silva begins to leave the cafe, in which there are only the faces of strange men. Her eyes have scanned all of these people; all of them are unimportant to her. She decides to get her brother and child. They drink coffee, or anything that might at once calm and embolden her.

The airplane has just arrived. It thundered mightily across the tops of the spruces and then landed.

"Mum, let's go, that one's for us!" Tonček exclaims.

"Just half an hour more and then …"

He won't be here. Tonček will leave without his father's goodbye and kiss. His kisses, which he had given so very many years ago, had been given in his stead by Rick. Everything that he had left behind … Rick had taken … But he could not entirely conquer her heart. Her thoughts again drift to the past.

Another twenty-five minutes. In these short, measured minutes, nothing else can happen, so Silva calms herself, drinks a double coffee and discusses something with her brother to avoid silence. Still, no mention is made of farewell.

The taxi makes an abrupt left turn and halts. A tall man with broad shoulders steps out, puts on his overcoat and begins to look for someone. His blue eyes look over the nervous passengers. Silva's voice suddenly emerges from the crowd:

"France, we're here!"

The words barely leave her lips, and her footsteps cease. Her legs are leaden and only get in the way.

Mere seconds now separate them.

The man is coming, only three more steps, now two. There is

an opening of arms, a quivering of lips, and, the sighs from the depths of her soul coalesce into a single word:

"Silva!"

The world begins to spin. Powerful arms grip her world, engulf it in their embrace, and Silva trembles in the knowledge that this is that incomprehensible thing that has been smoldering in her subconscious all along. Somewhere deep inside, she had always compared them: France and Rick, and she had always repressed France so that Rick might shine more brilliantly. And yet, France would time and time again rise to the surface - like oil on water; he would not be repressed.

"This is Tonček, our son!"

The child directed his fiery eyes upward at the tall figure that swiftly stooped. Its large palms enclosed his tiny face and drew him in for a kiss. The strong hands then lifted Tonček high, up toward the sun. The world became endlessly vast for Tonček. Everything became lost in its own littleness: the airport, the forest, the people ...

"We meet at last ... I had some car trouble, so I took a taxi. I see I've come at the last minute. As long as I'm not too late."

"Precious few minutes separate us, France. This is a bittersweet meeting, since we already must, in this very moment, consider our farewells."

"Our farewells, Silva? We haven't even properly said hello to each other and it's just to be "so long'? We've only just found one another."

"Maybe we've spent our entire lives looking for each other, then found each other, only to once more go our separate ways."

"Silva, only because that was what you wanted. I looked for you, and you avoided me; I wrote you, and you kept silent ... But now that we've finally met, I'd like us to stay together."

"Wait, I have to think this through. I wasn't counting on this."

"Silva, recall how cheerless was the song of the hills twenty years ago. It was us who began turning that sad song into a happy one. Some never even heard its resounding chorus. You were among those who lent it their voice, and now you want to leave here."

"Yes, Rick, and so does he."

"As you wish, Silva, this is the final call. If you can bring yourself to strike a line through our dark days and account only our bright ones, then stay."

Her legs remain rooted; her lips quiver. Her eyes look forward mutely. From somewhere comes Ivan's voice, which finally rouses her.

"Aren't you two leaving?"

Silva's gaze turns to meet France's eyes, blue, wide-open and inquisitive. The decision is made in the course of a second.

"We're staying! Tonček, your father came to meet us!" she says triumphantly, having overcome herself.

"And he's learned Slovene so that we can have a talk now," Tonček remarked with a smile, taking hold of his father's hand.

The plane roared and climbed in the sky. Three people remain by the fence. They shake hands and warm their fingers in one another's warm palms. In their souls, the very finest strings strum the reawakened melody of the hills that has sprouted into the love shared by three happy people. The sound of the plane fades fast. The white fog behind it dissipates over the blue of the sky.

"Thank you for staying, my dear. Today is the day on which my life takes on its real purpose. I shall begin to live for someone and for something. Until now I've lived merely for myself. The days and years have passed me by vainly …"

"Let's try to pick up where we once left off … Do you remember?"

"I remember. We were young, untamable. "

"And where to now?" Ivan inquires.

"Back to the car and then home … We'll all return home to our peak."

The airplane is now little more than a gleaming white dot. Silva stops for a heartbeat. The words, loaded with the juice of sweet grapes, were left unspoken in her heart.

"I'm sorry, Rick! Great things happened in this little land of mine. My heart sang because the right string vibrated. Gradually, your eyes fade, your kind words are lost. Someone else has taken your place.. he's stronger. Splendid is the moment when father and son meet. We are now inseparably connected. The grapevine has interlaced us. The song of the vineyards and of home has drowned out the swashing of your lake.

Once upon a time you were carried by a bird that made the sound of steel. You fell to the ground like a white butterfly with broken wings. We mended you and returned you home.

You fly without us, silver bird, but all the same—farewell and Godspeed!"

Karolina Kolmanič with her husband and sons in 1960

ABOUT THE AUTHOR

Karolina Kolmanič writes short stories and novels. Her first short stories were published in various journals. In 1968, she published her first short story as a book *The Sun Seeks Not the Lonesome Paths.* It was followed by her novel *Farewell, Silver Bird* (1972). Her novel *Marta, Daughter of the Wind* (1975) achieved great success and was followed by 21 other works:

- *Shadows on White Pages* (1980)
- *Dreams of Golden Buttons* (1983)
- *Your Distorted Image* (1986)
- *The Fruits of Early Blossoms* (1988)
- *The Silver Bicycle* (1990)
- *Vintner Ana's Hill* (1992)
- *I Am Returning You Your Spouse* (1993)
- *Late Summer* (1994)
- *The Sunflower's Blooming* (1997)
- *The Lotus Blossom* (1999)
- *No Sun Without Shadows* (2000)
- *Let Us Say It and Laugh* (2003)

- *Dawn of Hope* (2003)
- *Her Crossroads* (2004)
- *Alba* (2005)
- *I Wait for You, Dolores* (2005)
- *The Poems of the Unloved* (2007)
- *Nila* (2010)
- *Light in the Heart* (2011)
- *The School Bell Won't Stop Ringing* (2014)
- *Good Night, My Love* (2015)

INTERVIEW WITH KAROLINA KOLMANIČ

by Susan Smith Nash

It is very inspiring to read how and why writers began to write and how they developed and maintained their passion. Their circumstances may differ, and they may have had different experiences, but there are always a few things that seem to appear with some consistency. They include formative experiences in childhood, a fascination with nature, and a persistent need to observe and explain the world.

Welcome to an interview with Karolina Kolmanič, née Hari, born September 29, 1930, a Slovenian writer whose work spans several decades, and who has won many awards and inspired numerous writers to explore the human condition.

1. *What is your name and your relation to writing? Can you tell us a little bit about your background?*

   My name is Karolina Hari, and my married surname is Kolmanič. I was born in an idyllic rural place: my birth house sits amid fields and meadows - a world of freedom without fences and boundaries.

Karolina Kolmanič, Slovenian author

2. *When did you start to write and why?*

I went to elementary, middle and high school in Gornja Radgona. I graduated from the Teachers' College in Maribor and then from the Higher School of Education in Ljubljana. My favorite subjects were Slovene and Foreign Languages. In addition to German, I also learned Russian in school and Hungarian passively (from my mother). My father, 25 years my mother's senior, traveled a great deal and read a lot of newspapers, which helped me get into the habit of reading. In school, I already had the children's paper *Lučka in naš rod*. We would all read. Thus, I felt eager from an early age to read and write. I was inspired and encouraged more seriously at the age of fifteen by my professor of Slovene in my fourth year of high school. I am interested in social sciences, less so in natural sciences.

Karolina Kolmanič, Slovenian author

3. *What was your first book? How did the first book impact you? What made you want to continue to write?*

My first book was selected for publication at a 1968 Yugoslav festival and published immediately thereafter and is called *Sonce ne išče samotne poti* (*The Sun Seeks Not the Lonesome Path*). I translated it into German and it was published in the German magazine *Europapublikation* in 1978. *Srečno srebrna ptica* (*Farewell, Silver Bird*) in particular draws inspiration from real events in my life that motivated its writing: I had with my own eyes seen white parachutes gliding through the air like butterflies from beneath the plummeting, damaged plane in Graz. In writing the book, I allowed myself some literary and artistic liberties.

4. *What were some of the formative experiences that shaped the subjects you write about? How did they tie in with the plots of some of your works?*

My works enjoy a positive reception. Particularly well known is the novel *Marta* (starting circulation 5,000). The story centers on the problems of an expatriate working at a Volkswagen factory in Wolfsburg. I was invited there as an honored guest, so I was able to observe this worker in her work.

5. *What are you writing these days?*

I write short works of prose for various magazines at home, in Germany, Austria, the Hungarian Porabje and the Italian RAI. My latest book came out on 12/5/2015 with the title *Lahko noč, ljubezen moja* (*Good Night, My Love*).

6. *How has history shaped your view of the world? What do you predict for the future?*

The notion of a sunny future for humanity is an illusion. Human cruelty through conflict is timeless and has been expressed through religion and secularity alike throughout history. The world seems to strive to invent new methods of killing, but science should not be used as a weapon for the destruction of humans, animals or nature. Once a person's feelings, soul and heart die, evil awakens inside. Hope is ever there for the optimist, because melancholy and the grimness of reality can only be overcome by reason, love, light.

Source: E-Learning Queen
[http://elearnqueen.blogspot.com/2015/12/interview-with-karolina-kolmanic.html]

Karolina Kolmanič at a party for her 85th birthday.